AND THE CITY OF A THOUSAND PLANETS

THE OFFICIAL MOVIE NOVELIZATION

VALERIAN

AND THE CITY OF A THOUSAND PLANETS

THE OFFICIAL MOVIE NOVELIZATION

CHRISTIE GOLDEN

TITAN BOOKS

Valerian and the City of a Thousand Planets:
The Official Movie Novelization
Print edition ISBN: 9781785653841
E-book edition ISBN: 9781785653858

Published by Titan Books
A division of Titan Publishing Group Ltd
144 Southwark Street, London SE1 0UP

First edition: July 2017
1 3 5 7 9 10 8 6 4 2

A CIP catalogue record for this title is available from the British Library.

Printed and bound in the United States.

Did you enjoy this book? We love to hear from our readers. Please email us at readerfeedback@titanemail.com or write to us at Reader Feedback at the above address.

To receive advance information, news, competitions, and exclusive offers online, please sign up for the Titan newsletter on our website:
www.titanbooks.com

THIS BOOK IS DEDICATED TO ALL
THOSE WHO SEE WITH FRESH EYES
AND MANIFEST AWE AND WONDER;
THE MUSIC MAKERS, AND THE
DREAMERS OF DREAMS.

PROLOGUE

The stars were not eternal, but they were ancient nearly beyond reckoning.

Much had their judgeless gazes witnessed in the system ruled by Sol, especially the activity clustered around the third planet from that star.

By that world's calendar, in the year 1975, something momentous occurred above it.

From separate places on this planet, known to its inhabitants as "Earth," a pair of nations had launched what would later be deemed "primitive" space vessels. For the first time in Earth's history, two ships would be joined together, and the inhabitants could move freely between them.

The momentous "handshake in space," both a literal one and a figurative one, occurred between astronaut Brigadier General Thomas Stafford of the *Apollo*, and Alexey Leonov of the *Soyuz*.

There were smiles and joy and a sense of connection, and the two men became and stayed steadfast friends through the decades that unfurled.

What happened in 1998, at Alpha Space Station in orbit around the blue-green world, was not merely two nations meeting. When the European Hermes spaceplane, proposed in the same year as that first historic handshake, arrived to dock at Alpha, it represented a coalition of nations. Space was no longer the province of a few tiny humans, but was rapidly evolving to belong to humanity.

The space station grew as time went by. In the year 2019, China's massive *Tiangong-3* spaceship was warmly welcomed when it came to take its place at Alpha. The captain of the Alpha Space Station, one thirty-year-old James Crowford, enthusiastically greeted his Chinese counterpart Wuang Hu, who himself could not seem to stop smiling. Later historians would mark this moment as the end of international tension, and the beginning of what was the first Great Age of human cooperation.

What many on Earth had said could not happen, did happen. Humanity continued to work for peace and cooperation on Earth, while keeping their eyes and hearts attuned to the siren song of space. They continued to shake hands against the vast panoply of the starfield.

The station was fully established, and the distant stars looked on as Earth's united glory and passion fueled Alpha's boom. Eight short years later, the station had grown enormously. Its population had swelled to eight thousand. More nations had ventured into the stars, and wanted to be part of this symbol of unity. By 2029, every country on this third planet from the sun had at least one scientist on board to represent them.

In 2031, an artificial gravity system was installed. The station's denizens could now walk its corridors as easily as they walked on their home planet. Captain Crowford was now a distinguished man of forty-one years. He had the honor to welcome captains from India, the United Arab

Emirates, Korea, Africa, Australia, Brazil, and Japan—who, instead of the iconic "handshake in space," offered and accepted a traditional bow.

Still the stars, distant and silent, observed. The station expanded, its numbers swelled not just with military or official representatives, but families. And the stars watched as history—not just for humanity, but for the rest of the galaxy—was made in the year 2150; the international space station Alpha was now two miles long and home to over a hundred thousand people. But until this moment, all the construction and designs on the station, all the ships that had come to dock with it, and all those aboard them had all had a certain comfortable familiarity.

The vessel that was now approaching did not.

It looked more like a creature of nightmares than a spaceship—black, chitinous, covered with dozens of sharp, cruel-looking spines. It was lit from within—a dull crimson hue visible only from a few windows positioned on the ship's sides and two on its bow, if such a strange vessel could be even said to have so pedestrian a thing as a "bow."

Captain Joshua Norton, known for his somewhat rakish appearance with a neatly trimmed beard and piercing eyes, would later write in his memoirs:

> The ship looked like something out of a Jules Verne novel—more living entity than ship. The portholes positioned on its bow were located toward the top of the sloping vessel. The overall impression was of a huge, dangerous creature bearing down upon the hapless Alpha, its two red eyes glowing in anticipation. At any moment, I

expected an enormous mouth to open and swallow us all whole. The English word "alien" had never felt more apt.

Norton awaited the aliens in the station's ceremonial hall. "I tried not to be nervous," he recalled, some six decades later.

> *Our communications with the Kortân-Dahuks, whose species had originated in the Pleiades star cluster five thousand light years from our neighborhood, the Sol system, had been consistently civil. The shock of that first contact with them—our first confirmation that we were not the sole sentient race in the galaxy—has of course been articulated by historians and journalists, and captured by artists and poets. It seems old hat by this time, to be physically interacting with an alien. But you must remember, it was so shockingly, so bravely new to those of us who stood in that hall, sweating and no doubt silently uttering prayers.*
>
> *As I said, correspondence had been civil. They told us they explored the galaxy not looking for conquest, but in search of art and beauty, which was the heart of their species' culture. We hoped for the best. But we didn't know.*

The last airlock opened.

Three aliens stepped from their ship onto Alpha station.

They were slightly taller than their human hosts, and were roughly humanoid—"Such a telling, Earth-centric word," lamented Norton, "and we still don't have anything better"—but there the similarities ended. Norton and his fellow delegates recognized arms and legs, heads with eyes and mouths, but these were appendages affixed to reptilian bodies, and eyes and ears on faces without noses.

Their primary skin color was orange, with blue, yellow, and red blending in those large, noseless faces. Protruding blue-gray lips were set in hard lines. They wore armor on their torsos, lower arms, and legs, and their feet ended in what looked to human eyes like cloven hooves.

We all knew it was a pivotal moment. History in the making. But what kind of history? It seemed as though everything in the world—in ours, at least—was at stake, in the time it took for our hearts to beat... rapidly.

According to accounts, in the pivotal moment, Norton gulped. He offered a smile, and held out a hand that trembled, ever so slightly.

"Welcome aboard," he said.

One of the Kortân-Dahuks translated for its leader. There was a pause; the alien features were unreadable to humans, who had never before seen them in the flesh.

The leader stepped forward, taller than Norton. He seized the captain's hand—

—and pumped it up and down, vigorously.

The station—and the whole, watching world—breathed a sigh of relief.

Things moved briskly after that first contact. Species that were then unthinkably strange but who would later become old friends, household names, reached out to interact with humans and make their homes on Alpha.

Mercurys, beings that had transformed over time

from primarily organic into mineral beings. Analytical, bordering on emotionless, they were almost more alien than the Kortân-Dahuks. Their more accessible "ambassadors," the politically astute Doghan Daguis, were invaluable in smoothing out communications between humans and these beings also called the Mirrors.

The Palm Murets followed, gaseous beings encased in soft metallic exosuits and wearing elaborate, intimidating masks that belied their inherently peaceful nature. So, too, did the stars behold the arrival of the Arysum-Kormn, a nomadic race of explorers and travelers who prided themselves on familiarity with every species in the galaxy.

The KCO2s, beings who fed on the negative emotions of others, were received with mixed emotions. While they needed to be near beings who suffered fear, pain, or despair, their feeding on such things, as Norton would famously say, "sure cleared the air for the rest of us."

Martapuraïs arrived, introduced to the humans by their allies, the Kortân-Dahuks. They were aquatic beings encased in bulky full body suits that the captain who first met them, Ezekiel Trevor, likened to "old-fashioned deep-sea diving suits," which permitted them to live outside of their watery environment. They were large, benevolent, and ichthyoid with long, tentacular arms. Their round-eyed heads were set in the center of their chests.

Upon meeting them for the first time, balding but charismatic Captain Trevor smiled diplomatically and held out his hand. Blinking solemnly through the bubble of its helmet, the Martapuraï extended its tentacle fingers. Trevor kept the smile glued to his face as his fingers closed around the cool, gooey appendages.

"Welcome aboard," he managed gallantly.

Humanity, which had once scoffed at the very idea of extraterrestrial life, swiftly began playing host to not just a few, but dozens, and eventually thousands, of different species.

Over time, the thing that made Alpha so special—the welcome it extended to so many sentient beings—became a danger to the very planet that had symbolically opened its doors wide. But there was a way to stay hospitable and to protect the vulnerable Earth. And this, too, the stars saw.

It was time for Earth to say farewell and bon voyage to Alpha Space Station.

The speech the president of the World State Federation made was without precedent, and recordings of the historic moment would be seen in Earth classrooms for as long as there would be an Earth.

"The intergalactic space station has reached critical mass in orbit. It now poses a serious threat to Mother Earth," announced the tall, elegant statesman. He was in his early seventies, his once-gold hair now nearly silver. His piercing blue eyes gazed into the camera as he spoke. "In its great wisdom, the Central Committee has decided to use all resources necessary to release the space station from the Earth's gravity."

Shots of the president's recognizable, still-chiseled face were interspersed with the images of hundreds of ships that looked like fireflies with their wide rear engines and four grasping arms, attaching themselves to the space station. They activated simultaneously, and, slowly but steadily, the gargantuan space station shifted away from Earth, pushed to a distance where it would be able to escape the mother world's gravitational grasp. Then, the stars watched as the smaller ships disconnected themselves, permitting Alpha to drift to its future home.

"Its new course is set for the Magellan Current," the president continued. "Like the great explorer Ferdinand Magellan, the Alpha station will journey into the unknown, a symbol of our values and knowledge. It will carry a message of peace and unity to the farthest reaches of the universe! Our thoughts and prayers go with you… Godspeed, and good luck."

As the stars, and so many others, watched, the station was sucked into the current, and whisked away from Earth until Alpha Station, too, was to those on Earth no more than another tiny speck in the star-filled universe.

CHAPTER ONE

The living light above her waved its glowing filaments gently; in this it was, like all things in the world, in tune with the stars, seasons, sun, and sea. She responded to the gradually increasing illumination by opening her impossibly blue eyes, blinking peacefully, slowly awake, welcoming the new day with the same tranquility with which she had welcomed slumber the evening before.

Her soft, still-drowsy gaze took in the warm pink and coral hues of her bedchamber. Light spilled down the curving staircase, and the shiny surfaces of the enormous shell's walls and ceiling picked up the gleam and suffused the room with rosy brightness.

Her skin caught the light, too; a white that was so much more than a stark, single color. It was decorated with images that changed shape as her moods did: art of the spirit.

Pale and celestial-seeming as moonlight, her smooth, soft skin held every color of the rainbow blended into a pearlescent, ever-shifting, subtle glow.

She was Liho-Minaa, and she was a princess.

A soft squeak beside her drew her gaze from the familiar shape of the chamber to her favorite little friend, who always snuggled beside her while she slept. Līho-Minaa smiled as the creature snuffled at her neck happily with its long snout, offering its furry, impossibly soft belly for scratches. It was small enough to perch in her hand, but never feared being smothered by its mistress when she slept—the hard, bumpy scales on its back would wake her before any harm would be done.

Moving with the easy grace of a curling wave, she swung her legs to the smooth floor and stretched, before placing her little friend atop her shoulder. Rising, the princess padded barefoot to the giant clamshell affixed to the wall. It did double duty. The upper portion had been polished to create a reflective surface, albeit an imperfect one. Its base cupped dozens of large pearls, the one at the center as large as her own head. Above this base that served as a sink, a luminous, tendrilled creature, kin to the one suspended over the princess's bed, provided light, but the pearls themselves also emitted a soft, pulsing glow as multicolored energy shifted within their smooth surfaces.

Līho-Minaa smiled at herself and her small friend on her shoulder. He opened his slender muzzle for an enormous yawn, and she laughed. She dipped her long, elegant fingers into the shell's bowl, scooping up handfuls of small pearls. As if they were water in solid form, she brought them to her face and rubbed them on her skin. Any trace of sleepiness fled from her. Her blue eyes brightened, her skin became even smoother and tauter about her fine bones. She felt restored, refreshed, and energized, and she carefully let the pearls she had cupped return to their fellows in the bowl.

Before she departed, she fastened a simple necklace about her long, slender throat. It consisted only of a chain and a single exquisite pearl. Gently, the princess touched it, and the pearl thrummed, glowing gently at the caress.

Ascending the steps, she emerged outside into the dawning day. Lïho-Minaa was seldom sorrowful. Her life, and those of the rest of her people, was filled with rhythm and calmness and beauty. But if she ever did feel melancholy, all she needed to do was look around at what her world showed her.

She felt powdery white sand between her toes, heard the soft, endless sound of the languid ocean reaching up to touch the shore, then withdrawing its watery fingers. Enormous shells of different shapes and colors dotted the beach, some even sitting in the shallow aqua-turquoise water: homes to family and friends.

She set down her little friend on his perch outside her comparatively small shell-home, patting him gently before turning to stride toward the sparkling water. The playful ocean teased Lïho-Minaa's feet, pale as the sand, as she went to join the group of others.

Some were in the water up to their waists, gathering up filigree-fine nets laden with pearls of all sizes. They brought them to the shore, moving gracefully, their bodies pearls themselves. Children and adults clustered around the nets, eager to help remove the precious orbs and place them in large seashell-baskets that were then hoisted onto the backs of adults for carrying.

Further inland were small craters in the earth, about the size made when one extended one's arms and made a circle, fingers touching. Smiling, their faces bathed with the milky glow, those who bore the pearl-filled shells emptied them into the waiting earth.

The very ancientness of the routine was comforting. Lïho-Minaa turned her face up toward the rising sun and closed her eyes for a moment. When she opened them, she beheld a bright streak across the dawn-dappled sky—a shooting star.

It was not alone. Another joined it… and then another…

Fear closed around the princess's heart as the first chunk of something unknown—but definitely not star matter—slammed into the water. It smashed a shell house into jagged pieces. Others came too swiftly to count, sending spouts of water in the air as they struck the ocean making angry craters, wounds on the world.

Cries of terror erupted and people began to flee. But where could they run? The princess stared up at the sky, which had once contained nothing but stars and moons and sunlight, as chunks of metal ranging from the size of a fist to the size of a house rained down mercilessly upon the frightened populace.

She turned, helplessly, to gaze at another part of the sky—and then she saw it.

The scope of it was gargantuan, inconceivable, and she understood at once that it was not simply a vessel, but death.

Lïho-Minaa dwelt near the ocean, soothed by, and loving in return, its lulls and song and smell. Her family, wishing to be in the heart of the population they ruled with a gentle hand, lived in the village.

And the still-burning ship would crash directly into it.

All around her was the awful, never-before-heard cacophony of screaming.

But the princess did not scream.

She ran.

The village was a layered collection of shells, their graceful, sloping forms clustered companionably together around spiral steps and open plaza areas. The royal palace, home to Emperor Haban-Limaï and his family, was a collection of shells adorned with exquisite carvings and metalwork. It sat in a place of honor, at the highest point of the village, overlooking the shore and the ocean. In front of it was the largest plaza in the village. Once, it had been the sight of performances, both oratory and musical; it had showcased dancing and art, and had been a place for pleasant gatherings.

Now, it was crowded with frightened people, their eyes gazing skyward, round and terror-filled, as pieces of something that had once been huge and was now broken and alien and dangerous slammed down everywhere they looked.

The emperor was a calm individual, who had led his people wisely and with care. All eyes turned to him, hoping against hope that he would somehow be able to stop whatever was happening.

He turned to one of his guards as he emerged from his dwelling. The guard's forehead and eyes were black with fear. "What's happening?" he said in the musical tongue spoken by his people.

"There! Look!" The guard pointed beyond the elegant curves of the village at a huge plume of black smoke rising into the sky. Not everyone lived in the heart of the village. Many still lived close by.

Many lived where the ugly black tower of smoke was.

But that was not all that concerned him. He had lived a very long time, and he knew what a meteor impact was like. This was no such thing. This was much worse.

His own people would not be the only ones injured or dying.

"By all the stars!" cried the emperor. "Sound the alarm! We must contribute to the rescue effort!"

They ran, a sea of pale, pearlescent skin, foreheads dark with their distress and black, wide, worried eyes, toward the smoldering wreckage. The closer they drew, the less hope the emperor had of finding survivors.

It was massive, twisted, broken, burned black metal lying atop the pretty shards of smashed shells. There had been no war, no violence, on Mül for so long that it was the stuff of legends and folklore. The emperor had hoped that the ship had fallen from the sky because of some mechanical error, but he realized that it was a grim casualty of war, taking with it much more than the lives it had borne within its metal walls.

Closer they came, but saw no one staggering out, coughing or limping, wounded but alive. Only a single hatch was open, where a few of the ill-fated vessel's crew members had tried with bitter futility to escape the inferno.

Nonetheless, an effort had to be made. Surely not everyone aboard such a mammoth vessel was dead…

"Search for survivors and begin salvage operations," the emperor ordered. He took the first courageous steps himself, entering the doomed ship. He had no idea what he would find, only knew he had to see. Had to help.

The worried suspicion turned to cold certainty. Inside, they found only charred bodies that had once been living, laughing beings, who had never stood a chance. It was no longer a rescue mission, but those who had died so badly deserved more than to have their bodies forsaken.

He stepped outside, but as he began to tell the sad news, a shadow fell over them, as if something unspeakably huge was attempting to swallow the sun. Haban-Limaï looked up. His grief for the unknown aliens who had fallen to the violence of war was replaced by sick horror.

A ship about seven miles in length was falling out of the sky.

The emperor thought of the beautiful, but ultimately fragile, homes the debris from this ship had already crushed to sharp pieces. Without a doubt, their shell domiciles would never survive what was about to happen.

But perhaps this ill-fated vessel might have one final gift to offer those who had come to help its crew.

"Everybody inside!" he shouted. "Take cover! Hurry!"

There was not much time left before the end. The emperor kept one eye on the encroaching disaster and the other on his people as they rushed, carrying children, as fast as they could toward the only possible safety. Fear stabbed him when some of his guards ran up with his own family.

One of them held a terrified five-year-old Tsûuri in his arms.

Another bore the ominously still form of his wife, Aloi. Her beautiful flowing robes were torn and spattered with blood. Relief flooded him when she moaned slightly and her head rolled in his direction. She was injured—but alive.

"Get them inside! Hurry!"

The two guards hastened to obey. Fear still gripped the emperor's heart as he seized the arm of another guard and he asked, hoping against hope, "My daughter?"

The guard's eyes filled with sorrow as he shook his head. "I have not seen her," he said.

The emperor thought of the chunks of debris that had fallen like pieces of stars, and his heart cracked. But he could not afford the luxury of grief, not now, when he needed to stay calm and care for as many of his people as he still could.

In the distance, the ship finally fell. The earth shivered violently, as if it was a living thing in tremendous pain. Sounds that attacked the ears with the force of a sharp spike accompanied the ghastly spectacle as the ship plowed its way through the soil even as it cracked and exploded into a roiling fireball.

His eyes glued on the ship in its death throes, the emperor waited until the last possible minute, until the final few stragglers flung themselves inside sobbing and shaking, and then he, too, darted into the safety of the first ship and pulled the massive door shut with all his strength. His muscles strained as he gripped onto the strange latch, turning it until he felt it grind forward and lock into place. He leaned against it for a moment, panting.

His eyes fell on the survivors. Shivering, in shock, they stared blankly at him as they huddled on the metal floor. His wife was being tended, and his son looked up at him, tears streaming down his small, perfect face. The emperor scooped up the boy and held him tight, pressing his face into the soft flesh of the child's neck. Tsûuri clung tightly to his father, as if he would never let go.

There was a pounding on the hatch. The emperor went cold. He did not want to see who it was. He did not want to look into the frightened eyes of one of his beloved people who was a bitterly tragic few moments too late. Nonetheless, these *were* his people. He owed them what comfort he could, in this, their last moments.

He went to the porthole.

He had thought he could bear no more pain.

He had been wrong.

The frightened face of his sweet, beloved daughter stared back at him, her glorious blue eyes huge. Her face had been dark with fear, but now it receded as she gazed at her father, a soft pink suffusing her cheeks.

Was there time, even now? It would be but the work of a few seconds—

But her death, the death of the world, was approaching with vicious speed. A gargantuan fireball was on his daughter's heels, a cruel yellow-orange wave of incineration. If he opened the hatch now—if he let her in, saved her life—he would put everyone else inside at risk if he could not get the door closed in time. The fireball would scamper greedily through the faintest crack, and then everyone on board would join the burned, motionless shapes of the vessel's original crew.

She saw it in his eyes, and hers flew open wider. She struck the portal window with her small fists. All he could do was look with profound grief at her, his first-born, the embodiment of all the goodness he saw daily in the world.

After a few seconds, the pounding slowed, stopped. Tears poured down her face, but there was no longer terror in her expression. Only understanding, and sorrow.

Oh, my little girl...

Shaking, she pressed her forehead to the circular window.

"Liho!" he cried, brokenly.

"Dadda!"

They wept, father and daughter, a few inches apart, a universe apart. Though a benevolent ruler, Haban-Limaï had a staggering amount of power at his disposal. There was very little he could not do.

But he could not save his precious child.

Unused to utter helplessness, the emperor pressed his hand to the porthole. The princess gulped and lifted her own hand. It was not real contact, a loving connection of flesh to flesh, but it was all he could give her. Even so, the feeble gesture seemed to calm her. She blinked back the crystal tears and swallowed hard, straightening. Haban's heart, so battered this day, shattered into pieces at the expression of resolve on Lïho's exquisite face.

The wave was coming, an orange, hungry beast, ready to devour anything in its path. Ready to turn her to blackened bones and charred flesh, or worse.

Lïho gave her father one last smile. Not tremulous, not fragile. It was strong, and peaceful, and certain, and he thought he had never admired anyone more in all his long years.

She turned from him, to face her death. She would make it count.

Lïho-Minaa spread her arms and tilted her head back, opening herself to the fiery embrace. Her father did not want to watch, but he could not avert his gaze. He needed to honor her courage. He needed to bear witness to what would come.

And in the instant before the flames engulfed her slender form, before they rendered her into ash and memory, a powerful blue wave emanated from Lïho-Minaa's body.

The wave raced at staggering speed, whirling up from the beleaguered planet Mül, sweeping up into the stars, soaring across the immensity of space, luminous as the girl whose death had birthed it, rushing straight into—

CHAPTER TWO

The young man bolted upright, his heart slamming against his chest, gasping for breath. He blinked, rubbing his eyes with one hand as the welcome realization penetrated his brain: *A nightmare. Just a bad dream. Not real.*

He forced his breathing to slow as he took in his surroundings—perhaps not as ethereally, magically beautiful as the ocean and seashore of the nightmare, but a good deal less... well... terrifying.

He looked out at the rolling, peaceful waters of a turquoise sea as the waves lapped gently against a pristine white sand beach. The sound was calming, and Valerian took a deep breath and let out the last bit of tension that still lingered in the knot of his muscles and watched the slow sway of green-fronded palm trees.

His mood brightened as he watched the slowly swaying hips of a young, fair-haired woman who was, in his opinion, even more gorgeous than the lovely princess of his dreams.

Like him, this vision was dressed for the beach in a swimsuit. But he was pretty sure his swimming trunks used up more fabric than the young woman's black bikini—top *and* bottom—did.

She had studied ballet when she was a child, developing

an interest in martial arts as she grew older. As she moved, her grace and the sleek strength promised by her slender but athletic form announced that biographical fact to anyone with eyes. And he *definitely* had eyes—eyes that were very appreciative at this particular moment.

Her long legs halted their gliding stride in front of him. One hand held a sweating glass of something bright orange and topped with a straw and a tiny, flower-patterned umbrella.

"You okay?" Laureline asked, lips curved in a frown of slight concern. She lifted the glass and pursed her lips around the straw, her high brow furrowed in worry as she stood in front of him as he lay on the lounger.

"Yeah. Just a bad dream." Valerian grinned, now that he was in her proximity. "I feel better now."

"Well, good. Maybe now you'll be up for running through our assignment." She took a long pull on the straw, regarding him seriously.

It seemed to Valerian that Laureline never let her hair down. Well, not figuratively, at least. But even literally, she presently had it pulled back in an efficient, sleek ponytail. He imagined it unfettered, blowing softly around her perfect face and practically begging for him to tangle his fingers in the soft length.

"That's the *last* thing I feel like doing," he said in reply to her statement.

"We really should prepare," she insisted.

Valerian pretended to consider the prospect. "Well..." he mused, "that's thirsty work, you know."

Quick as a thought, Valerian seized her drink in his right hand, grabbed her left hand with his own, and tugged her around and down, flipping Laureline so she lay beside him while he propped himself up on his elbow and grinned down at her. He took a sip of the too-sweet beverage and said, "Ah, that's better."

Laureline eyed him as one might eye a toddler whom one found particularly trying. "Not very professional, Major," she said, her voice heavy with mock disappointment.

"Don't worry, Sergeant, I scored a perfect two hundred on my memory test."

"When was that? Ten years ago?"

"Yesterday!" Valerian said, defensively.

"Impressive. But the major still forgot something today."

"Oh, I doubt that," Valerian replied airily. Then, as doubt flickered in his expression, he asked with careful casualness, "What?"

"My birthday."

Worst. Thing. Ever.

"Oh, no!" Valerian sagged, mortified and kicking himself from here all the way back to Earth.

Laureline took advantage of his distressed state to link one long, lovely, and deceptively strong leg around his waist, used Valerian's own weight against him, and to his surprise flipped him as neatly as he had her a few moments ago. Smirking slightly, she relieved him of the cool beverage.

He gazed up at her as she took a sip, not at all unhappy with the moment. Laureline was at once both completely dependable and highly mercurial—a neat trick, one he'd never seen anyone other than her master. They had worked together for two years, and in that time, she had blown all his previous partners out of the water. There was quite literally nothing he didn't admire or respect about her. Even as he had the thought he amended it; Laureline appeared to be completely immune to Valerian's charms, which were considerable, even if he did say so himself.

But for the present moment, all was well in his world. Laureline made no move to change her position, continuing to sip her drink and peruse him with blue eyes bright with humor.

"They say memory blanks are the first sign that you're getting old," she said. Her eyes narrowed, focusing in on something. "After gray hairs," she corrected. With the comment, she reached out to stroke his hair—and plucked one.

"Ouch!" he yelped.

She brandished it toward him like a weapon, with a triumphant, "See?"

His hair was dark brown. The treasonous hair she showed him was most definitely not. He stared at it for a moment, then his gaze slid to Laureline, dark with suspicion.

"You dyed it while I was sleeping!" Valerian said.

Laureline laughed. "Right," she said, still grinning. "Like I've got nothing better to do."

Gray hairs. He was getting old at twenty-seven. It was not a happy thought. He returned his focus to the gorgeous woman in front of him, her own hair shining in the sun, glorious and most definitely *not* gray.

He reached up and brushed a small, rebellious strand from her face, lingering on her skin. "I feel horrible that I forgot," he said. Then, with a slightly lascivious smile, he asked, "What can I do to make it up to you?"

"Beginning descent in three minutes," came a clipped, polished voice. Next to them, a small black pod started to flash a red light. Valerian closed his eyes in misery. *Talk about bad timing*, he thought.

"Nothing that you can get done in three minutes," quipped Laureline, her grin broad as she slipped out of his grasp.

Valerian reached out, both playful and pleading. "C'mon…" he wheedled, under no illusion that she would acquiesce but, apparently, incapable of not trying anyway.

Laureline scolded him, pretending to be serious, though her slight smile betrayed her. "Now, now, don't start something you can't finish!"

"Who taught you a dumb saying like that?"

"My mother."

"Oh… sorry." He was batting a thousand today, wasn't he? Gray hairs, forgetting her birthday—how the hell had *that* happened?—accidentally insulting her mom…

Laureline pressed the flashing red light, and reality intruded upon their private paradise.

The languidly waving palms and the ocean itself ceased their motion instantly. Clouds paused and the seagulls that had been wheeling froze in mid-flight. The blue sky that arched above splintered, like ice that had been struck, melting away swiftly to reveal the familiar black metallic interior of their spaceship, the *Intruder XB982*—or, as Valerian liked to quip, "Alex's House."

Still in their swimsuits, the two agents padded barefoot along the *Intruder*'s hallways, Laureline striding briskly, ready to get to work, and Valerian tagging along after her like a still-hopeful puppy.

"Come on, Laureline," he wheedled as they passed rows of monitors, empty space suits, and various pieces of equipment. "I know you're attracted to me. Why deny the obvious?"

She shot him a look that was both scathing and mirthful. He never knew how she managed it. "It's *obvious*?" The acidic sarcasm that dripped from the words could have eaten its way through the bulkhead.

But Valerian was uncowed. "Sure," he continued. He was joking, of course. Well, a little, at any rate. "Don't feel too bad. It's only natural. Little goody two shoes with an Ivy League education are always attracted to galaxy-hopping bad boys like me."

"My Ivy League education taught me to steer *clear* of bad boys like you," Laureline retorted, having no visible problem sticking to what she had allegedly learned.

But Valerian continued like a used shuttle salesman who knows he has about thirty seconds left to make his pitch. "You won't find better than me on the market," he promised. "Straight up. Take a good look."

He darted in front of her, but as she refused to slow, he had to walk backward while he tried to interest the potential customer. He spread his arms, indicating his regulation-fit physique. "Handsome, smart—"

"Modest!" exclaimed Laureline. He noticed that she was smiling despite herself. This was a game they played… well, almost constantly. Valerian always enjoyed it—even if it never ended with what he wanted—and he knew she did, too. Laureline was no pushover. If she disliked the game, she'd have put an end to it the first time he'd started flirting. With, say, a right hook that left no question as to her sentiments.

So he continued. "Brave," Valerian reminded her in a serious voice, striking a heroic pose—which, damn it, was impressive considering that he was walking, backwards, fast.

"Suicidal," Laureline corrected.

"Determined." She could not possibly argue that one, given what he was doing this precise moment.

"Pigheaded."

Yeah, okay, he supposed he had to admit that one.

"Faithful," he said.

The word was there, lobbed out by some impulse Valerian was now utterly flummoxed by. It hadn't been what he had intended to say. It had come out, unbidden... real. For a moment, they both dropped the act and stared at each other, their eyes wide.

Then Laureline lowered her eyes and pushed past him, muttering under her breath, "To yourself."

Valerian was annoyed, and angry. He wasn't sure why. With her? With himself?

"Why don't you speak with your heart not your head for once?" he asked.

She threw him a cold look over her shoulder. "Because I don't feel like being just another name on your list of conquests."

"Who are you talking about? What list?"

"Alex? Can we see the playlist?"

Dozens of images flashed up on one of the many screens: pictures of attractive humanoid females, one after another. Slightly panicked, Valerian stared at the images, as if the women were about to attack him.

One attractive woman who was standing right in front of him just might. Laureline advanced past him, her jaw

33

set. Valerian felt his face grow hot. How the hell had she known about this?

"Hey!" he protested. "Most of them are coworkers, that's it!" It was true.

Well, mostly.

Laureline turned, arching a brow. "Really? Coworkers?"

He nodded.

"Well, in that case, where's *my* picture?"

Valerian had no answer for that, and so simply stared at her like a woodland creature in a beam of bright light.

"Yeah," she said, and it seemed to him that there was genuine emotion in her words, "that's what I thought."

Valerian grasped her arm. "Laureline, those girls mean nothing to me. Okay, I admit it, I took a few… detours… when I was younger, but so what?"

The sergeant pointed to one of the pictures. It was of a stunning young woman with dark skin and laughing eyes. "Your last 'detour' was one week ago."

Valerian was a superlative pilot. But even the best pilots didn't always bring their vessels in without taking damage. He knew when a ship was about to crash and, likely, burn. He was experiencing that realization at this moment and, desperate to divert the course of his vessel of romance, he turned up the charm full throttle.

"With you, it's different. You know it. My heart is yours and nobody else's!"

Laureline was unmoved by his plea. "My heart will belong to the man who will have only *my* name on his playlist."

"That's what I'm saying! I'm that man!"

Laureline smiled, her face softening. The anger in her blue eyes was gone. But her words were no less devastating for being spoken gently.

"Your illogic is adorable. You know, you're quite the lady-killer," she admitted, and for a glorious second he thought the prize won. Her next words proved him wrong. "But how come you lose interest in a girl as soon as you win her heart?"

"Because I'm looking for the perfect woman."

She rolled her eyes. "Since I know who you really are, you'd better just keep on looking!"

"That's not a crime!"

"Your crime is to be scared of commitment!"

Valerian laughed. "Me? Scared of commitment? With seven medals of honor?"

Laureline stopped. "Medals of honor aren't for sticking with something day in and day out. They're for moments of outstanding courage. Recklessness, maybe. Running in and saving the day and then getting out before you pay the price for that courage. You do running well, Valerian— into and out of things. That just might be all you know how to do. How old were you when your mom passed away? Six?"

A volley of unfamiliar emotions surged through Valerian. "Oh, please!" he said, his voice almost— almost—cold. "Spare me the pop psychology. This has nothing to do with my mom, okay?"

The day that he had received the news was permanently seared into his memory. He'd been Valentin Twain then, and his mother, Sarah, was a part of a diplomatic entourage visiting the Boulan-Bathor world. The giant, lumbering species was becoming increasingly hostile toward the idea of expanding Alpha Space Station, and

Sarah had been aboard a diplomatic vessel when it had been bombed. Valerian's world had been upended. He'd gone to live with his grandmother, while his father—

He swallowed and licked his lips. "I was five, if you must know. Five years and three months, to be exact."

There was no humor or playfulness in his response. Laureline's face softened and she looked slightly guilty. She shifted her weight from one bare foot to the other.

"I'm sorry," she said, sincerely. "I didn't mean to dredge it all back up."

Valerian gave her an awkward smile, and tucked those uncomfortable, unfamiliar emotions of vulnerability and old sorrow away deep inside, where they belonged.

"It's okay," he said. "I forgive you. In return for a kiss."

Laureline smiled. He did, too. The flash of discomfort between them was gone, replaced by their congenially familiar, if fruitless, chase. She reached out a hand and touched his cheek gently, with affection, and a small electric thrill went through Valerian.

"We're going to be late," she reminded him, and turned to enter the *Intruder*'s bridge.

As with every other area of the vessel, the bridge was a study in blue lighting and black metal. Oval in shape, it was large enough to house a slightly sunken, two-person cockpit, a large table that provided a map of everything from a single street to the entire known galaxy, and two small, individual transports known as Sky Jets. The pair had spent countless hours here, working as a team, and it felt more like home than their quarters.

Valerian heaved a sigh and dutifully followed, feeling like a schoolboy who's just heard the bell announcing the end of recess. As he eased himself into his chair, he spoke to Alex, the ship's onboard computer.

"Hey, Alex," he said.

"Hello, Major, Sergeant," Alex replied, her voice warm and deep. "I trust you enjoyed your relaxation time?"

"We did, thanks," Laureline said.

"Yes," Valerian said, adding, "although it was a bit... frustrating."

"Was there something wrong with the environmental simulation?"

"It was fine," Valerian dodged, and changed the subject. "Have you entered the coordinates?"

"I did take that liberty, so you could both enjoy the beach a while longer."

"Aw, thanks," said Laureline.

"You are welcome, Sergeant," Alex replied politely. "We will be leaving exospace in thirty seconds."

The two agents buckled themselves into their harnesses. Valerian found his thoughts wandering from the beauty beside him, vivacious and most definitely human, to the luminous, languid, tragic beauty in his nightmare, who most definitely was not.

It had felt so real. The sense of peace, then the fear and horror. It didn't feel like an ordinary dream. Valerian made a decision. To Laureline, he offered, "You want to take us down?"

"Yes, sir," Laureline responded at once.

Valerian nodded to himself. "Alex," he asked the computer, "pull up my brain charts for the last ten minutes, please. I had a weird dream." *Yeah... that doesn't begin to cover it.*

"My pleasure."

A flurry of diagrams appeared at once on the monitor, flashing past in rapid succession. Though they were incomprehensible to Valerian, Alex absorbed the information at lightning speed.

"See anything abnormal?" Valerian asked, shifting slightly in his seat. He was more worried than he'd thought.

"Your cerebral activity is a little more intense than usual," Alex confirmed, adding almost blandly, "You received external waves."

What the hell was that?

"Explain."

"These waves don't come from your memory. Somebody is sending you the images."

Valerian went a little cold inside. "Do you know who? And where they came from?"

"Negative," Alex replied, her voice holding regret. She wasn't a person, but she had a personality, and she disliked being unable to answer any question the agents threw at her. "They could come from the present or the past, and from anywhere in the universe."

"Leaving exospace," Laureline called over to Valerian. The young major did not respond. He was too busy pondering Alex's unsettling analysis. Why would someone want to direct images into his sleeping brain? Specifically, *those* images?

"Three…" Alex counted down, "two… one. Exit!"

The cockpit shuddered. The black expanse of space visible on the enormous view screen exploded into thousands of filaments, out of which emerged the image of the planet Kirian.

It was smaller than Earth, and no clouds softened the red, rocky image it presented. It took a stretch of the imagination to think that such a place could support life, let alone give birth to it. But it had, and Valerian and Laureline would be interacting with it soon. The place was certainly uninviting, but on its desert surface was where their next assignment lay.

Laureline swiveled in her chair and grasped the joystick.

"Manual," she instructed the computer.

"Affirmative," replied Alex. "You now have command, Sergeant. Rendezvous coordinates are shown on B4."

"Thanks."

The spaceship hurtled through Kirian's atmosphere, approaching the desolate, bleak, and very hard surface with unsettling rapidity. They hit turbulence and the ship began to buck. The two agents bounced wildly about in their seats. Valerian was almost ninety-two percent certain his teeth were rattling, but Laureline didn't seem to care. She looked forward with those intent blue eyes, totally focused, both hands gripping the joystick as if trying to arm-wrestle it into submission.

"Easy," Valerian cautioned. The bouncing made his voice waver.

"We're running late," Laureline retorted, her own voice somehow managing to stay steely even though it, too, was wobbly from the ship's erratic motion.

Valerian muttered under his breath, "Better late than dead." Of course, as soon as he said it, he realized that "late" could also mean "dead," but he shoved the thought aside, preferring to focus on the speed with which Kirian was approaching and the hope that he'd survive the next few minutes.

Exasperated, Laureline released the joystick and threw her hands up in the air. "*You* want to drive?"

"Keep your hands on the wheel, please!" Valerian tried not to yelp the words.

Laureline, stony-faced, appeared not to have heard.

Sweat broke out on Valerian's brow. With the utmost politeness, he said in a calm voice, "Laureline, will you please put your hands back on the wheel?"

"Will you stop complaining about my driving?" she retorted.

"Yes, I'm sorry. You're a great driver. You're the best driver in the entire universe!" Valerian wasn't sure who he was trying to convince—himself or Laureline. Probably both.

She beamed at him, but her eyes were sly. "Aww, thanks!" She'd won this round and they both knew it.

But at least she'd grabbed the joystick again and had gained control of the ship.

CHAPTER THREE

"Touchdown on Kirian in two minutes," Laureline announced. There was a trace of pride in her voice as she added, "I saved us some time."

"Perhaps I should take over for a moment," Alex said, "so you can both utilize that time to put on something more appropriate?"

While Valerian had certainly not forgotten that Laureline was in her bikini, he'd forgotten that he was sitting in the cockpit of a cutting-edge ship in nothing but swimming trunks.

"Good thinking," Laureline said, to Valerian's quiet disappointment. "Leaving manual."

"Manual disarmed," Alex replied.

Laureline rose and left to change. Valerian watched her retreating figure with all the appreciation it deserved, murmuring under his breath, "Wow! Man…"

"Do you want me to regulate your hormones, Major?" Alex offered helpfully.

For a brief instant, Valerian actually considered it. Then, "No thank you," he replied, and rose to change as well.

* * *

They walked down the ramp to the surface of Kirian, a plain of soft, powdered sand interrupted by craggy, jutting stone. In the end, their attire was a bit more modest, but otherwise not that different. The major was in shorts, closed athletic shoes, and a yellow mesh undershirt overlaid with a gaudy flower-print shirt. The sergeant followed clad in a short, gray, flowing dress, waving at the six unsmiling soldiers who had been awaiting their arrival.

They were, at least at this moment, unmistakably that—soldiers, despite their efforts to blend in with the populace. They wore loose, somewhat messy sand-colored clothing. Their heads were wrapped with cloth—except for one soldier, whose bald pate and long, thick beard set him apart and, frankly, probably was a better disguise than a head-wrapping. Voluminous ponchos served double duty, concealing their excellent physical condition and also conveniently hiding various pieces of equipment and weaponry. Their disciplined military bearing was obviously being sorely tested by the heat of the planet, which had reddened the paler faces among them and dewed all of them in sweat.

Kirian was every bit as unwelcoming on its surface as it had looked from space. Some of the huge boulders had been contorted and shaped by time and weathering, their tops looking like the wrinkled folds of brains propped up on narrow stalks. Others erupted at angles from the ground and looked more like sharp, flat arrows. Both types reared up over flat desert like ancient witnesses to a time of tremendous chaos. The sand was soft, but hot, and it was already starting to creep into clothing and skin.

The commando unit further emphasized the incongruity of the situation by lingering near an old bus that looked almost as weathered and solemn as the boulders. It was painted in what had once been a bright yellow and was now a dull ochre, and it was decorated with insanely tacky rust-hued flames. Along its top were emblazoned the words "Kirian Tours."

Valerian responded to the absurdity of it all by gleefully snapping a picture of the soldiers. The glowers of some of them were priceless, and would make fantastic souvenirs.

"Hey," he asked, looking about and spreading his arms. "Where's the band?"

Major Gibson, the officer in charge of the operation, looked at him askance. "What band?"

"To welcome us," Valerian answered cheerfully. The soldiers looked at one another, utterly at a loss for words.

Gibson, a tall, lean man with sharp features, eyed the pair critically, his mouth turning down in an expression of distaste. "You plan on going on a mission dressed like that?"

"Hello Major Pot, I'm Major Kettle. Have you looked at yourselves in a mirror? We're supposed to mingle with the tourists, aren't we? What do you expect us to wear? A panda suit?"

Gibson sighed. "I'll make this short and sweet, as we're running late."

Laureline threw Valerian an *I told you so* look as they climbed into the bus, settling in as best they could.

"Major Valerian," Gibson said briskly, "your contact is Sergeant Cooper. He is in position and will be waiting with your equipment in the back of the suspect's store." Without another word, he turned to take his seat.

"Hey!" Valerian protested. "I'm only working with my partner here!"

"Is that so?"

"Yep. We're a team."

Gibson glanced at Laureline, raising an eyebrow. She shrugged. "Funny. Because Sergeant Laureline will arrive at the drop in precisely twenty minutes, and you will have ten seconds to make the transfer." An unpleasant smile quirked his lips. "Or didn't you read the memo?"

"Of course I did," Valerian lied, with just the right combination of annoyance and weariness.

"You better have." Gibson's tone of voice and skeptical, slightly worried expression gave Valerian the distinct impression that the major wasn't fooled.

The two agents were bumped and jostled as the vehicle made its way across the desert to their destination, moving over the endless sand and passing through shade provided by the enormous rock formations. Laureline pulled out a tablet and quipped wryly, "Hey, how about we look over the memo? You know—*one last time*?"

Valerian, feeling his face getting hot, shrugged nonchalantly. "Can't hurt," he said casually, stretching and slouching in the uncomfortable bus seat.

Laureline pulled up a map on the tablet, pointing to it with the tip of one long, elegant finger.

"Section four. Aisle 122," she stated. "Suspect claims to be a bona fide art dealer. His name is Igon Siruss."

She called up the suspect's image. Valerian, like most humans, had gotten used to aliens of nearly every shape and size imaginable. Even so, he had a sneaking suspicion that in this case the suspect had a face even his mother would be hard-pressed to love.

Bald, with reddish, slightly shiny skin, Igon Siruss was

jowly and sullen-looking, with eyes so tiny they were all but swallowed by rolls of extra flesh. But that was not what had caught Valerian's attention.

"Wow!" he yelped. "What's with the three sets of nostrils?"

"He's a Kodhar'Khan," Laureline explained. "There are three seasons on his planet. The dry season brings suffocating sandstorms. The rainy season results in clouds of noxious sulfur dioxide fumes. And then there's winter, when you can breathe pretty much normally. Each nostril set has developed separate air filtration capabilities and can be sealed off voluntarily, just like we can close our eyes."

Not for the first time, Valerian looked at his partner with open admiration of her beautiful brain. "How do you know all this?"

"*I* paid attention in school," she said archly, then grew serious. "When you head in there, you should take extra precautions. Igon's right-hand man is his son, goes by the name of Junior. He has a list of crimes almost as long as his father's."

"How bad can someone named 'Junior' be?" scoffed Valerian confidently. "Bet he got picked on at Kodhar'Khan school."

Laureline's lips thinned. "In addition to Junior, Igon's said to have quite a lot of private bodyguards, and Kodhar'Khans are reputed to be very aggressive due to a lack of females on their planet." Private bodyguards were often encountered on Kirian. The native population known as Siirts allegedly provided security, but they often did not measure up to others' standards.

"Really?" Valerian grinned. "Aggressive because there's

45

competition for females, or aggressive because they don't have to deal with them?"

"You know," Laureline said in a conversational tone, "another thing I learned in school is that planets where women are in charge are usually eighty-seven percent more likely to be peaceful, prosperous worlds where art and education flourish, and the males think before saying really stupid things."

Laureline patted his thigh, then, to his disappointment, rose to settle into another seat by herself. Valerian shrugged and made the best of it by stretching out more fully in his seat, fishing out a pair of sunglasses he settled over his eyes, and grabbing a catnap.

He hoped he wouldn't dream.

Valerian blinked awake as the bus arrived outside a long, high wall of red stone that marked the parameter of Big Market. As it chugged along, Valerian could see a gargantuan ornate gate soaring into the air, covered with what looked like gold. This gate marked the main entrance to Big Market.

Valerian sat up, yawning and stretching, and watched as they pulled up beside hundreds of other tourist buses. The vast majority were similar to the decrepit workhorse of a vehicle that had ferried the two spatio-temporal agents through what looked like an empty spot in the desert. A few buses, though, were of radically different design, meant to accommodate aliens of equally radical design.

Valerian had never been to Big Market, but had heard

about it, of course. Few sentient beings in the known universe hadn't.

Nearly every civilized world had its tourist clusters, and where there were tourists, there was money to be made. And there were few better ways to make money from tourists than by providing shopping opportunities. Judging from his experience, Valerian had formed a theory that the desire to shop was the driving force in the universe. Even more important than another certain driving force that most species in the galaxy shared. Not everyone procreated in pleasurable ways, but everyone *did* seem to enjoy returning home after traveling laden with souvenirs that were often outrageously priced and wholly unnecessary.

"So," Valerian said to his partner as they hopped off the bus, "think you can survive twenty minutes without me?"

Laureline rolled her eyes. "Could anyone?" she replied, melodramatically. Then she sobered and touched his arm gently. "Go. Be careful. I wasn't kidding when I said this species was aggressive."

Valerian nodded and walked away toward the gathering crowd of tourists. He slowed and came to a stop, considering something very intently. The decision made, he whirled and briskly trotted back to a perplexed Laureline.

"You're right," he said. "I must be getting old."

Her eyes sparkled. "I agree, but what makes you admit it now?"

He squared his shoulders and looked her in the eye. "I completely forgot that I have a question for you."

She eyed him. "Okay," she said, curious.

"Will you marry me?"

The expression on Laureline's beautiful face shifted, darkening with a thunderous frown.

"Not funny!" she snapped, turning, but Valerian grabbed her arm.

"Laureline, I'm serious," he said. "I was thinking about what you said earlier and—" he swallowed hard. "You're right. I need to move onward and upward." Then the words: "I need to commit."

Laureline blinked in confusion, caught utterly off guard. She looked around, at the overheated crowds, red dust clinging to them, at the guards who were too far away to hear the words but were definitely watching with curiosity. At the rickety old bus and the soldiers in and around it.

"Here?" she said. "Just like that?"

"Why not?" He grinned suddenly. "They sell a zillion things here. I'm sure we can pick up a priest who'll be happy to oblige."

His grin faded at her expression.

"Marriage is no laughing matter, okay?" she stated flatly. Coldly. "Not for *me*, at least."

Oh, shit. She assumed he was kidding. His throat constricted with the sudden awful thought: *I just blew this.*

"I'm not joking," he protested.

Laureline continued with her flinty stare for a long moment, searching his eyes, then she softened ever so slightly.

"Valerian," she said, not angry this time, "you and I get on just great. The best team ever, you've said. And I agree. We get along. You flirt, I smile. It's light and it's fine. Why reconfigure what we've got?"

Words tumbled out of him, erupting from some place

deep inside, nearly as surprising to himself as he uttered them as Laureline seemed to be at hearing them: "Because I've been working nonstop since I was seventeen. I've fought in battle, and I've killed and I've protected. I've spent my whole life going on missions where I've saved entire worlds and peoples. But when I think about it, all I've got is the mission. I don't have a world of my own. No home. No family."

"You have coworkers," Laureline deadpanned.

That zinger stung, and he twitched slightly. "I don't want coworkers," he said, honestly and intently. "I want *you* to be my world."

Laureline smiled at him. His words seemed genuine, but they were almost impossible to read. She further confounded him when she leaned forward and gave him a quick peck on the cheek. Her lips were warm and soft, and Valerian trembled inside, just a little. Gently, he again caught her arm as she turned to leave.

"Hey," he said, "a kiss is not an answer."

Her inscrutable smile suddenly turned impish. "You'll get your answer at the end of our mission."

For a second, Valerian wanted to tear his hair out in frustration, and then he realized: She was not saying no.

Oh.

All at once, everything in the universe seemed possible, and he smiled back at her. "Works for me."

A large uniformed Siirt, bulkier than was usual for the spindly-bodied species native to Kirian, came up to them. Valerian didn't understand the words, but his hat that bore the word POLIZ, a red and black decorated baton, and a variety of gestures toward them, the bus, and the horizon made his request very clear. Laureline threw Valerian a last smile, then climbed back on the bus.

Valerian watched the ancient transport cough and chug on its way for a moment, then turned back toward the throng of tourists.

He was going to get this mission done in record time.

CHAPTER FOUR

Valerian threaded his way through the crowd, moving toward Big Market's main gate. It really was pretty impressive—tall, wide, with gold stones on one side and a sturdy metal door open in the center. Valerian wondered how many people thronged through it daily.

He ambled amiably toward a group of tourists, nonchalantly attaching himself to the edges of the cluster. The slender Siirt employees of the tourist trap were handing out the equipment necessary to fully appreciate "the premiere place for galaxy-sized bargains," as Big Market brazenly advertised itself. Valerian accepted his own set of shopping gear: a lightweight yellow and black helmet with a large visor, gloves equipped with sensors, and a bulky belt. The employees were loaded down with sets designed for humans, as his species was among the most avid tourists and, apparently, extremely fond of tchotchkes.

The herd of eager shoppers that Valerian had joined tramped through the gate, and it closed behind them. They were within the market's walls, along with other clusters of shoppers, but the four walls that enclosed several square miles contained absolutely nothing else.

"Welcome, everybody!" came a cheerful voice. Valerian turned to behold one of the most outlandish things it had been his honor—or misfortune—to witness… and it was a human. A thin, tall, lively man with an enormous smile, wide eyes, scrawny beard, and an outfit straight out of a third-rate theater troupe, lifted his arms expansively. His robes were long and flowing, striped in orange, yellow and red… because, you know, *desert*. Huge hoop earrings dangled from his ears.

But what was most arresting about him was his turban. It was about three times the size of one that was usually utilized in hot climates, and presently it perched atop his head like a brightly colored beehive. He was now waving for silence, and the excited murmuring of the throng died down.

"Welcome, everybody!" His voice could not be any more cheerful. "I am Thaziit, and I have the honor of being your guide for today." He bowed, hand on his heart. "So, whose first time is this at Big Market?"

Half the tourists raised their hands, tentacles, or other appendages, but not Valerian. He listened with half an ear as he frantically examined the market's map, prominently displayed on a nearby wall, trying to locate Section 4, Aisle 122.

"Wonderful!" Thaziit exclaimed. "Let me remind you that there are nearly one *million* stores in Big Market, so, I'm so sorry—we won't be visiting them all!"

He feigned sorrow and a chorus of *awwwwww* went up. Then he brightened.

"But! But, but. But we will try to get to the most interesting ones! But before we go, just a few reminders so you can stay safe and shop happy! Remember that for each section, you will pass under a portal."

Valerian saw no portals. The living giant turban continued. "Important safety tip! Watch the letters on the top and verify that the 'U' for human is full green. That's for your own security. Big Market cannot be held liable for any mishaps humans encounter if the U is not green. Now!"

He clapped his hands together and rubbed them excitedly, his eyes so wide open the pupils were completely encircled by white.

"There are *seventy-eight sections* and more than *five hundred streets*. We're going to see amazing sights! Find incredible bargains! But above all, we're going to try not to get lost!"

Knowing laughter rippled through the crowd and Thaziit laughed the loudest. Valerian, still perusing the map, felt the hairs on the back of his neck prickle, as if he were being watched. He spun around, staring through the visor of his helmet, but he saw nothing.

"So!" the ebullient guide was saying. "Everybody needs to keep together right behind their guide, whose name is…?" He spread an arm expectantly and held his other hand to an ear completely enveloped by the brightly striped turban.

"Thaziit!" the tourists replied in unison, exchanging smiles and chuckles.

"Glad to see that *some* of you are paying attention," Thaziit approved, glancing around meaningfully at others whose eyes were fixed on their gauntlets or busy reading the map—like Valerian. Again, there came the friendly ripple of laughter that conveyed that this was a group of happy people filled with anticipation.

"You can activate your systems… *now!*"

Valerian, along with everyone else, hit the button in the middle of his belt buckle. Light streaked and sparkled across his field of vision as he observed Thaziit, the tourists, and the walls that enclosed the empty Big Market compound.

Then, suddenly, the guide, the tourists, and Valerian appeared to be surrounded by a staggering variety of stalls, run by vendors who seemed to represent every alien species Valerian knew.

A murmur of delighted amazement rippled through the crowd of bargain-hungry tourists.

"Welcome to Big Market!" announced Thaziit, and grinned.

Laureline sat with her cheek pressed to the grimy window of Major Gibson's bus. The view was of the massive red wall that delineated the space of Big Market, but she didn't see the stone barrier, and she wasn't thinking about shopping.

She wasn't even thinking of the mission right at this moment, which was completely out of character for her.

She was thinking instead about what Valerian had said, and wondering if her next step after this mission would be to kiss him on the lips, or kick him… elsewhere.

If you're joking, Valerian…

The smart money would be on that, she mused. Laureline knew, after serving beside him for two years, that there was much more to the young major than met the eye. She was well aware that despite his antics, he took his position very seriously and with a great deal of respect. He was courageous, dedicated to his job, and more intelligent than his frequent goofiness would let on to those who didn't know him well.

But there were also things that he didn't take seriously or with respect, and the sort of traditions and rituals that Laureline valued deeply were among that number. Relationships for him were so fleeting and insubstantial that Laureline didn't think she could even grace them with that name. *Flings*, she thought, *would be a better word*.

Not that Valerian was cruel or manipulative; despite his nigh-constant wheedling, he never had—and never would—try to force himself on or bully any woman. Most girls were more than pleased with his attention. As for the sergeant and the major, their flirting was established, familiar, and Laureline had to admit, she always enjoyed it as much as he did.

Until today.

His proposal, if it truly was such, had come absolutely out of the blue, and she had no idea how to respond to it. He knew she was old-fashioned and that, despite her occasional aloofness, a false proposal would wound her deeply. Not to mention she'd find a way to show him in no uncertain terms what a terribly bad idea that would be.

So that meant...

Laureline lowered her face into her palm for a moment. A fake proposal would be awful, but a serious one just might be worse.

She sighed and looked out on the desert once more. They had almost reached the eastern gate of the empty Big Market compound, and ahead she could glimpse the shape of a water tower—their initial objective. With the ability to seemingly effortlessly compartmentalize things that so often exasperated her partner, Laureline folded the whole married-to-Valerian idea into a tidy little box, closed the flaps on it, tied it up neatly, and put it into a distant corner of her brain.

Time enough for that later, as she had told Valerian. Right now, her part of their mission was about to begin.

The bus lurched to a halt at the base of the tower. Laureline smoothed her dress, fluffed her hair, put on a vacuous smile, and flounced out of the bus. She walked toward the tower, shielding her eyes with one hand as she waved cheerily with the other.

There was a single figure standing guard at the watchtower: a Siirt who peered down at them anxiously, its gaze flitting from Laureline to a few of Gibson's people, draped in ponchos, as they too climbed off the bus.

The half-humanoid, half-reptilian Siirts were a gentle people, if rather low on the intelligence scale. They were employed by the Big Market Corporation as guards and police, but generally were too easily distracted and too friendly to be terribly effective. Laureline knew that many of the merchants who wanted reliable security simply hired their own—like Igon Siruss. Siirts loved meeting new people, and their culture was based on a philosophy called *Unbugalia*, which essentially meant: "The more happy people there are, the greater the happiness." The throngs coming to Big Market, Laureline mused, doubtless made these rather kooky beings ecstatic. They didn't see any of the profit, though. Their species had nothing resembling "currency." As a result, it was difficult to keep them employed.

On the tower, a yellow skinned Siirt guard watched Laureline getting out of the bus. His gaze moved to the men in ponchos following her. He lifted a three-fingered hand—to wave, Laureline thought. He did precisely that, but then a thought seemed to occur to him, and he placed his hands down on the very impressive rapid-fire weapon standing beside him and moved it in their direction.

CHAPTER FIVE

Laureline smiled brightly and shouted up at the anxious Siirt, "Hi there! No need for that! I know, no idling here. Not to worry, we won't be long!"

Her friendly greeting made him hesitate. She reached behind her, grasped her weapon, and took aim at the guard. A shockwave emerged from the barrel of the gun that securely planted a small dart in the Siirt's scrawny bare chest.

At the same instant, the men removed their ponchos, revealing bulky hardware strapped to their bodies. Captain Zito—though Laureline had heard him called "Captain Z" from time to time by his team—stood beside her, carrying a flat computer with a wide screen. Swiftly Laureline detached part of her weapon and flipped it onto the screen's back. Zito turned to the left, and then the right.

The Siirt in the watch tower mirrored his movement.

"Okay," said Zito, "I've got control of our skinny friend here. We'll be able to see everything he can."

Laureline had seen this before, of course, but she could never quite suppress a flicker of amusement whenever a Con-Dart was utilized not just to render the enemy harmless, but also to, essentially, conscript him. How efficient the resulting "forced friendly" actually turned out to be was dependent on two factors—how easy the target was to manipulate, and how proficient his controller was.

Siirts, not being the sharpest knives in the drawer, were extremely malleable, and Captain Z was clearly an old hand at this. Laureline suspected that the captain was an old hand at a lot of things, and she wondered why he wasn't a higher ranking officer. She looked at the sharp face, the determined jaw, and cool eyes and decided she didn't really need to know.

Laureline turned her attention to the target, impressed with how smoothly—well, comparatively smoothly—the gangly Kirian native returned to his weapon and, as far as anyone watching was concerned, resumed his loyal watch over the compound.

"Let's go," Captain Z ordered, and the team returned to the bus.

A few moments later, they had rejoined Major Gibson. He and his men stood around the steel door of the eastern gate. A soldier was scanning the door as Laureline jumped off the bus, frowning as he examined the readout.

"It's as we expected—the doorframe is booby-trapped all the way around, sir," he reported.

Gibson nodded. He turned to Laureline, handing her a large, long carrying case, and then checked his watch.

"Drop in twelve minutes, Sergeant," Gibson said.

Laureline nodded. The taciturn, focused Zito stood next to her as the rest of Gibson's team pressed flat against the rough red stone of the outer wall, and Laureline glanced over at his screen.

Zito was now seeing through the eyes of the puppet Siirt

up on the watchtower, who was gazing at the compound on the other side of the wall. Laureline smothered a grin, an expression that wasn't really appropriate at this tense moment, as she watched tourists in virtual reality gear amble about haphazardly, pointing at marvels invisible to her gaze and picking up things that weren't there. It looked like some kind of amateur improvisational theater performance.

"Adjusting view," Zito informed the group. He turned the dial. As Laureline continued to watch the Siirt-Cam, the actual desert inside the stone walls disappeared, to be replaced by the busy consumer paradise and colorful chaos of Big Market.

"Excellent," Gibson approved. "Activate the guard's monitoring camera and locate Major Valerian."

"Aye, sir," Zito replied promptly. The point of view shifted as the Siirt's head turned to regard the controls. He—and now Zito—were seeing through the point of view of a camera drone the size of a small bird, which rose, hovered, darting about, then dove downward, zipping through the unreal souk in search of Valerian.

One of the soldiers stepped forward and marked the outlines of a rectangle on the enormous metal of the gate's door with a laser. With a quick tap of a button, the rectangular portion of the iron barrier vanished, becoming a human-sized doorway.

"Time for you to go shopping," Gibson said.

Laureline nodded. She donned the helmet and gloves two of the soldiers held out to her. Gripping the carrying case she had been given earlier, she slipped through the door.

And then she, like Valerian, was in Big Market.

* * *

Big Market, Valerian thought, was overwhelming. He had no idea how anyone could focus long enough to purchase anything. It filled the vast enclosure to overflowing with nearly a million merchant stalls and millions of things one could purchase. He was presently on the Market's main street, open to the sunlight, but a quick glance around revealed that there were not just myriad shops, there were myriad levels. A lift zipped by to one side, ferrying beaming customers to new sights.

The cacophony of aliens of every description hawking things that Valerian couldn't even imagine filled his ears. Here, under a carved stone arch, a pale humanoid with an elongated head was selling small clouds, securely fastened by small rope lassos about their forms. A little storm was gathering inside one of them as Valerian passed.

A large blue alien with tiny eyes on large stalks stood wearing very human-looking clothes upon which were affixed an inordinate number of buttons. His entire shop, in fact, appeared to consist of nothing *but* buttons, and as Valerian passed, the merchant waved to him and held up a small button that had an image of Earth on it. Valerian felt an unexpected tug; most of his youth had been spent on Earth, but he hadn't been back in years. If anyplace was home to him now, it was the *Intruder*.

"Monoliths!" shouted a merchant, an alien about three feet tall, squat, with eyes the size of Valerian's fists on either side of his head and a shock of wildly frizzy hair. "Get your monoliths here!"

Valerian frowned, seeing about a dozen solid black rectangles propped up against a wall. At first glance they were just slabs, but he found his gaze being held by them.

He felt oddly drawn to them, wondering what it would feel like to touch them.

Abruptly Valerian shook his head, snapping out of it. He had a job to do.

The flow of the tourist group ferried Valerian to the vicinity of a middle-aged couple dressed in clothing that managed to be both garish and frumpy. Their faces were largely obscured by their helmets, but the woman's shocking candy-red hair peeked out from beneath. Valerian thought he could imagine their appearances just fine judging simply by their body language.

And their conversation.

"Just think, baby!" the woman gushed. She was practically vibrating with the thrill of the hunt. "A million stores! Let's buy a few trinkets!"

"We discussed this," the man began to protest. "You said you just wanted to see it!"

"Well, yes, but we'll need *something* to remember the experience by, won't we?" Her voice was plaintive.

The man sighed. "All right, honey, but only stuff we can carry, okay?" He wagged his finger at her.

"Deal!" she replied. She actually clapped her hands and skipped before letting out an excited squeal and hugging her husband. Beneath the visor, the man gave a broad, happy grin. Valerian found himself smiling as well.

Thaziit turned to face his group, walking backwards with practiced ease as he said, "Remember that the sensors embedded in your equipment enable you to be fully present in Big Market and have the total experience. You can touch objects, the walls…"

Not looking where he was reaching, Thaziit's hand

closed on the enormous proboscis of an alien merchant with tiny eyes and two sets of arms. One of his four hands came up to slap Thaziit's.

"Watch it, buddy!"

"Oops! Sorry!" Thaziit apologized. The alien muttered at him and rearranged the items on his table, still glaring. The items on his table glared, too.

Thaziit took off his glove and held it over his head, so everyone could see. "As I was saying, you can touch objects in Big Market if you have your gloves on. But if you remove your sensors, you will lose contact and all sense of touch." He reached out, and this time his hand went completely through the alien's head. It sputtered in annoyance, clearly fed up with the annoying human guide.

"Then you'll lose the chance of snapping up bargains! So keep your equipment on at all times!"

The group headed deeper into the market. Thaziit slowed, allowing some time for everyone to wander a bit and peruse tables and carpet displays more carefully. Valerian pretended to show interest in an ancient piece of furniture that the vendor assured him "every household needed," then, once he was certain Thaziit's attention was on helping another tourist, he fell back and melted into the crowd.

He slipped discreetly down a narrow street, checking the street and vendor numbers he'd seen on the map. Further away from the center area, the real estate grew distinctly seedier. Instead of large, airy plazas with statuary, fountains, and awnings, the architecture went up—and down, into the earth—instead of out, and the shops were smaller and darker, becoming not much more than a warren of holes.

Valerian hastened down seven sets of stairs, then he turned into another street, slowing as he approached the appointed site. Light filtered down from a series of grates overhead, both from artificial illumination and from some round, glowing, floating creatures harnessed for just this purpose. He passed a tentacled being juggling about twenty bright metallic balls, and then found himself a few shops away from Igon Siruss's "antique store."

Slightly amused, Valerian thought it was completely nondescript, looking like any one of the thousand other stores he'd passed. Modest columns rose on either side of the door, and an arched entrance with a red curtain shielded the interior. There was nothing special about it— if you excluded the pair of heavily armed Kodhar'Khans flanking the door and the leashed Pit-Ghors that sat beside them.

The Kodhar'Khans were slender, a little taller than Valerian. They did not look nearly as imposing as Igon Siruss, but they were clearly members of the same species; Valerian made note of the three sets of nostrils.

They wore dark orange hoods and were heavily armed, but otherwise did not look particularly dangerous. Valerian decided that Laureline was probably overestimating their aggressiveness. Which was kind of sweet.

The Pit-Ghors, however… These were two of the larger ones Valerian had ever seen. He regarded them with healthy appreciation. They were four-legged and very solidly built, reptilian, red in color. Their heads were enormous, their sharp-toothed mouths equally large, and they seemed to be obedient.

For now.

Valerian continued at a reasonable pace, regarding the store and the other shops on the street with a casual *oh hey I'm just looking* amble, then turned left down another street as if looking for more shops.

Sergeant Cooper was waiting for him. Valerian had never met the sergeant, but he decided that if he ever wanted to get into a bar brawl, it wouldn't be with this man. Not so much because he was larger or more muscular, or even that he looked particularly scary, but because there was just something about the way he held himself that promised that such an encounter would end badly.

Cooper eyed the floral shirt with distaste. Valerian found that highly amusing, considering that Cooper, who was also attempting to blend in, wore a floppy, shapeless hat and a bulky necklace that was of obviously cheap craftsmanship.

"Major Valerian," Valerian introduced himself.

"Sergeant Cooper," the man replied, nodding at him. He handed a gun to Valerian, who inspected it while Cooper pulled the cover off a rectangular metal box that had the words "The Sleeve" written on it. The metal was dinged, and the brown paint on it grimy. It had seen better days.

"Put this on," instructed Cooper. With the weapon gripped in his hand, Valerian thrust his right arm into the Sleeve up to the shoulder. Cooper fastened it securely over his arm. The Sleeve swallowed Valerian's lower arm, hand, and weapon.

"Ever used one of these before?"

"Nope," Valerian said. He hadn't had many missions involving virtual reality. He preferred his reality to be… well… real.

"Enter your genetic code on the front keypad, here,"

Cooper instructed. "To come back, you enter your code on the back keypad here. Clear?"

"Crystal," Valerian replied.

Cooper reached into a pocket of his outlandish garb and brought out a small canister. "This will let you infiltrate the VR scenario completely unnoticed."

"I'll be invisible?"

"In the virtual world of Big Market, yes. Here in the compound… not in the slightest."

"Got it."

Cooper spritzed him twice with the concoction. It had a faint floral scent. *They won't see me, but they'll get a lovely whiff of springtime freshness,* Valerian thought, amused. He looked down at himself and grinned. Through the visor, in this virtual world, he now couldn't even see himself. It was disorienting, to say the least, but kind of fun.

"Good luck," Cooper said.

Valerian moved to the front of the store and took up position.

He didn't have to wait long.

CHAPTER SIX

Two tall, willowy humanoid figures approached the storefront. They wore gloves and hoods and kept their heads ducked down, so Valerian couldn't get a glimpse of their faces. They strode right up to the store, making no pretense at being ordinary tourists out for a day's shopping. Parting the hanging red curtain, they stepped inside. A Pit-Ghor growled at them, but one of the guards reprimanded it and yanked on the creature's chain. It subsided, unhappy but obedient.

Valerian was forced to follow the two customers almost immediately, lest further movement of the curtain at the entrance betray him. Again, the Pit-Ghor reacted, baring its ugly teeth.

"Fluffy, what's with you today?" the Kodhar'Khan guard said, glaring at the animal.

"I told you," the other one replied, "he needs more exercise. Big healthy boy like him. Don't you, Fluffy? Huh?"

The creature wiggled happily at the guard's tone of voice.

"I give him enough exercise," the first guard said, "but every time I ask *you* to take him out…"

While they were bickering and both Pit-Ghors were

staring directly at him, Valerian slipped inside. He spared only the barest glance for his surroundings, noting exits, entrances, and the locations of civilians, of which there were only a few. Fortunately for them, they appeared to be getting ready to leave.

The store was piled high with a variety of bizarre-looking antiques—books, lanterns, and candles, rolled-up carpets, carvings, jewelry, hats and headdresses, pipes of all varieties, animal saddles—but Valerian's attention was focused on the two newcomers and the back room they were heading for.

Igon Siruss stood there, a massive presence, clearly expecting them. Behind him, arms folded across his large, muscular chest, stood a tall Kodhar'Khan in the prime of his life. He wore armor on his shoulders and down one arm. He had stripes on his bare skin and head, and a vicious scar from a previous fight that had taken his right eye and cut a line down his face. Fit and lithe where his father was obese and trundling, "Junior" nevertheless bore a strong resemblance to him.

Okay, so he probably *hadn't* been picked on at Kodhar'Khan school. If anything, Valerian was willing to bet Junior had instigated any bullying that had taken place.

"Hey, Tsûuri! Good to see you again!" Igon boomed. His jovial voice was several octaves below a human's speaking tones, and it all but rumbled along Valerian's bones. One of Igon's guards held the door open for the hooded pair to enter. Moving quietly, and wishing he didn't smell quite so sunshine-fresh, Valerian entered hard on the strangers' heels. The closing door missed him by an inch.

70

The two newcomers halted at the sight of no fewer than six guards standing against the walls of the room. Valerian's gaze flickered over the slender shapes, noting their locations and their weapons. He was beginning to revise his estimate of their species.

"Please, sit down!" Igon invited. He had moved to stand behind a large table. There was one gargantuan seat to accommodate his enormous behind, and two ordinary-sized chairs at the front of the table. His "guests" would be forced to sit with their backs to the door—a psychologically vulnerable position. The newcomers exchanged glances, and slowly sank down into the proffered chairs.

The one Siruss had addressed as Tsûuri asked, coldly, "Do you have what we asked for?"

"Yeah, sure, of course," Siruss replied genially, "but I have to tell you, it was a toughie." He shook his grotesquely large head. "I lost an awful lot of personnel getting it for you."

He nodded to one of the guards, who placed a rectangular metal box on the table. The front end was not solid, but grated, and Valerian heard a slight shuffling sound from inside.

Then a small creature pressed its face to the bars.

Valerian started. *It looks a lot like the pet the princess in my dream had*, Valerian thought. Where had that weird dream come from? Alex's "answer" had raised more questions than it had answered.

The creature's eyes widened and it squealed gleefully, wriggling in excitement and extending a small forepaw through the bars.

"We will pay you!" cried Tsûuri. His voice trembled with emotion.

"I'm sure you will," Igon said, with false kindness. "You're honest, valiant people." One hand went to his chin as he added, "But this... thing... is priceless. What can you give me in exchange that could really be worth giving this up?"

Tsûuri hesitated. Then he took a small white spherical object out of a pouch at his side.

Her pale fingers cupping radiant spheres and bathing her perfect face with them. Fishermen, harvesting pearls in tiny nets, bringing them joyfully to shore—

Valerian angrily wrenched himself out of the dream recollection.

Tsûuri held the object in his gloved fingers for a moment, then set it down in front of Igon. The "antiques dealer" delicately picked it up in one great hand. The other reached for a large magnifying glass lying on the table. Siruss peered at the pearl through the lens, which made his tiny, beady eye appear enormous.

"Amazing!" he murmured. His voice was hushed and filled with awe, and he was obviously forgetting the first rule of haggling: don't seem impressed. That spoke volumes to Valerian. His gaze fell again on the box on the table, and the small creature within. What the hell *was* this animal? And why were these pearls so valuable?

Siruss continued to gaze at the small white object, compounding his violation of the first rule of haggling. "I never thought I'd see one in my lifetime!"

The unknown alien snatched it deftly from the other's large palm.

"You'll have hundreds of them," he promised Siruss. "Just as soon as you give us what we came for."

Igon regarded him with mock sorrow. "Ah, now... that's where I have a slight problem, my friend. You see, I've been thinking. I'm a big fan of cutting out the middleman." He indicated the pearl Tsûuri held.

"If you're going to knock out copies of this baby for me... why shouldn't I do it for myself?"

He smiled. It was ugly, cruel, and intelligent, and Valerian abruptly hated him with an intensity that surprised him.

Too late, the slender aliens realized their mistake.

Both leaped to their feet, drawing weapons, but Igon's six mercenaries had beaten them to it. While everybody leveled their gun at everybody else, Valerian slipped behind the Kodhar'Khan crime lord.

"Easy, my little lambs!" soothed Igon.

A female voice snapped, "We absolutely *need* this converter!" Now she, too, had broken the first rule of haggling. "You told us you could help! You *know* we are fighting for a noble cause!"

"I know," Igon said solemnly. "I'm fighting for a noble cause, too." He grinned. "Mine. Here's the deal."

Igon casually pulled a gun and pointed it at the female. *Time to end this.* Valerian lifted his visor so he could see himself again, and began to type in the code at the end of his Sleeve.

"I get the converter and this pearl," Siruss was saying. "You get to stay alive. How about it? A good deal, right?" He guffawed at his own feeble humor, then sobered. His voice was utterly without warmth as he said, "You have ten seconds to accept."

He began a countdown as the muzzle of his gun split in two, with each muzzle curving away, as if with a life of its own, to point at each of the aliens.

"Five, four…"

Valerian quickly punched the last figures of the code into the keypad.

"Three…"

Valerian flipped down the visor—

"Two…"

—and saw his arm manifest in the virtual world as he jabbed his gun into the smuggler's neck.

Igon abruptly ceased the countdown, but his gun did not waver. Nor did those of the mysterious aliens. Those of Siruss's guards, however, immediately turned to take aim at Valerian. Or at his Sleeve-encased arm, at least.

"Federal Agent Valerian," he introduced himself. "Sorry to interrupt this great deal, but I'm *also* here for a noble cause called the *law*!"

The unknown aliens flipped back their hoods—and it was all Valerian could do not to gasp.

Pale, luminous skin. Eyes as blue, bluer than the sky. Delicate features, now drawn in anger and fear, their foreheads black with it. The beautiful faces did not carry such expressions comfortably.

Pearls, came a thought, drifting and easy as a summer zephyr. *They are called… Pearls.*

"Wrong place, my friend," drawled Igon confidently. "There is no law around here."

"There is law wherever I am," Valerian stated with surety. Even as he spoke, though, his gaze drifted back to the aliens. "Haven't I seen you guys somewhere before?"

The alien named Tsûuri—*the Pearl*, Valerian thought—looked very ill at ease.

"Hey," grunted Igon, "I'm not running a tea room here. What do you want from me, Mr. Law?"

"Igon Siruss," Valerian stated, "you stand accused of stealing a Mül converter belonging to the Human Federation. But before I drag your sorry ass in, I've got to recover stolen property."

The moment stretched out in silence. No one moved.

Valerian continued to press the muzzle of his gun to Igon's neck. The Pearls kept their weapons trained on the guards, looking increasingly panicked.

"Valerian," came a familiar and welcome female voice in his ear, "I'll be on your right, three o'clock, three feet away."

He smiled, slightly. "Got it."

"Huh?" Igon said. "What do you mean?"

"You," Valerian retorted, pressing the muzzle even more firmly into the thick neck, "don't move."

A moment later, as if by magic, a large carrying case appeared at Valerian's right—at three o'clock, three feet away.

Laureline.

"Now," said Valerian to Igon, "take it nice and easy and put the critter's carrier into this box." Even before he spoke, Valerian saw growing horror on Igon's face as it dawned on him that he was about to A) lose the converter, B) get arrested, and C) could do nothing to prevent either misfortune.

"That converter is ours," blurted Tsûuri suddenly. Fear and determination mingled on his face. "We are prepared to buy it back. Name your price!"

"I'll double it!" yelped Igon.

Despite the illogical, bizarre, but very real dream connection Valerian had with the Pearls and the critter, he shrugged slightly. Whatever was going on here was no concern of his; he had his orders.

"Sorry, guys, I'm not into sharing. Move it!"

Slowly, reluctantly, looking almost as if he wanted to cry, the smuggler placed the converter into Laureline's case.

Gibson's voice spoke into Valerian's ear. "Guys, move on, now."

"Converter in the box," said Valerian to the listening Gibson.

"Copy," said Laureline's disembodied voice beside Valerian.

Valerian kept his weapon trained on the smuggler. A moment later, Gibson's voice spoke in his ear. "Good job, Sergeant. Undetected. Back to base."

"Affirmative," Laureline's voice replied promptly. "Valerian? We're good. Get out of there."

"I'm on my way," Valerian responded. He hesitated, then grabbed the pearl from the table. It, too, was evidence. Igon watched, helpless, fuming.

"I'll find you, Federal Agent Valerian," he sputtered, almost choking on his rage. "Wherever you are in the universe, I'll find you! And I will *kill* you!"

Valerian grinned. "Good luck with that!"

He was done with this. The whole thing with the Pearls was too weird for him to handle right now, his arm was itching inside the encasing Sleeve, and Laureline still owed him an answer to his question.

Keeping the Sleeve-hidden gun trained on Igon, Valerian slowly moved around the table back toward the door, punching the code into the rear keypad of the Sleeve as Cooper had instructed.

The Sleeve should have disappeared.

It did not.

Valerian glanced at the guards at the door, who were staring in utter confusion as a disembodied arm holding a gun floated toward them.

"Tell your guards to step aside," Valerian ordered. Igon, still seething, did not obey immediately. "*Now*. Or not. I think removing your head would do wonders for your looks."

Igon growled in anger, sounding almost exactly like the angry Pit-Ghor straining at its leash. "Let him pass," he snarled, finally.

The Kodhar'Khan guards obeyed reluctantly, taking a few steps backwards. So did one of the Pit-Ghors, though it snarled.

The Pit-Ghor named Fluffy, however, wasn't as well trained.

Just as Valerian had stepped through the curtain, out into the street and had almost finished a second attempt at keying in the code, the animal gave a great bellow of frustration and lunged after him so violently the leash snapped.

Its massive jaws closed on the enticing floating metal box that covered Valerian's arm.

"Ahhhh!" Valerian shouted. "Bad dog! *Bad dog!*"

The Sleeve was not just a piece of cutting-edge technology, it was also made of very strong metal, so Valerian's arm was not in danger of being severed in a single bite. But the beast had put the rest of him in jeopardy. He tried to turn the cumbersome Sleeve against the animal, squeezing the gun's trigger.

The sound of gunfire was like a spark of flame to an old-fashioned powder keg. Suddenly everyone was firing. Bullets whizzed past Valerian, and he threw himself into an odd, contorting dance so they wouldn't be able to guess where his invisible body was.

The sound of combat was coming from inside, too, and out of the corner of his eye, as he continued to attempt to detach a ravening Pit-Ghor from his arm, Valerian saw that the two Pearls had taken advantage of the chaos to flee.

The female glanced over her shoulder as they ran down the street, and even in the midst of the madness Valerian was struck by her ethereal beauty and wondered again just what the hell was going on.

"Valerian's in trouble!" Laureline's voice, in his ear. Valerian dropped to the ground, flailing wildly, trying to dislodge the monster-dog.

"Your mission takes priority," Gibson replied. "Keep going. Cooper? Cover him!"

Finally, with a well-placed kick to the Pit-Ghor's belly, Valerian managed to wrest free. Dodging the hail of bullets, he raced around the back of Igon's shop to join Cooper.

Cooper had already "armored up," wearing two Sleeves and carrying a machine gun in each hand.

"The keypad's broken!" shouted Valerian. "I can't get my arm back."

No sooner had he gotten the words out than Igon's goons came pelting around the corner after him, guns blazing.

"Get back to Gibson!" Cooper shouted. "I'll cover you!"

Valerian obeyed, sprinting off as fast as he could while Cooper opened fire and the guards returned it.

He wanted to believe that Cooper—he who would win a bar fight against anyone, any size, any time— would survive the attack. He had two machine guns and military experience.

But the Kodhar'Khans had guns, too, and they had more of them.

Cooper, if he fell, would do so in the line of duty.

Valerian had experienced a plethora of bizarre things in his twenty-seven years. But this situation was right up there in the top few. He was in one world, and his arm was in another, and the result was comical and potentially deadly chaos.

His body, firmly grounded in the "real" world, was invisible and untouchable thanks to Cooper's spray earlier. He wasn't about to bump into anybody or anything in Big Market other than tourists—or, he amended, real bodyguards and those they guarded. But his Sleeved arm, trapped in the virtual part of the current reality, was completely uncooperative. Try as he might, that damned exposed arm kept smacking unreal heads, catching on non-existent merchandise, and in general putting the rest of the real body at high risk.

Normally Valerian was on good terms with his appendages, but not today.

Definitely not today.

CHAPTER SEVEN

Lumwak's duty shift at Siruss's "shop" was not due to begin for over an hour, and he was permitting himself a much-needed break. The pay was good, excellent in fact, but Lumwak could not help but notice the high attrition rate of the crime lord's "staff."

Lumwak considered himself a bit of a philosopher—something unusual among the Kodhar'Khans. And after three years of working for Igon here in Big Market, he had formed a philosophy about it. He leaned back in the café seat, sipping something sludgy and potent and wonderful while his enormous gun—which ensured his privacy; few wanted to chitchat with someone who had his weapon out and obvious—lay on the table within easy reach, and examined his thoughts as he watched the tourists bustle and buy.

There were three kinds of people who came to Big Market per Lumwak's philosophy. One was the original, intended customer base: tourists, with too much money and too much room in their homes, who wanted the delight of visiting a thousand worlds without the hassle of, well, actually *visiting* a thousand worlds.

The second group was composed of those who made

money off the first group. This group had subsets. The first was the merchants, who supplied the goods to the eager, greedy tourists. The second was comprised of those who preyed on them—pickpockets, muggers, that sort of riffraff.

The third group was physically located in Big Market—and this made Lumwak chuckle to himself, because "physically" was a relative term—but had little or nothing to do with the business conducted within the confines of the compound. His employer was one such member of this group. Oh, Igon sold antiques, yes, and made a respectable income through the legitimate business. But his primary business was smuggling, and at that, he excelled.

Lumwak took another contented sip, musing on the concept of what was real, and what was not. Was this drink real? This café? In a manner of speaking, yes, but one could make the argument that it wasn't.

Was *he* real? What about the theory of the soul, of—

An alert began to beep on the small screen he wore around one wrist. Reality asserted itself quite solidly as the words flashed up with the urgent order: *Seek and destroy. Top priority. Target's photograph follows.*

On the tiny screen, a photo of a humanoid Sleeve appeared. The Sleeve presumably concealed a hand with fingers—probably five, or fewer—curled around a gun pressed to the throat of Lumwak's employer. Lumwak recognized the angle—this image had been taken from Security Camera 4A in the boss's back room.

He looked up just in time to see the selfsame Sleeve float down the street in front of him.

Lumwak was a philosopher. And his overriding philosophy was entirely centered around what was best for Lumwak. He fully intended to be the one to slow this running Sleeve—and the person attached to it—way, way down.

He grabbed his weapon with both hands, sprang to his feet, and took off after the disembodied Sleeve.

Valerian was fit, but he had been running at top speed—as top a speed as he could reach while his Sleeve-encased arm slammed into unwitting merchants and knocked over virtual merchandise—and he really hoped that he had shaken his pursuers. He risked a glance over his shoulder. There was no sign of the Kodhar'Khan thugs. Panting, but still moving, he said, "I think I lost them!"

"Good," came Laureline's voice.

Valerian allowed himself a smile. He glanced down at himself, and the smile faded—because he *could* glance down at himself. The spray was wearing off, and parts of his body were now becoming visible.

He swore.

"What was that?" Laureline again, a hint of humor in her voice. "I didn't quite copy."

He looked up from the sobering sight of his left foot, right kneecap, and three of the fingers of his left hand and his heart kicked.

One of Igon's guards was in hot pursuit—and carrying an enormous weapon. Valerian knew exactly what it did, and all of a sudden he felt up to running at top speed again. But even as he turned to flee, the guard opened fire.

Valerian was struck, and he knew he was about to go down.

The weapon was specific and, in a way, merciful. Law enforcement often used it to bring down criminals, enabling a speedy capture that ensured little to no harm befell either party. But it would be no mercy to Valerian. Igon Siruss obviously preferred him alive... and that was not a good thought.

It fired thousands of steel ball bearings at the target—the cumulative weight of which would eventually cause the unfortunate target to slow and eventually collapse, unable to move. Valerian knew he was lucky. The goon could only target the Sleeve, not his entire body.

But it proved to be enough to get the job done.

Abruptly, his arm felt as though it weighed a metric ton. He kept running, stubbornly, doggedly. At first he was able to lift the arm on its own, then he had to hold it up with his good hand, and, finally, his body surrendered. His weighted arm plunged down to the ground, and he followed, lying flat and gasping as he struggled to lift the unliftable.

The guard approached, taking his time. *Well, why should he rush, I'm not going anywhere,* Valerian thought with morbid humor.

"You know," the bodyguard said affably, his deep, growling voice almost pleasant, "the way this weapon functions can serve as a metaphor. One of these tiny metal spheres would be completely unnoticeable. A few hundred will slow you down. A few thousand—well, now, here we are, aren't we? The right number will slow anything. Which illustrates the point that so often, when we stand alone, we cannot succeed. When several join together, however, that's an entirely different story."

Valerian couldn't believe the bodyguard was taking the

time to spout such platitudes. Stuck where he was, unable to move, he imagined he was a captive audience in all senses of the word. Maybe that was why. Probably no one else listened to this guy.

But even as Valerian mused, the guard had given him an idea. For all his words about how one alone couldn't succeed... the guard was trying to take him by himself.

In the time it took for Igon's goon to meander toward him, Valerian had already spotted a means of escape. A grate a few inches away opened to something below. He didn't know what, and right now, he didn't care. Slowly, both to not attract notice and, well, because he couldn't move quickly even if he had wanted to, Valerian forced his Sleeved arm over the grate.

Then, with an effort that made him grunt and the sweat pop out afresh on his forehead, he lifted the Sleeve with his other arm as high as he could, and then let it fall.

"Perhaps my friend, had you not been acting alone, you and I would not now be—*hey*!"

For the briefest of instants, as his superweighted arm smashed through the grate, Valerian allowed himself to snicker in triumph. But, too late, he realized that not only did the Sleeve pull him down to the next level—it took him through the next level.

And the next... and the next...

Crash.

Crash.

Crash.

By the fourth floor, Valerian had figured out that he needed to align the rest of his plunging body with the implacably weighted Sleeve arm. By the fourteenth, he had almost mastered the position. But by the time he landed hard on the twentieth, and had realized, somewhat to his surprise, that he wasn't going to be treated by a twenty-first floor awaiting him, he was more than grateful that the unexpected and painful ride had come to a halt—jarring though that halt had been.

Valerian caught his breath and looked around. Still slightly addled from the twenty-story-floor-smashing spree, he tried to orient himself and get his bearings. Which, Valerian discovered, was kind of hard to do when you were in the middle of a virtual reality toy store, which in itself was a whole other world.

He felt positively bombarded by color. Swirls of purple, blue, green, fuchsia, bright yellow, orange, and every single combination of color therein assaulted his eyes. Clothing that he assumed to be costumes of some sort hung on a rack on one wall. Mimic masks, which took a scan of one's face and turned it into a variety of alien faces, were piled on another shelf. A floating scooter of some sort hummed along six feet over his head. Figurines of various galactic heroes cluttered one wall, while toy weapons were stacked up against another. Games, balls, spaceships, candy, you name it, if it appealed to anyone under the age of ten—and, he had to confess while looking at some of the figurines, a little over ten—it was here in rainbow-vomit glory.

His dizzy gaze and bemused brain were both sharply redirected when something soft, squishy, and foul-smelling landed on his visor with a *plop*.

A sound that was unmistakably alien, and also unmistakably giggling, reached his ears as he wiped it off, wrinkling his nose at the stench. It was, lamentably, exactly the substance he had suspected.

He turned to regard the small Da child, who gazed at him, still giggling. He looked like a toy, too, about two feet tall, round, soft, and peachy-pink. His eyes were very tiny, as was his mouth, and there was no noticeable nose. He wore a yellow hat, and orange and yellow overalls. His three-fingered hands were closed about a bright orange and red toy gun. It operated, on a much simpler scale, the same way as the Mül converter did. You put something in the top, and it came out the barrel of the gun in large quantities.

In this the "something" was—

"I got you!" the child said triumphantly, his tiny mouth barely moving. "You're all poopy now!"

Valerian forced a smile. "Very funny," he said, wiping his hand on the floor, "but I've got something even better. Watch *this*."

Fishing inside his shorts pocket, he took out a small device. One-handed, he maneuvered the scanner. In two seconds, it had analyzed the cluster of ball bearings on his arm and reproduced one. Valerian tossed the small metallic ball to the young prankster, who caught it deftly with his mitten-like hands.

"Here you go, kid," he said, grinning. "Put this in your gun. It's way more fun."

Elated, the child did exactly that, and just in the nick of time.

Junior came barreling through the door. Almost three times as tall as the small Da, he was fast and he was angry. His small remaining eye glowed with rage, and he would be on Valerian in a heartbeat. Junior was so focused on killing Valerian with his bare hands—or at least roughing

him up pretty severely before handing him over to Pops—
that he didn't draw his weapon.

But the kid, the wonderful, marvelous, poop-gun-
toting child, turned to the intruder and gleefully opened
fire. Though much healthier looking than his father,
Junior appeared to lack Igon's sinister cunning, because
all he could do was stare in slack-jawed confusion as
thousands of tiny ball bearings sped through the air to
fasten themselves on his metal armor. He grunted, baffled,
as the weight forced him to drop to his knees.

"So long, Junior!" Valerian exclaimed cheerfully.

He hit a switch on another small piece of equipment he'd
fished out from his kit. All the ball bearings on his Sleeve,
every last one of the tiny, cursed things, flew across the
room to latch onto Junior's already laden shoulder plates.

The weight of two rounds of ball-bearing fire,
plus Junior's own weight—which had to have been
considerable—was too much for the floor. With a crack
that sounded like a groan, it gave way, and Junior dropped
down to the floor below. Valerian strained to listen and
heard the satisfying sound of another crack, and then,
more faintly, another.

After being so horribly weighted, his muscles were
quivering on the Sleeved arm, which felt like it was about
to float away. Valerian got to his feet and went to the kid,
clapping him approvingly on the shoulder.

"You're right! That was fun! Who do we shoot next?"
the child exclaimed gleefully.

"Hey now," said Valerian sagely, "there's a time for
everything, son. Don't you have homework to do?"

The child's face fell. On impulse, Valerian wiped

another stinky gob from his visor and dabbed it onto the child's face. The child gaped, then took a deep breath and let loose a mighty wail and began to sob.

"Go on. Go on home. Run to mommy. Get yourself cleaned up!"

He heard a sound behind him. Turning, Valerian looked up…

…and *up*. Before him towered a being that was obviously the same species as the poop-anointed, sobbing child. In fact, its proportions were almost identical—right down to the soft shape, large head, and tiny eyes and mouth.

Except it was seven feet larger and probably weighed as much as Junior.

Valerian felt the blood drain from his face as he blurted out, "…Mommy?"

Her tiny mouth went from the size of a fingernail to the size of Valerian's—no, Junior's—fist. It occupied the entire lower half of her face, showcasing an impressive set of sharp fangs.

From that enormous mouth came an equally enormous bellow that left Valerian's ears ringing. He wasted no time pelting out the door as fast as his legs would carry him.

CHAPTER EIGHT

The next several minutes or... however long it was, were a blur.

Igon Siruss's team was highly coordinated, restricted, apparently, only by the fact that they seemed to want to take the spatio-temporal agent alive. For now, at least. Siruss struck him as someone who could easily change his mind about such niceties.

So for now, Valerian ran. He scrambled onto the virtual representations of expensive antiques, launching his rubber-soled feet off the heads of ancient alien rulers to scrabble atop a roof. He ran across illusionary old tiles, unable to see his own body—well, most of it, anyway. He tried to judge if his single available arm was strong enough to grab onto a thick, dangling creeper and swing from one faux rooftop to another—or in one case, crash through a window right in the middle of what appeared to be a formal ceremony involving priceless dishware, which he shattered.

"It's okay," he shouted back over his shoulder, "remember, they're only virtually real dishes!"

This appeared to be of no comfort to the six-legged gray-green alien merchant, who waved four of her legs at him and grated out something blistering.

Valerian had not had a lot of time to study the map, but it had been enough to let him know this place had vertical subway cars—and where they were located. He wasn't sure exactly where he was at this point, but "up" was an excellent direction as it would be at least somewhat harder for Igon's henchmen to give chase. "Up" would also get him back to the main level, which was the only way to reach the gate and safety. He couldn't risk getting into a car—but he sure as hell could get *on* one.

And there was one of the lines, not too far ahead. No convenient car was in sight, though—not yet. "Keep the faith," Valerian muttered to himself as he kept running. And sure enough, when he was only a few strides away, he was rewarded with the sight of a car crowded with tourists, all with faces—or what served as faces—pressed to the clear sides of the car and oohing and aahing at the view.

They were not oohing and aahing thirty seconds later when Valerian leaped and clung as best he could with his own face pressed to the side of the car. They drew back, startled. Some started to laugh and one of the kids made faces at the Sleeve with both his mouths.

Valerian couldn't risk craning his neck to look around, as any movement might dislodge his tenuous grip. Nonetheless, he found the fact that he was not being fired upon an encouraging sign indeed.

He made it to the top and leaped off, threading his way through the unexpected volume of tourists. This level was obviously the equivalent of a checkout line. Bored-looking aliens and several humans wrapped up objects of all shapes and sizes. Once wrapped, each item went into a gray box bolted into the flooring.

"What's this called again? A transmitter?" came a familiar voice. Just before he high-tailed it in the other direction, Valerian recognized the distinctive voice and bright red hair of the female half of the tourist couple he'd seen earlier.

"A transmatter," the checkout person said. He was human, angular and tired-looking, with thinning hair and a forced smile. He'd probably had to repeat the words a thousand times a day. Valerian wished him well with the thousand and first.

"Oh, a trans*matter*, sorry," apologized the red-headed human female. She and her husband were among the throngs of shoppers that Laureline passed, scanning the crowd for Valerian.

"It allows any object to be sent from one world to another," the checkout person said in a monotone. "Please punch in the code you were issued with your ticket, and it'll be waiting for you safe and sound upon your return after your exciting visit to the magnificent Big Market, the premier place for galaxy-sized bargains."

The male tourist punched his code into the machine, and the object disappeared, dispatched to Earth, or Alpha, or wherever else the couple called "home."

"Amazing!" cried the woman. "And so practical!"

The man did not look as enthusiastic as his wife. His face was red and sweating beneath the visor of his yellow and black helmet. "So useless, you mean," he grumbled. "You don't even know what you'll do with the darn thing!"

"Oh, don't be such a grouch, honey! It's…" the female fumbled for a word, "…decorative. Try to be civilized for once!"

Her husband looked around. Briefly caught by the domestic drama, Laureline noticed his gaze fastened on one group of aliens, then another, then a third.

"Civilized?" he sneered arrogantly, his lip curling in barely concealed disgust. "Yeah, sure."

Major Gibson's voice sounded in Laureline's ear. It was a diversion from the unpalatable display of bigotry she'd just witnessed, but the instructions were not welcome.

"Sergeant?" Gibson snapped. "Back to base, Sergeant. Immediately."

"I can't abandon my partner out here," Laureline replied, still scanning the crowd.

"That's an order, Sergeant."

Laureline bit her lip in frustrated annoyance and concern. Her gaze traveled back to the outer wall. Reluctantly, she started heading in that direction. But as she maneuvered through the press of satisfied, and most likely broke, tourists, she asked, "Valerian? Do you copy? *Answer me!*"

"I hear you loud and clear," came a welcome voice. Laureline let out the breath she hadn't realized she had been holding.

"There you are!" she exclaimed with equal parts annoyance and relief. "It's about time! What the hell are you doing?"

Laureline headed back toward the outer wall, casually taking a gun off one of the Siirt guards so smoothly he didn't even notice.

"Shopping," came Valerian's voice.

Laureline glanced at the gun she'd just filched and thought it more likely that she was the one doing the "shopping."

"Are you safe and sound?"

There was a long pause—long enough for Laureline's heart to resume its previous position in her throat.

"...Almost!" His voice wasn't quite a squeak, but it was definitely higher than usual. The words were immediately followed by gunfire.

Without breaking stride, Laureline immediately turned around and headed back to help.

But Gibson had, of course, been monitoring her, and her abrupt U-turn had not gone unnoticed. His voice came to her, clipped and angry.

"Turn around, Sergeant. The mission takes priority. We need the converter!"

Laureline lowered her chin in a gesture of stubbornness her wayward partner would have immediately recognized, had he not been, it seemed, in dire need of rescue, and kept going.

"Agent Laureline! What are you doing?"

"I won't be a minute," she promised.

"Sergeant! Back to base—it's an order!"

Agonized, she obeyed. Valerian was close; he'd said so. But she'd be ready to spring into action if she heard anything more from him that warranted it.

"On my way!" she replied, trotting back to the wall, thinking, *I hope I just haven't made a terrible mistake...*

Valerian raced to the end of a street that led to a wall that was wonderfully, magnificently solid. Not just any wall—

the wall, the outer wall of the compound. He had never thought chunks of rocks piled atop one another could be so beautiful. He almost wanted to kiss it.

He perused the wall, wondering if he could get over it in time. It was old and weatherworn, if thick, so he could easily find footholds…

And then he thought of the oversized shoebox attached to his arm and realized it would be impossible to climb with just his right hand. He swore, colorfully. Nonetheless, he gave it a try. He had no other option. He extended his left arm and pulled himself up, scrabbling for toeholds and bracing himself with the Sleeve-encased arm while attempting to cling and release with the other. It was every bit as frustrating as he had anticipated.

Frustrating, and potentially deadly. Could he reach the gate? He turned, intending to start following the wall, to see how far away it was, and his eyes widened.

The bright sunlight that marked the end of the street was blocked by two familiar silhouettes: the tall, angular shapes of the Kodhar'Khans, and the shorter, compact, scampering ones that meant Pit-Ghors. Even as Valerian stared at them, they saw him, too. They lifted their weapons and began to fire.

Desperately, Valerian turned back to the wall, and his eye fell on something dark. A shadow… in the wall.

A hole.

A beautiful, glorious square hole where someone had removed one of the carved stone bricks. And with a little luck…

He crouched down beside it. *Yes!* He wriggled inside it. For an instant, he used his free hand to help maneuver, and immediately realized he'd lost the pearl. As if in slow motion he watched it roll back toward the entrance. Swearing under his breath, Valerian lunged forward, his fingers closing around it. He yanked his hand back, feeling hot breath on it as a Pit-Ghor's gargantuan teeth snapped a bare inch away. Just then he heard a voice next to his ear.

"Need some help?"

Laureline!

She slid down next to him and they pressed tightly together in the hole. Normally, that would be a pleasant thing, but at the moment he had something a bit more important to worry about. "Just want my arm back, thanks."

The Pit-Ghors made horrible sounds as they were unleashed and hurtled toward Valerian. He squeezed the trigger and a volley of bullets sped toward the creatures. They gave the Pit-Ghor equivalent of a whimper and fled back the way they had come.

Laureline opened a small flap in the side of the Sleeve. A bunch of fibers spilled out. She hunkered down and took hold of the jumble of wires and immediately began to repair them.

She was smiling as she said, "I suppose if you're going to ask for my hand, you'd better get your own hand back first."

He'd been peering down the various avenues of attack, but now his head whipped back to look at her, a hopeful smile on his face. "Is that a yes?"

Laureline looked up at him with those eyes and said only, "Don't move."

He attempted to oblige, but then he realized that the Pit-Ghors hadn't actually retreated. They had simply run around the block and were now charging at the object they could see—the Sleeve—from the other side. Valerian swiveled his arm and fired at them.

"Cut that out!" Laureline reprimanded. "How can I fix you if you keep moving?"

"If you don't hurry, there won't be anything left *to* fix!"

Valerian fired into the charging pack. They dropped, but then he heard an awful, final *click-click* and realized with a sinking feeling he'd just run out of ammo. If there were any more, or if the guards came after him—

"There, that's better! Don't move!" said Laureline, peering deep into the mechanical entrails of the Sleeve.

Valerian's gaze darted to each place where an attack might come. It had flickered back to the pile of dead Pit-Ghors when one of them shuddered, gnashed its sharp teeth, and started to drag itself to its feet. It shook itself, then its eyes refastened on the Sleeve, and it started to lurch toward them, gathering speed with every step.

"Faster, Laureline!" Valerian yelped. "There's one coming this way and I'm out of ammo!"

"I'm doing my best, Major!"

"Do it faster!"

Laureline threw her hands up in the air. "Want to do it yourself?"

"Laureline, dammit, they are *coming*. Put your hand back on that thing!"

Somehow that didn't come out sounding quite right.

"All right, so stop complaining and hold *still*."

Valerian's mouth was dry. He didn't mind facing danger. He minded facing danger with an empty weapon. Major Gibson's voice sounded in his ear.

"You've been detected," the major was shouting. "Split up!"

Splitting up was pretty much impossible at the moment. Valerian's heart jumped into his throat as he saw that the wounded Pit-Ghor heading for him had company. Some of his buddies had also recovered sufficiently to get to their feet and were closing in on Valerian.

"There's three of them now!" he told the major. "I can't hold them much longer."

"A few more seconds, Major," Laureline chimed in. Her fingers were flying over the snake pit of wires, and her face was still and set in concentration.

"Attack!" shouted a guard.

Laureline snapped the case closed. Her eyes blazed as she looked into Valerian's.

"You're good!"

"Thanks!"

Even as he spoke he was rolling to one side, dodging the attack from the first Pit-Ghor. It overshot him and wheeled around, lunging at the oh-so-tempting Sleeve with its fangs bared. Valerian stopped breathing as he jabbed his fingers down, punching in the numbers on the keypad.

His arm disappeared and the Pit-Ghor sprawled pathetically in the dirt, its great jaws snapping down on only air.

Valerian pulled his arm out of the Sleeve and touched it. He'd had so much of virtual reality today he felt he had to make sure it was still there. He grinned and squirmed out of the hole, then pulled off his helmet, throwing it away and shaking his hair.

"Okay? You got everything?" asked Laureline, following him and grabbing the case that contained the converter. "Can we go now?"

Without waiting for an answer, she hastened back toward the eastern gate, and Valerian was hot on her heels.

"Your cover's blown," came Gibson's voice in their ears as they ran. "Zito's friend's screen just flashed your images. Keep moving. Don't change course."

"We don't intend to," Laureline stated.

Igon Siruss did not often move swiftly, and even when he did, it was not particularly fast. His guards had notified him that they had Agent Valerian trapped, and he had come with mild rapidity. Now he stood at the end of the street, but all he saw were some unhappy-looking guards and some dead—or baffled—Pit-Ghors, who scampered around, futilely sniffing the ground.

"Sorry, boss," one of his Kodhar'Khans said.

"He made it to his world," another supplied. "We're not sure how, but he did."

Fury welled inside Igon. His first impulse was to rip the guards apart with his bare hands. He could; it was messy and he preferred to leave that sort of thing to others, but he certainly could.

But no. There would be time to deal with them later.

He had learned a human saying a long time ago: *Revenge is a dish best served cold.* Most of the time, Igon found this to be true. But not today.

Today, he wanted his revenge swiftly, speedily, and preferably bloodily.

"Bring me a Megaptor!" he roared.

CHAPTER NINE

Major Gibson gave the orders to his unit to exit the brightly colored bus and stand ready to cover the team's escape through the gate. It sounded like Major Valerian's mishap with the Sleeve had resulted in half of Big Market following in hot pursuit.

Gibson had heard nothing but good things about Sergeant Laureline—a fast thinker, a good fighter in a combat situation, a stickler for details, respectful of the chain of command. He had heard good things about Major Valerian as well, but unlike that bestowed upon the young sergeant, Valerian's praise had come with qualifiers.

A bit impulsive, some had said. *Arrogant, but damn good at what he does*, someone else had put in. *Reckless... but he's got seven medals and he's not even thirty yet*, a third party had said.

Gibson suspected that the kid hadn't even read the mission instructions. And now, Valerian, the very respectable sergeant, and the priceless converter were all on the other side of the thick red wall.

His eyes were on Zito's screen, flickering occasionally, irrationally, to the eastern gate. Then they widened as Gibson saw a large spot on the screen. Something very,

very big was chasing after the two agents—and closing the gap with sickening speed.

"The Siirts on the other watch towers have primed their weapons," Zito reported.

"Attack! Level red. I repeat, attack! Level red!" the Siirt puppet shouted.

"Cops are closing in on them, sir," Zito added.

"Cover them!" Gibson shouted.

"What do we do now?" came Laureline's voice in his ear.

There was only one answer Gibson could give them. "*Run!*"

They did.

Small dust clouds appeared behind them, stirred up by each frantically placed footfall as the two agents raced toward safety. Gunfire was erupting all around them. Valerian glanced up to see the puppet Siirt controlled by Zito was opening fire on his buddies. The poor guy looked horrified at what he was being forced to do. The gate was just up ahead. The pair hurled themselves through it at top speed, not slowing as they raced toward the bus.

Like the people conducting the mission, the vehicle that had ferried them here had also been undercover. Now, though, it was already well into abandoning its camouflage of a rickety old tour bus. The front portion, including headlights and bumper, was opening like a book, its two sides coming together to form a defensive and decidedly uninviting shield. Twin lights rolled out to either side. Similar armor was being provided to each wheel, folding over it protectively as heavy metal plates slammed down on the bus's side.

The old, grimy windows lowered, to be replaced with grates with holes precisely wide enough to admit rifle barrels spaced at militarily perfect intervals. Similar grates with longer, horizontal bars scrolled over the windshield. With a grinding whir, a turreted gun emerged and folded itself into position. Other weapons appeared along the now heavily armored military vehicle, bristling and ready for action.

Bullets spattered around Valerian and Laureline. Gulping in air as she ran, clutching the case and its precious cargo tightly to her chest, Laureline heard the sound of *something* on their heels. Despite her better instincts, she looked behind them—and lost the air she'd just inhaled in a horrified gut-punch realization.

"Faster! Now!" she cried, and she and Valerian sprinted even harder.

It was a Megaptor, and it was the stuff of nightmares.

The thing was gargantuan. Four times the size of the largest Pit-Ghor that had been snapping at Valerian's heels, it was even uglier than they were. Laureline had not imagined such a thing possible. A third of its reptilian, bulky body appeared to be its head, and at least half of its head was teeth. It seemed too big, too muscular to be as fast as it was. And yet it was closing the distance, propelled forward by giant forepaws with claws easily large enough to close about Laureline's slender frame. Black, sharp spikes jutted up from the ridge of its spine, and Laureline could only pray that it was her imagination when she could have sworn she felt the heat of its breath.

She forced herself to focus on the rapidly approaching

metal door of the Eastern Gate. The portion of it that had been opened for the day's round of tourists was far too small to permit such a monster to follow.

And she and Valerian were not alone. She heard Major Gibson give the order to fire. While Zito blazed away at the other towers attacking the pair, the remaining commandos closed ranks around Valerian and Laureline, firing at the monstrous creatures. The bus had almost completed its transformation; by the time the two dusty, sweaty, adrenaline-saturated spatio-temporal agents reached it, all that was vulnerable was the folding door through which Laureline and Valerian flung themselves.

The others were not far behind. The door closed and barricaded itself with four-inch-thick metal.

"Let's get out of here!" Gibson barked at the driver. He obeyed immediately. The plated vehicle peeled off and, exhausted and shaking with relief, Laureline and Valerian tumbled into the seats.

They'd done it! They'd—

A terrible sound reached their ears.

Laureline brought her eye to one of the small holes. The bus-turned-tank was wheeling around, and in the center of the gate's metal door, she saw not the tidy, small exit through which she and Valerian had escaped, but a jagged circle of sharp metal edges. She turned to Valerian. They stared at one another, eyes wide.

Then there was another loud, frightening sound, and the bus lurched violently.

The Megaptor was on the roof.

Laureline heard the *rat-tat-tat* of the gun mounted on the roof as it swiveled and began to fire at nearly point-blank range. But judging by the violent rocking of the bus and the terrible noise of claws tearing metal, and the angry, deep bellows of the creature, the powerful weapon was having little-to-no effect.

"Get that thing off our backs!" Gibson had to shout to be heard over the din.

The driver yanked the bus this way and that, jouncing everyone inside, but his serpentine maneuvering appeared to be as ineffective as the weapon that was still spitting bullets at the thing. Suddenly the desert landscape glimpsed through the rear windshield was filled with the horrifying sight of mottled yellow-brown skin, a single baleful golden eye, and then a mouthful of teeth bared in a furious roar.

Three of the soldiers opened fire through the bars, trying to concentrate on that awful eye and the open mouth. The Megaptor clung on with its hind legs and one of its gigantic forepaws and brought the other one back, then slammed it forward. The bars bent as easily as if they had been made of saplings. The black claws closed around one of the soldiers, piercing his body effortlessly. He screamed and jerked as blood spurted. The Megaptor hauled him out, bit at him, then tossed the body back inside as it reached in for more, murderously swiping at the men with a forepaw now dripping scarlet.

Over the screams and the firing, Valerian shouted into his mic, "Alex! We need you!"

"On my way, Major," Alex replied. Laureline thought she had never been so happy to hear a computer's response in her life.

The Megaptor appeared to be unstoppable. It turned

its attention from the windshield to the roof, rending it with teeth and claws until, with a protesting groan, the roof at the rear of the bus peeled back, as if the beast were opening a metal can. It let out a higher pitched cry of pleasure, shoving its arm in and again plucking out a hapless soldier. Laureline thought for an instant that it was all over now, but the creature stopped only partway inside. Its roaring turned to growls of frustration as it realized it could only get the one arm and its bulbous head through the gap it had created.

Everyone had clustered toward the front of the bus and was firing at the beast, but their bullets seemed to simply bounce off its hard skin.

Laureline, who was doing her best to fire while using a bus seat as cover, noticed the play of shadow over the bloody scene and risked a glimpse back through the front windshield. It was the *Intruder*—the cavalry coming over the hill. Just in time, too.

"I'm out of ammo!" shouted Laureline to Valerian, panic creeping into her voice.

"Me too!" Valerian replied.

"Go on!" shouted Gibson. "Take the converter and get out of here!"

The two agents shared a quick glance. They didn't like the idea of leaving everyone else behind to be ripped to pieces by the slavering Megaptor.

"That's an order, agents!" Gibson shouted. "Go!"

Valerian's lips pressed into a thin line as he grabbed the converter. "Alex?" he called out.

"I'm in position, Major."

Seizing a gun from the lifeless fingers of one of the

fallen commandos, Valerian shot out the glass in the windshield as the driver slammed a button. The metal bars retracted. The way was clear.

Slightly ahead of them was the *Intruder*, matching their speed and dropping down to their level as Alex extended the ramp. The two tossed their weapons aside and crawled through the broken windshield, balancing precariously on the front of the speeding bus. Behind them they heard screams, roars, and an awful crunching sound.

The *Intruder* and the ramp to safety drew closer... closer...

They leaped, flinging themselves forward. Laureline felt hot breath on her exposed legs, which this time absolutely *was not* her imagination, and heard a ripping sound and the bellow of a thwarted monster.

Valerian and Laureline hit the ramp hard, got to their feet, and charged up into the cockpit. Alex retracted the ramp behind them. Laureline leaped into her seat. A horrible fear seized her, but eased as she saw Valerian set the converter down in one corner in its carrying case. Her gaze fell to her lap as she exhaled in relief.

Her dress was in tatters. "Dammit!" she exclaimed. "He ruined my last dress!" And then she thought about Gibson and the others, and felt horrible about being even remotely upset about a stupid dress. She began decoding their coordinates.

"Thanks for the rescue, Alex," Valerian said, ignoring Laureline, "I'll take over on manual." He checked the monitors, tapping quickly on the controls. "Prepare to enter exospace." He glanced over at her. "You have the coordinates for the rendezvous?"

"I'm just deciphering them," Laureline replied.

A sudden jolt ran the length of the spaceship.

"Alex?" Valerian asked. "What was that?"

Alex's voice was anxious as she replied, "I fear we have a stowaway."

Laureline didn't feel quite so bad about Gibson and his team anymore.

The Megaptor was no longer the commandos' problem. It was theirs.

"Shit!" Valerian swore, then to Laureline he said, "Hold on!"

She barely had time to strap herself in before he pulled back hard on the joystick. Laureline's back slammed against the black upholstery as the *XB982*'s nose pointed skyward, soaring up almost vertically.

A screen flickered to life in front of Valerian, revealing the face of one of the Federation ministers. And he looked really, really unhappy.

"Major Valerian," he snapped in a tight, irritated tone, "you're running nearly twenty minutes late!"

"Really?" Valerian tried to put on his best innocent face. Despite the situation, Laureline smirked; she knew that expression very well indeed. With a quick glance up at the roof where, presumably, a thoroughly pissed-off Megaptor was trying to claw his way into the cockpit, he added, "Time flies when you're having fun!"

"We have the Mül converter, sir," Laureline chimed in. Unfortunately, this did not seem to placate the minister as much as she had hoped it would.

"Excellent," the minister replied, curtly. "Now perhaps you could tell me what you're doing seventeen light years from your rendezvous?"

Valerian winced. "It does sound pretty bad if you put it like that," he admitted. "But if I say we'll be there in…" He turned to look at Laureline, eyebrow raised in query.

"Nine minutes," Laureline supplied.

"Nine minutes," Valerian echoed, "does that sound better?"

The Megaptor was losing patience, it seemed. The *Intruder* hurtled into space as the creature slammed about, shaking the vessel in a desperate effort to get inside.

"I'll inform the commander that you're behind schedule… and pass along your apology," the minister said, archly.

"You do that," Valerian said with false cheer. The minister disappeared from the screen and Valerian exhaled.

"Exospace in five seconds," Laureline said.

"Somebody's going to hit the ground with a bump!" Valerian said, and grinned.

The Megaptor was hungry, and the small things that had peppered his skin stung a little. He was angry with his prey for being so elusive; he had not been fed all day. Normally prey was soft and juicy and easy to eat, but this prey hid in a strange box and had been so hard to catch.

This box was very large, but the Megaptor had seen them leap into it, so it knew they were there. It roared, angrily, but could not smell their fear. Could not smell them at all, only the metal of the box.

Fresh irritation made him bite and scratch vigorously again at the large box.

Then, all at once, the box was no longer beneath it.

Nothing at all was beneath it, and as it started to fall, somehow it understood that it was a long, long way down.

CHAPTER TEN

Once they had lost the unwelcome stowaway and confirmed with Gibson that there had been no further casualties, Laureline changed out of the few ratty strips of cloth that was all the Megaptor had left of her dress and decided it was time to take care of their new guest, the converter. She was concerned about what effect all the action might have had on it. She hoped it wasn't injured, but at the very least it would likely be shaken up. Nobody liked to be in a small box, getting jounced around while subject to the bellows of a Megaptor.

Laureline set the perforated box containing the converter down on the table in the *Intruder*'s sickbay. She could hear it shuffling around in the back of the box. Using a remote, she deciphered the locking code and the front end clicked open slightly.

"Okay," she said sweetly. "Come on, little guy, let's take a look at you."

The overture was met with a growl as the creature backed up against the rear wall. Laureline hunkered down and peered into the box. She made an appealing clucking sound with her tongue, her voice coaxing. "Come on, Tiger, it's okay. I'll look after you."

More growls, though less certain.

"That's it… come on…" She smiled at it, and placed her hand down. It hesitated, its eyes darting about and its long muzzle twitching with uncertainty. Laureline was patient, though, and after a long moment, it moved hesitantly to the front of the carrier and placed a tiny, four-digit forepaw on her palm. It looked like a reptile on the surface, but as it moved, Laureline could see that its belly was covered with fur.

"That's a good fellow," she cooed. It brightened at the tone of her voice and moved out trustingly. It was small enough to fit in her hand. She saw now that the underbelly fur was bright blue, but patchy and scabby. There were scabs on its back, too, but the eyes it raised to her were blue and gentle.

"You have eyes to die for, you know that?" At her words, the creature's scaly form flushed to a bright red and it puffed up slightly. Laureline couldn't suppress a smile.

"Hey, are you flirting with me, little guy?"

The smile faded as she stroked it with a finger, examining it gently. "Your back and tummy are all scabby. How about some intensive skincare to get your mojo back?"

The little creature purred with pleasure. It was a soft, pleasant sound, and Laureline abruptly felt very protective of the small creature. The purring increased as she opened the door to a square compartment in the wall, placed the little animal inside, and closed the door behind it. It looked at her through the circular viewing window, suddenly concerned, as she lightly tapped in a code.

"No need to fuss," she reassured him. "A little high-grade uranium and you'll be as good as new. Hang on!"

She hit the button. Four nuclear beams filled the regenerator with a powerful blue light. As Laureline watched, the animal doubled in volume, and beamed contently. When she opened the door to take him out, he looked much healthier and clearly felt better. As he snuggled up under her chin, Laureline melted.

"You know, I remember studying you guys at school," she told him, placing him down on the table. "I'm dying to find out if everything in the textbooks is true."

She patted him once more, reassuringly, then reached to remove a diamond stud from the outer rim of her ear and held it out to the animal. His long muzzle twitched as it sniffed at the gem, then he opened a mouth lined with tiny, sharp-looking teeth, and gulped it down.

Laureline watched, fascinated, as the converter puffed up and changed color. Two seconds later, it delicately raised its lizard-like tail and deposited hundreds of diamonds on the table.

Laureline stared at the tiny pile of glittering gems. "Wow!" she said at last. "I need to take you shopping with me." She picked up the converter and kissed him on the top of the head.

It blushed.

Like his partner, Valerian, too, had cleaned up and dressed in his regular uniform. He sat alone on the bridge, gazing at the precious pearl he'd recovered, turning the smooth, perfect sphere over and over in his hands. He was wondering about the strange dream. Wondering about the beautiful beings who had held this object, who had seemingly manifested in the flesh today, fully formed from his sleeping thoughts.

At length, he placed the pearl down gently in a small well on the console.

"Alex?" he said to the ship's computer. "Analyze this, please."

"Certainly, Major," Alex said obligingly, activating a bright, slender beam of light and directing it on the pearl. Impossibly, it was even more beautiful as it caught the light. Slightly mesmerized, Valerian had to force himself to breathe as the light scanned the pearl. Data flashed up on the screen.

Valerian read the information. Size, weight…

He blinked. "Power—*twenty megatons*?"

"Indeed," Alex replied, almost blandly. "There's ten times more power in that pearl than in the entire ship."

Baffled, Valerian eyed the object with new respect. "Where does it come from?"

"From Mül, a planet that was located in the constellation QN34."

Valerian caught the usage of the past tense. "Was?"

"Yes. The planet has not existed for thirty years."

Valerian leaned back in his chair, intrigued. "Let's see what it looked like."

"Of course."

A magnificent blue-green planet came up on the screen. It was comprised of mostly water, but here and there lush landmasses jutted up out of the embracing ocean. Gentle wisps of clouds seemed to caress the tranquil world.

"Abundant vegetation, a few primal species, but of no particular interest," Alex said.

"I don't know about that. The one I saw in my dream was pretty interesting," Valerian countered. He leaned forward. "Zoom in."

The image started to enlarge, but was abruptly frozen. A message flashed up on the screen: ACCESS DENIED.

Valerian frowned. "Use our access codes," he instructed Alex.

"I fear that won't be enough, Major. Access is restricted." *This just keeps getting stranger.* "To what rank?"

"General. Five stars."

Five stars? Valerian reached for the pearl again, enjoying the smoothness of it as he held it in his fingertips. "The princess, in my dream… she wore a pearl just like this around her neck."

"Noted, sir," Alex replied properly.

Laureline entered, and she was smiling.

"How's the converter?"

"He was in fairly bad shape, but the regenerator helped. He's so cute! And a real charmer. I have to tell you, you have onboard competition."

She smirked at him, hands on her hips, as she stood by his chair. Valerian reached up and took her by the hand.

"I'm fine with competition," he replied, running his thumb over her fingers. "But I'm still waiting for your answer."

"The mission is not over yet, Major," she replied professionally, although she made no attempt to remove her hand. "There's still the whole 'top secret' part to come. Or is your perfect memory failing you again?"

Valerian tugged gently on her arm, pulling her down into his lap. She settled in, draping her arms around his neck.

"Come on! Don't keep me hanging like this," he

protested. "What's going on?"

She regarded him searchingly. For a moment, she said nothing. "Valerian, you're a great guy, and we make a good team."

A knot developed in Valerian's stomach. There was a *but* in there somewhere.

"But…"

Dammit, there it was.

"—Love isn't just about being good partners. It takes a lot more than that."

"Okay," he said, then asked, very reasonably, he thought, "Why don't you tell me *exactly* what it takes?"

The pause lasted precisely long enough to be awkward. Valerian was acutely aware of the warmth of her body against him, the curve of her throat, the fall of her hair as she glanced away, gathering her thoughts.

Then she spoke, in a calm, soft voice. "We spend our whole lives learning who we are, so we can be stronger, and able to defend ourselves. Then, out of nowhere, love comes along. And then all at once we're supposed to just… open up, to lower our defenses. To let someone into our hearts, into our DNA even. Just like that."

A shiver ran along Valerian's skin, and his heart started to race. He'd never seen Laureline like this, not in the two years they'd been at each other's side almost constantly. He'd seen her be cool, and then hot with a burst of anger; he'd seen her smart, professional, kind.

But not like this. Not… shy. Not fragile. He realized, with a humbleness that caught him off guard, that she was more exposed to him now than she had ever been while wearing a bikini or an alluring dress.

Laureline continued to look away from him as she spoke. "All of a sudden we feel vulnerable," she said, her voice barely a whisper. "Defenseless. And we tell ourselves that's why we never really fall in love. Because we're afraid to be weak. But in fact, it's the opposite."

And then she turned her head, and he was startled anew by the intensity of her blue-gray eyes as he tumbled headlong into their depths.

"Love makes you stronger, because you have to learn to trust someone else, even more than you trust yourself." Laureline paused, leaned in and whispered, her breath soft against his lips, her voice so quiet he had to strain to hear, "Valerian... do you think you can do that?"

He swallowed, hard, and then opened his mouth to answer her.

"Leaving exospace in one minute," Alex announced. Valerian groaned in disappointment as Laureline eased out of his embrace.

The moment was lost.

"Saved by the bell!" the perfect woman quipped, and moved to sit at the console.

"Alex," Valerian said through gritted teeth, "I hate you right now."

"Do you want me to regulate your hormones, Major?" Alex asked politely.

"No, thank you!" Valerian snapped.

"As you wish. Leaving exospace in thirty seconds," Alex counted. Valerian slumped into the copilot's seat. Then, determined not to let the moment be completely lost, he turned to face Laureline sitting beside him.

"You know what?" he stated. "I'm gonna put in for

ten days' leave right now, and I'll take you to the most beautiful beach in the universe. A *real* one this time!"

"Ten seconds," Alex continued.

Valerian ignored him. "It would be the perfect place for a honeymoon!" he insisted.

Laureline eyed him. "The honeymoon comes *after* the wedding. You know that, right?"

Valerian regarded her, skeptical. "Really?"

She smiled. "Yep."

Oblivious to their banter, or perhaps inured to it by this point, Alex continued, "Decelerating…"

The stars seemed to explode.

Time stretched out, simultaneously eternal and within a millionth of a heartbeat, as the *Intruder XB982* winked out of exospace, the non-time, non-space where faster-than-light travel was possible, and dropped right into the midst of a traffic jam composed of tens of thousands of other transport spaceships. His heart rate rising not at all, Valerian casually steered past them with the expertise of nearly a decade of experience, just dodging a collision here, zipping over a line of ships there. Most of the vessels were large, bulky cargo ships, jostling to get ahead of everything else as they waited to dock at Alpha Space Station.

"Well, traffic didn't get better," Valerian complained. He swerved in and out of the cluster of cargo ships until the City of a Thousand Planets, as it had come to be nicknamed, seemed to burst onto their screen.

From the station's humble beginnings in the 1900s Earth reckoning, it had swelled far beyond what anyone could have imagined at its inception. To an eye beholding it for the first time, it resembled an actual planet, albeit one hidden by shadows. But in reality, it was nothing as natural as a planet. It had grown, ship by ship, year by year, as millions had come to sightsee, negotiate, seek refuge, or ply their trades, docked, and never left. From small single-person crafts to vessels that could host thousands of individuals, nearly every sentient species had come to visit or dwell, linked together to form the greatest space station in the known universe.

It had been some time since the two agents had been asked to report to their home base, and Valerian was curious to know exactly how much the gigantic space station had changed during that time.

"Alex? Can you update us?" Valerian queried.

"I'd be delighted to." Alex sounded like she truly meant it. This sort of thing was what she was programmed for. "Alpha Space Station has grown seven percent this year, and now has a diameter of twelve point four miles." As she spoke, images on the monitors showed the station's architectural evolution as more and more vessels became a part of it.

"What's the population these days?" asked Laureline.

"Approximately thirty million," Alex replied promptly. "Three thousand, two hundred and thirty-six species from the four corners of the universe—metaphorically speaking, of course, as to the best of our knowledge the universe *has* no corners—inhabit the station, pooling their knowledge and cultures. Over five thousand languages are currently in use, not counting the various computer languages."

A list of languages scrolled up on the monitors.

"Current demographics?" asked Valerian.

"In the southern part of the station, the submerged portions are located. There are presently eight hundred species situated there, which live in a variety of liquids."

Various aquatic creatures appeared on his screen. Valerian recognized most of them, such as the Toinul, who were both gaseous and aquatic and resembled a human brain, the fishlike Martapuraï, who had been among the first few aliens to make contact with humans, the benevolent Poulong farmers who harvested cobalt, and the enormous, generally pacifistic creatures known as Bromosaurs, seventy yards from nose to long tail who inhabited the depths of the Galana Plains. But there were even more that he didn't recognize. That didn't surprise him. Alpha Station was always growing.

"In the north, we have gaseous lands, which continue to be dominated by a large colony of Omelites," Alex continued. These guys, Valerian knew. Everyone did. The Omelites, rather scrawny beings with oversized heads and long, dangling arms, were greatly valued by the station. They were both organic and metallic, and had developed a society based on information technology.

"To the east of them, of course, the Azin Mö still have their nuclei fields, which have grown eighteen percent since our last visit." The Azin Mö, too, were honored and respected at Alpha. They had the unique ability to produce any kind of cell, and were invaluable physicians and masters of neuroscience.

"Finally, to the west, in a pressurized atmosphere, we have nine million humans and compatible species."

"Home sweet home," Laureline said sardonically.

Alex ignored her tone, continuing her role as tour

guide. "The transit halls that connect the districts to one another now total seventeen units."

"What a mess," said Laureline, sighing.

"The economy has been in shambles for a year. Would you like a quick summary?" Alex inquired.

"No," Valerian said quickly, adding sarcastically, "enough excitement for today."

A brisk voice came over the controls. "*Intruder XB982. Authorization to dock in Section 1. VIP access.*"

Laureline turned to Valerian with a look of exaggerated astonishment on her face. "Hey, we're famous!"

"Took them long enough," Valerian replied.

CHAPTER ELEVEN

General Noïntan Okto-Bar awaited them in the Alpha
Space Station control room. The room was familiar to
Valerian and Laureline. This was the nerve center of the
station, and nearly every square inch of space except for
the floor was covered with screens. Monitors of a variety of
colors set against a black background displayed everything
from the temperature of any given locale on the station to
the number of inhabitants, from the chemical makeup of
gases and liquids in the various districts to which doors
were locked. From here, systems could be monitored and
overridden if necessary. Life or death decisions were made
by dozens of expertly trained technicians every second.

It was dizzying to look upon, even for spatio-temporal
agents like the two who now entered. But they were used
to the technology on display inside. What bothered them
was what else was on conspicuous display this time: troops.

Valerian and Laureline exchanged glances. Something
was definitely afoot.

Valerian was really starting to regret not reading the
briefing on this particular mission. But even if he had, it
was becoming abundantly clear that there were quite a lot
of pieces missing.

General Okto-Bar turned to regard them, his lips pressed together in disapproval, his always-cool blue eyes now icy with displeasure. He was a tall man, fit but slim, with reddish-blonde hair and a controlled demeanor. Valerian knew that although the general had come from a long line of famous soldiers, he himself had no spouse or children; Okto-Bar had said more than once that his soldiers were his family. Everyone who had served under him knew the general always had their backs.

Except, perhaps, when he was annoyed with them. Like now, for instance.

"You're late," Okto-Bar said without preamble.

"Sorry, sir," Valerian apologized. "The mission was a bit more complicated than we expected."

"Always expect the worst," the general stated. "You'll never be disappointed."

"I'll keep that in mind, sir."

"Did you check the converter?" the general asked.

Laureline smiled. "He's in great shape!"

"Sir," said Valerian, "we didn't get all the info on this mission. May I ask what's going on?"

For answer, the general turned to the main screen. "Declassify," he instructed.

A layout of the entire station appeared on the screen. This was also familiar to the agents. But something was different.

Amid the cool blue lines was a hazy red spot located in its center.

"What are we looking at?" Valerian asked. His gut was already tightening in anticipation of the answer, which he was pretty sure he knew.

"This is an image taken a year ago. The red area is a

radioactive zone," Okto-Bar said grimly.

Shit.

"We discovered it growing right in the middle of the station," Okto-Bar continued. "No signal of any kind could get through it. We sent in several probes, but none came back. So, last year, we sent in a special unit. Its mission was to get as close to the zone as possible and define the nature of the threat."

The general paused. "And?" Valerian prodded.

"Nobody made it back from the mission alive," Okto-Bar said bluntly.

Valerian and Laureline stood in somber silence. *An entire special unit…*

"Any idea who attacked them?" asked Laureline.

"None whatsoever," the general replied. He couldn't quite keep the anger out of his voice, and Valerian couldn't blame him. "As I said—that was what it looked like a year ago." He paused, seeming to steel himself, then said, "This is the situation today."

He nodded at the technician, and she hit another key. A second image appeared alongside the first.

The red radioactive zone was ten times larger.

Beside Valerian, Laureline shivered, almost imperceptibly. Valerian himself felt slightly sick to his stomach.

Okto-Bar continued implacably. "The air in the affected zone is unbreathable and highly contaminated. And this… thing… keeps on growing. Like a tumor." He practically spat the last word.

Another voice joined the conversation—masculine, strong, certain. "A tumor that we have to cut out as soon as we can. If we don't, and the cancer keeps spreading, it will destroy Alpha in under a week."

The speaker entered the control room. He was a striking figure in his blue-green uniform, his posture straight and his expression concerned but confident. There was not a crease in his uniform that wasn't meant to be there, nor a hair out of place, and he radiated a sense of leashed energy. Valerian had never met him, but he recognized him at once as Commander Arun Filitt.

Filitt's reputation preceded him, of course. It always did. He had blazed through the ranks and become a genuine war hero, promoted to general at the young age of thirty. Since that time, he had been redirected from active military duty in order to inspire humanity in other areas. His current position was commander of Alpha Station. It was whispered that he wasn't overly fond of aliens, which, in Valerian's mind, made him an odd choice to head up a space station in which aliens outnumber humans about a thousand to one, but it was not his job to question his superiors.

He knew that Okto-Bar had been a shoo-in for the position and had to be smarting at seeing Filitt in the role, but both men were behaving professionally toward one another.

Filitt was flanked by two of the K-TRON combat androids that served the station as police officers. While their bodies, which towered nearly ten feet tall, were somewhat humanoid, their designers had made no attempt to humanize them otherwise. Their heads were featureless, save for a light that blinked in two colors that all denizens of the station had come to know: blue for "move," red for "eliminate target." Their nearly impenetrable armor was shiny black, banded with yellow at the areas that corresponded to upper arms and thighs. Despite their massive size, they moved with fluid grace, speed, and efficiency.

Valerian and Laureline saluted smartly. "Commander," Valerian said. Filitt nodded in acknowledgement. Valerian returned his attention to the screen, searching for and finding no clues there about the ominous red spot.

"Sir… this doesn't make sense. Who'd have any reason to destroy Alpha? Practically every living species is represented here."

Filitt turned his eyes to the screen and his mouth hardened. "This radiation is a weapon of mass destruction. And behind every weapon, there is a killer. So no matter who it is, Major, it's a threat to us all, and must be eliminated."

Valerian took in the news. He could see by Laureline's expression that she liked it no better than he. Even so, he had to say something.

"Of course the radiation must be stopped, but if we could determine—"

He was interrupted by the appearance of the Federation's defense minister on one of the screens.

"Minister," said the commander, nodding a greeting. "I hope you have news?"

"I do, Commander," the minister said. He was in his early seventies, but his black hair bore no trace of gray and the lines on his dark skin were well-earned. The ones on his forehead were accentuated as he frowned with concern. "The Council has given you the green light. But we strongly recommend that international law and the civil rights of all concerned should be respected."

"Thank you, sir. And of course. I shall see to it personally," the commander assured him.

"Also, I've assigned agents Valerian and Laureline to be responsible for your physical protection," the minister continued.

That bit of information seemed to surprise Filitt, but he recovered quickly. "That won't be necessary," the commander assured him. He indicated the pair of silent robots beside him. "As you can see by the presence of my companions here, I have a unit of K-TRONs and I personally trained for—"

Frowning more deeply, the defense minister cut him off in mid-sentence. "It's a direct order from the government, Commander. The two agents need to report on the outcome of the operations."

A muscle twitched near the commander's eye. But, "As you wish," was all he said.

"Major, Sergeant," the minister said, looking at each of them in turn, "good luck!"

The minister's face disappeared. Filitt turned to look at his two new guardians with thinly disguised annoyance.

"Since we have to join your team, do you mind updating us on the operation?" Valerian inquired with perfect politeness.

The commander gave him a penetrating glance. "I am going to speak to the Security Council in a few minutes," he said crisply. "You will have all the details you need to know at that point."

All pretense of pleasantness abandoned, the commander turned and strode out of the room, followed by his K-TRONs.

Laureline watched them go. "Boy," she drawled, "this is going to be a lot of fun!"

Commander Filitt walked through the station briskly, but he was not heading to his meeting with the Security Council. Not yet, anyway. There was something he needed to follow up on.

The area was secured, but his clearance permitted him entry. He ascended in a small lift that was tight quarters for him and two K-TRONs. At least he was not forced to make small talk. In so many respects, robots were superior to living beings, even humans, he mused.

He emerged from the lift and went down another corridor, which was dark save for blue lighting along the floor. The corridor ended at the door of a single room. Filitt keyed in his code and the door slid open. The two K-TRONs waited outside for their commander as he entered.

A K-TRON captain was stationed just inside the room, perfectly motionless, carrying his weapon untiringly. The room, like the corridor outside, was dimly lit, and the figure at the end of it was swathed in shadow. Its stats were monitored on a screen. It sat slumped in a chair, prevented from falling out of it only by the bindings that went around its thin frame. What faint light there was caught the gleam of medical instruments and various drips sticking out of the silhouette's arms.

One of Filitt's men was leaning forward, shouting into the creature's face, demanding information. The figure in the chair remained infuriatingly silent.

Another subordinate was at the controls, observing.

When the door opened, he stepped away from his station to stand beside the commander. Filitt watched impassively as the interrogation continued.

"Anything?" he inquired.

"We've tried everything we know," his subordinate replied, "but for now we haven't got a peep out of him."

The commander grimaced. This was not good. Torture was a fine art, he had learned. With aliens, it was often so hard to know what they'd respond to. You couldn't do too much, or else any confessions would be completely false or, worse, the subject would die without revealing any necessary information. On the other hand…

"Increase the dosage," he ordered. The man nodded and returned to his station, touching a few buttons. Various liquids oozed through their tubes into the subject's flesh. The subject arched its back, the hood it wore falling away to reveal a pale face contorted in agony. Its skin was almost luminous, like the luster of a pearl, save where it was discolored from beatings.

And although its mouth was open and twisted in pain, the creature stubbornly remained silent.

Damn you, Filitt thought. *I'm running out of time.*

He made a decision. "If he hasn't talked within an hour, finish him off."

"Yes, sir."

The commander turned to leave, pausing to whisper to the K-TRON captain as he walked out. "If the operation goes wrong, you know what you have to do."

The K-TRON captain nodded its inhuman head once. Before he left, positioning his body so that no one else in the room would see, Filitt discreetly gave the

130

robot a small data storage device.

On to the meeting, Filitt thought, and squared his shoulders as if he were preparing to head into battle.

Because, in a way, he was.

CHAPTER TWELVE

The converter was waiting for them patiently in the regenerator, but as soon as it spotted Laureline it started to bounce up and down excitedly. Despite the seriousness of what they'd just learned—and what they were about to do—Laureline found herself smiling as she switched off the machine and opened the door.

"Aww, did you miss me? Come here," she said as the creature scampered happily into her arms. She cradled it affectionately, and realized she was growing quite attached to it. "Isn't he a cutie?" she said to Valerian, holding him out to her partner.

Valerian patted the creature's head absently, but his face was hard. "Somebody's holding out on us," he said bluntly.

Laureline's own heart sank, and even the happy snuffling of the converter underneath her chin couldn't move her. "I agree. Setting off like that without the faintest idea of who we're fighting is suicidal."

"Of course it is, but I don't mean that. I meant planet Mül," Valerian said. "You remember that dream I told you about? The images I was fed?"

She nodded, stroking the cooing converter, wondering where Valerian was going with this. "The planet was inhabited," her partner continued. "There were creatures on it. I saw their houses and children. And there was a young woman calling to me for help."

Laureline stopped petting the converter, bridling slightly. "Really?" she scoffed. "And you call that a bad dream? Knowing you, it's more like a dream come true." She widened her eyes and pitched her voice higher as she said in an exaggerated voice, "Oh, Major Valerian! Help! Save me!"

She was startled when he said with uncharacteristic sharpness, "Knock it off, Laureline—this woman had a Mül converter with her."

Laureline became serious. Scratching the converter under the chin, she asked, "Like this fellow?"

"Yes, almost exactly like him. And this morning I ran into two of the planet's inhabitants in the flesh!"

She stared at him. "You mean—at Big Market?"

Valerian nodded. "We were sent to retrieve the stolen converter from Igon Siruss, but they were there trying to get it from him too. Actually, I suspect they paid him to steal it from us."

Laureline peered at the small creature she cuddled. "Whoa," she said to him. "Sounds like everybody is after you!"

The converter chirped.

"That may be. But what I want to know is, why do we need him for this mission?"

Laureline grinned. "Let's find out," she said. "Come on. Let's gear up."

* * *

They approached Commander Filitt's quarters to find two K-TRONs standing on either side of the door. "Agents Valerian and Laureline. We're here to guard the commander," Valerian informed them. He wondered if this was going to be a problem, but somewhat to his surprise they stepped aside and permitted the team entrance.

Filitt was adjusting the last of his ceremonial regalia and eyed their battledress as they stepped inside.

"Wow!" the commander said sardonically. "You two look most impressive. I can see you're taking my protection very seriously."

Laureline held up the box containing the converter. Its small face was pressed to one of the slats in the front. He stuck his narrow muzzle out and his nose twitched as he sniffed.

"*His* protection, actually," she corrected. "He's one of a kind. Extremely precious."

"Precisely," Valerian said, then asked the commander, "Given that, are you sure there's any purpose taking him along with us on such a dangerous mission?"

Filitt adjusted his jacket as he spoke, eyeing himself critically in the mirror. "The Mül converter is capable of producing any conceivable product in record time. It will come in very handy if we have to negotiate."

Satisfied with the jacket, he reached for the large traditional belt that would encircle his waist. In the center was a circular ornamentation that was hollow inside. It was common military issue to have such a centrally located, small pack. Over the years, though, it had become regalia rather than a practical accoutrement, and its contents were reflective of rank. The commander's, Valerian noted, was currently empty, and he had a sneaking suspicion what Filitt wanted to put inside.

As the commander turned, fastening the belt, Valerian said, "With the army of K-TRONs you've got, I'm surprised negotiating is on your agenda, Commander. They're not really trained for that, seeing as they can't talk."

That appeared to irritate Filitt. He replied tersely, "You take care of my security, Major. I'll take care of the negotiations."

He went to Laureline and reached out toward the container she carried. Opening the door, intending to grab the small animal, he stuck his hand inside.

The converter promptly bit him. Valerian thought that the creature exhibited excellent judgment, but somehow managed not to voice the sentiment.

"For your personal security, sir," he said instead as Filitt snatched back his hand and inspected his finger, "how about you leave the animal to Agent Laureline for safekeeping?"

Filitt stared at him, his eyes narrowed. "You mean wear the belt with nothing in it? That's against protocol, Major. I am the highest ranking officer on this station!"

"And this animal, as far as we know, is the last specimen of its species. The whole universe is after it. And by carrying it, you automatically become a target," Valerian pointed out.

Laureline added wryly, "That's why Major Valerian would rather *I* carried it."

The commander hesitated. He glanced again at the converter, who was displaying its admirable discernment by growling and baring its small teeth.

"All right," Filitt said at last, "but do not leave my sight, Agent Laureline."

Laureline beckoned to the converter in the carrying case. It hopped into her arms, purring, and Filitt looked even more irritated. She opened the front of her own belt and slipped the converter inside.

The door opened to reveal General Okto-Bar. He, too, was formally dressed.

"Your guests are waiting, sir," Okto-Bar said to Filitt.

"All right," said Filitt, with one final look at Laureline's belt. "Let's make it fast."

"Stay on backup," Valerian ordered Laureline.

"Yes, sir," she replied.

The two were twenty feet behind Commander Filitt as he entered, but on Valerian's command, Laureline dropped back into the corridor while the major continued to follow the commander into the ceremonial hall. A crowd of extraterrestrial dignitaries who comprised the membership of the station's Security Council stepped forward to shake the commander's hand as he entered. Filitt was the picture of calm military decorum as he looked each of them in the eye—or what passed for it— and firmly shook whatever appendage was proffered.

As the commander made his way to the podium, Valerian and Okto-Bar followed. Gravely, not a hair out of place, Filitt lightly jogged up the steps and stepped behind the podium, taking a moment to look out at the sea of alien faces turned up to him. Okto-Bar stood off to the side, while Valerian took up a position beside and slightly behind the man he was guarding. He busied himself with scanning the crowd, alert to anything that might pose a potential threat. His HUD also had two transparent screens constantly feeding him information. He might not like the commander much, but he was not about to let the man die on his watch.

"Where's Agent Laureline?" Filitt asked in a soft voice.

"She's down the hall at the far corridor, sir," Valerian reassured him quietly.

"Her orders were not to leave my sight," the commander said. There was an edge to his words, though his voice was still pitched softly.

"Yes, sir, but she and I are your security, and I placed her where I thought best."

"But—"

"Sir, the sooner you speak, the sooner we can get this over with," Valerian reminded him. The look that his superior officer gave him could have melted steel, but the commander merely tightened his jaw and turned back to his audience.

"Good evening," he began. "I want to thank you all for answering the call at such short notice. As the elected representative of the Human Federation, I have called this meeting of the Station Alpha Security Council to update you regarding the state of emergency in which we find ourselves.

"As you all know, the historic heart of Alpha Station has been contaminated by a power whose origin remains a mystery to us. What's not a mystery is that this is a deliberate act of absolute evil. We have already conducted several military operations in an attempt to ascertain and understand the nature—and severity—of the threat. But these have ended in failure, and have resulted in significant losses among our troops."

He let that sink in. There was a rippling of dozens of languages throughout the vast hall. Filitt continued. "The affected area of this epidemic measured approximately thirty feet eight months ago." He paused for effect, then said, "It is now one point two miles long."

More concerned murmuring. "In light of this alarming and growing threat to us all, the Human Federation seeks your permission and support to launch a comprehensive and decisive military attack to eradicate this phenomenon once and for all. I am sure you will appreciate that time is of the essence, and I'm here to answer any questions you may have about the details of the operation."

"Which troops will lead the operation?" a Chrysokar asked. The tall insectoid beings had once been bellicose and masters of warfare. Over the centuries, they had turned their skills and nature to peacekeeping, but many of them, apparently including their ambassador, still had an interest in things martial. Valerian had a particular respect for the species. His first post out of the Academy had been with the infantry, where he had spent a year working for a Chrysokar military engineer named Prek'Tor, who shared with the eager young human his formidable knowledge about military strategy.

"Thirteenth Battalion, Special Assault division," Filitt replied. "It is a unit of about two hundred."

"Will any weapons be employed that could pose a potential threat to our troops?" an Azin Mö inquired. As the primary doctors on Alpha Station, naturally their first concern would be for the safety of the troops.

"No chemical or liquid weapons will be used during the assault," Filitt assured it.

"What is the main goal of that mission?" That came from the representative of humanity's oldest friends, the Kortân-Dahuks; the first aliens to shake hands in space with a human.

"We intend to destroy their defense system, which has shut down all our mediums of communication."

"Why are *you* the one organizing the mission?" the Toinul ambassador inquired. They were highly respected on Alpha Station, as their scientists had contributed a great deal of knowledge and information as well as assisted with discoveries and inventions. They were always ready for intellectual discussion, and clearly the ambassador thought this mission warranted one.

"The Central Committee has entrusted me with this mission, and it will be an honor for me to complete the task successfully."

Valerian was scanning the crowd when he heard Laureline's voice in his ear.

"That's all we need!"

"What?" he asked.

"Doghan Daguis."

"Oh, great," he replied, rolling his eyes.

CHAPTER
THIRTEEN

Three squat aliens, all about four feet tall, stood in front of Laureline. Their stubby, four-fingered hands were in the air, and their small, beady eyes were wide as they stared down the lengths of their elongated, trunk-like muzzles at Laureline. They were brown and wrinkled and stooped, with sparse hair sticking up here and there.

Laureline had drawn her weapon, startled at having someone come up behind her, but now she lowered it, and they lowered their arms.

"Nice to see you again," one of them said. He had a smudge of blue around his eyes.

"Agent Laureline," the second chimed in. This one, too, had markings around his eyes, except his were burgundy-colored.

The third Doghan Daguis, whose markings were yellow, completed the sentence. "As resplendent as ever."

"What the hell are you doing here?" Laureline snapped.

"We go where work calls—"

"—We can speak over five thousand languages—"

"—which can come in handy—"

"—at a party like this," the first finished. The second one added, "Need our services?"

Laureline patted the gun she'd just replaced on her hip. "No thanks. I have my own personal translator," she said acidly. "Now, scram!"

Valerian's voice came over the radio. "Ask them if they have any intel on Mül."

He's really obsessed with this dream, Laureline thought, *but I suppose I can't blame him*. She grimaced, but obeyed. Sighing, she said to the three, "Okay. Major Valerian does want some intel after all. Planet Mül? Ring any bells, guys?"

"A highly sensitive matter!" exclaimed Blue.

"The best person to speak to—" continued Burgundy, and the yellow-marked Doghan Daguis finished up, "—would be Major Samk."

"Alex?" said Valerian. "What have you got on a Major Samk?"

A picture of a dark-complexioned, handsome military man with a neatly trimmed beard came up on Laureline's screen, along with his stats. *Samk, Major Aton. 33. Deceased.*

"Major Samk died a year ago," Laureline said accusingly to the trio.

The Doghan Daguis appeared to be unruffled. The first one produced a small device and showed her his own picture of Samk—stone dead at his desk. Laureline's eyes widened.

"Yes," Blue began, "a most curious demise—"

"—that was never fully explained," added Burgundy.

"Murder, some might call it," Yellow said in a melodramatic tone. Laureline fought the urge to punch him right in his long nose, but refrained.

"I'm listening," she said.

"Major Samk was an expert on planet Mül," Blue continued.

"He took all that precious information—"

"—to the grave with him," said Yellow.

"What a waste," sighed the first Doghan Daguis.

"If you learn anything about the planet," Laureline told them, "we're interested."

"It would be a pleasure to work for you, Laureline," enthused Blue.

"Before we go," the second began.

"—allow us to give you—"

"—some info—"

"—for free," finished Burgundy.

Laureline eyed the three aliens skeptically. "For free?" she echoed. "Are you not feeling well?"

"The converter is precious—"

"—and highly sought after." Burgundy nodded sagely.

"Mercenaries will come—" said Yellow.

"—to retrieve it—" Blue continued.

"—sooner than you think," Burgundy finished solemnly.

"What kind of mercenaries?" Both Laureline and Valerian spoke at the same time.

They all eyed her with a smug expression. Blue actually wagged his finger at her. "The first tip was free."

"You must pay for more," Burgundy said.

Yellow added, "You get a discount, of course."

Valerian's voice came over the radio. "Alex? What's that?" Laureline, too, could see a flashing red light on her own screen.

"A dozen individuals approaching," Alex informed them. She added, "They are *not* on the guest list."

"What kind of individuals?" Valerian pressed.

"Undetectable for now," Alex responded.

Laureline looked at the Doghan Daguis wryly. "I get the feeling your info just lost its value. Go on, get out of here!"

The three headed for the exit, looking dejected. Valerian anxiously noticed the red light blinking faster.

"Valerian," Laureline said, "this doesn't look good."

"No, it doesn't. I want you back in the room near the commander, right now. Alex? Where are they coming from?" Valerian demanded.

"Everywhere," Alex responded. "They're going through the walls."

Laureline picked up her pace, threading her way through the packed hall and heading toward the podium. She met Valerian's gaze, and he seemed to make a decision.

"Laureline, evacuate the commander! I'm going after these intruders!"

Laureline shoved aside the last few audience members blocking her path, leaped onto the stage and rushed toward Filitt. She seized his arm and began to haul him away.

"Agent, what—" he began to protest, but she cut him off.

"Sorry! Emergency protocol!"

General Okto-Bar, who had been standing off to one side, instantly sprang into position to offer cover for the commander's exit. His gun was drawn and his face was resolute. The crowd was starting to panic.

I really hope this is a false alarm, Laureline thought. But she didn't expect they'd be that lucky.

Valerian's gaze darted from the screen to the crowd and back again. The red warning light was flickering faster now, and the adrenaline was kicking in.

"Alex? Dammit, I need to know the attackers' identity! Who is it?"

"I'm sorry, Major, but I cannot read their DNA," Alex replied.

"What?" exclaimed Valerian. That simply couldn't be. The *Intruder XB982* was programmed with the DNA of every known sentient life form. Alex couldn't possibly—

The far wall of the reception hall exploded.

Cries of terror went up as several of the guests were knocked off their feet. Valerian stared, stunned at what he was seeing.

A dozen slender, gray-robed figures suddenly poured into the hall. Beneath their hoods, their blue-eyed, bone-white—*pearl*-white, Valerian realized—faces were set in expressions of determination. They lifted something that looked like gracefully fashioned glass or ceramic vases, except instead of being carried upright, they were held so the opening faced forward. In their bulbous lower parts, pale blue light glowed softly.

But they were not vases, of course. They were weapons, and the aliens began firing indiscriminately into the crowd.

Valerian braced himself for carnage of the worst sort, but what emerged from the muzzles of their weapons was not bullets, but a gelatinous substance. It spread rapidly over the victim's body like some kind of webbing or cocoon, sealing them up inside and completely immobilizing them.

Valerian's mind flashed back to when he had asked Alex to analyze the pearl. The computer had assured him that Mül had no inhabitants. But Valerian had dreamed them, and then he had seen them on Kirian, and here they were again.

Alex hadn't been able to analyze the Pearls' DNA *because the Pearls didn't exist.*

He snapped back to himself, but by then the commander's men were already firing at the slim, pale figures. But in addition to being non-existent, the Pearls seemed also to be untouchable. They leaped and dodged, their movements agile and flowing and as beautiful as they themselves were. Before Valerian could even react, Okto-Bar, Laureline, and Commander Filitt himself, in addition to most of his men, were encased in the strange, gelatinous cocoons.

Valerian dove for cover behind a large white marble pillar. "Alex," Valerian hissed, "give me something with a bit of bite." He glanced down at his gun, watching the LEDs flashing.

"A new generation weapon," Alex replied. "Running analysis. Plasma bullets. No counter before thirty seconds."

"Great!"

Valerian pulled a tube from his pocket, activated it with a quick snap, and stuck it between his lips, gripping it with his teeth. By this point, the Pearls had reached the stage. They seized the cocoon that encased the commander, hoisted it, and were carrying it off when Valerian leapt out from behind the pillar and opened fire on them.

He never saw the Pearl that had managed to sneak up on him from behind, but he did see the blue gel from their weapon ooze over his face and body and felt its gooey warmth envelop him, as it had done with all the others. He struggled against it for about a nanosecond before it totally wrapped him in its embrace and he toppled to the floor. Fortunately, the goo also provided plenty of padding.

"Thirty seconds," Alex intoned. "Plasma bullets operational."

Well, that's nice, Valerian thought. *But I can't do so much as wiggle my little toe right now.* The seconds ticked by, but Valerian wouldn't give in to panic. Then, thankfully, the tube he'd stuck into his mouth started flashing red and then split in two.

A small mechanical spider emerged from the tube. Through the blue of the gel, Valerian followed the little trail of blinking red light as the robot extended a knife blade from its back and plunged it into the cocoon. It scurried down along Valerian's body, cutting upward through the goo and slicing a tidy little line all the way down.

Valerian gulped in fresh air and sat up, squirming free of the sticky second skin. Stumbling forward, he rushed over to Laureline, drawing out a small knife from his kit and slicing open her cocoon. Her eyes fluttered open, and she inhaled deeply.

"What was *that*?" Laureline asked.

"The Pearls from Mül," Valerian told her. "And they've got the commander! Free the general and get to the control room. You can track them and me both from there."

She nodded. Goo was on her face, clumping in her hair. And he wanted nothing more than to kiss her. But he didn't.

Instead, Valerian sprinted after the Pearls. He had worried that, since Alex wasn't able to track their DNA, he might have trouble following them, but it turned out it was child's play.

He just had to follow the enormous holes they'd blown in the walls.

CHAPTER
FOURTEEN

There had, surprisingly and fortunately, been no casualties among the extraterrestrials gathered in the security hall. It seemed that the commander's soldiers had been good enough shots to avoid collateral damage, and the weapons the Pearls had used only incapacitated. The converter had been completely unharmed, and a quick check revealed that it had slept through the whole ordeal. Within a few moments, Laureline and General Okto-Bar were back in the control room. Both of them placed their hands on the ID screen.

"Status on Major Valerian. Level Five. Emergency," Laureline stated, keeping her voice calm and cool.

"Accepted," answered Okto-Bar.

Laureline called up a map of the space station on the screen and typed in the code. A red light appeared on the map. It looked like Valerian was deep in the heart of the technological section of the station. He was right in the middle of a major intersection.

"Valerian? I've got you on visual," she said.

"Okay, but I've lost track of them. Try to locate the commander!"

Laureline typed in the message, but instead of the location of the missing Filitt, the face of the minister of defense appeared on-screen.

"Agent Laureline here," Laureline said. "I need to access the genetic code of Commander Arun Filitt."

But the minister was shaking his head. "Those codes are strictly confidential, Agent Laureline," the minister chided. "You know very well I—"

Laureline had no time for this. She placed her hand over a scanner that glowed red when she touched it. "The commander has been abducted," she stated. "If we don't get a lock on him in the next minute, we'll lose him."

The scanner turned green.

Okto-Bar read the result aloud. "Lie detection result: negative, sir. And I can confirm that the commander's been taken."

The official hesitated. Then he nodded. "Very well. Access granted."

Laureline entered the code as soon as the minister of defense sent it through, and another red dot appeared on the virtual map. She exhaled in relief.

"Thank you, sir. Okay, Valerian, I've got a fix on him. He's near the docking bay. The intruders must be headed for their vessel."

"Okay! What's the shortest way there?" asked Valerian.

"North-northeast," Laureline replied. "One hundred thirteen degrees."

Valerian spun around, following the digital compass on his wrist. He lifted his head and blinked.

"North… East… Laureline, that leads me straight into a wall!"

"You said you wanted the shortest way!"

Valerian sighed. He *had* said the shortest way, hadn't he? He hit a button on his sleeve. With a series of snapping sounds, his combat suit morphed into a solid shell. He took a moment to steel himself for the experience, then he started running.

He'd done this before, so he knew it didn't physically affect him in any way. Even so, he found his stomach tightened every time he ran into a wall full tilt.

But that very normal human reaction didn't slow him one bit. Valerian sped up and crashed through the black metal wall, and the chase was on. He was in the west part of the station—the humanoid area. He continued his straight, shortest path, crashing through corridor halls, into private domiciles, and charging through public recreation and shopping areas.

He was so focused on what was ahead of him that at one point he almost didn't see what was underneath his feet—or, rather, what *wasn't* underneath his feet; he exploded through a wall and into open space. Various small spacecrafts went about their business as Valerian plunged downward, the surrounding buildings black monoliths sprinkled with lights here and there. Streams of magenta and blue lighting marked walkway tubes that connected the buildings. His suit's default setting was to operate at all times as if he were in normal gravity unless specifically reprogramed. He was therefore hurtling downward directly at one of the walkway tubes right now, and he frantically tapped in the key that changed his suit from one that smashed right through solid matter to one that didn't.

He had to get the timing just right—

Valerian crashed through the clear top of the tube and, just in time, his suit transformed so that he landed safely on the corridor's floor instead of continuing right through it, albeit on his hands and knees.

There were several other humans in the corridor, understandably startled by his appearance. They cringed back as they ducked the falling chunks of clear debris, but no one looked hurt. They'd be fine; already the breach Valerian and his suit had made had sealed with a protective force field.

"Alex," he yelled, "give me the surfacer setting!"

"Right away," Alex replied promptly. "Reconfigured," she said an instant later.

Valerian took off again. "This may be the shortest way, but it's sure not the easiest one," Valerian said to Laureline, panting. The suit protected him from physical damage and gave him added strength, but any speed was still his own.

"Keep going," encouraged Laureline's voice. "You're losing them!"

"I said, I'm doing my best!"

"Do it faster!"

Valerian bit back a retort. Right now, he needed his breath to keep running. He sprinted down the enclosed translucent passage as long as it took him where he wanted to go. It opened up onto a building of small apartments, continuing straight as the hallway turned left. He was vaguely aware that one wall of an Arysum-Kormn family's home was of a translucent material as he raced through it, but he didn't realize that it was actually a window until he'd shattered it into a few hundred shards and found that he was, once again, hurtling downward.

This time, though, he was prepared. Alex had reconfigured his weapon to produce a deceptively thin, glowing plasma disk with a diameter of about four feet. Valerian struck it with his right foot and launched off, firing ahead of himself before every leap.

He sprang forward from the last plasma disk into the Azin Mö nuclei cluster field. He winced as he did so. The station's doctor race crafted orbs of various genetic materials for emergencies, and there was no way Valerian wasn't going to step on quite a lot of them. Well, that was Arun Filitt's problem as the commander of Alpha and the one being rescued, not his, Valerian thought as he stormed through the cluster field shouting "Sorry!" and smashed his way out the other end. It was some consolation to him that the Azin Mö tended hundreds of cluster fields, and this one looked to have tens of thousands of soft, radiant orbs.

The nuclei field was the demarcation between the humanoid section of the west and the gaseous environmental part of the station. Valerian continued onward. His "shortest" path took him directly through an enormous, glowing, golden wall of intricate computer technology that was currently being upgraded by a group of Omelites, bio-metallic species with large, bulbous heads, several spindly appendages, and laser eyes. The destruction this particular move caused bothered Valerian more than the damage he'd done to the nuclei fields. He hoped he hadn't done anything irreparable. The Omelites had developed the ability to communicate telepathically, and the messages being fed into his brain quite vividly conveyed their displeasure. He didn't think they'd hurt him, but he was glad to get out of range of those laser eyes.

"Hurry," came Laureline's voice. "Looks like they're making for a docking station and you're nearly there!"

"I'm doing my best!" Valerian snapped. He smashed through the other side of the giant computer banks into a freefall, firing plasma disks to step on as he made his way through a sea of translucent floating creatures that looked like jellyfish of the air.

"Hang on," Laureline said. "They've boarded. Ship has no tags, a totally unknown model. Change of plan. One hundred forty degrees east! Just keep going straight and look for a door marked eighty-one. Alex will pick you up!"

Valerian didn't break stride as he glanced at his wrist and made the correction. Each section, no matter the inhabitants who had settled there, had a docking area that could accommodate a variety of vessels and environments. He was heading toward one of those now. It hadn't seen much use in the last several years. Doubtless the Pearls had chosen this one so as not to attract unwanted attention.

He reached it now, running on metallic flooring instead of the softer plasma disks. Valerian smashed through another wall, and found himself in a ventilation shaft. He kept going.

"Alex?" came Laureline's voice in Valerian's ear. "Sending you the coordinates. Pick him up."

Valerian was starting to tire, but he couldn't afford to. Not now, not when he was so close.

"*Intruder* in position," came Alex's voice.

"That's good news!" said Valerian, panting. Seldom had words been more sincerely meant. He sprinted straight for an iron door with the numbers eighty-one prominently displayed on it.

"That's it!" said Laureline. "Keep going!"

Head down, Valerian charged through a steel wall and found himself in space.

Unfortunately, the *Intruder* wasn't there to catch him, and he started to plunge downward past levels of empty docks.

"Hey, Alex! Where the heck are you?" he shouted as he fell.

Puzzled, Laureline glanced at her map. She turned the dial. The map spun. She gasped, horrified, as she realized that eighty-one became eighteen.

"Alex? You are on eighty-one?"

"Affirmative, Sergeant."

"Sorry, my mistake," said Laureline. "It's number eighteen!"

"Great!" came Valerian's voice. "See? I trust you more than I trust myself, and look where it gets me!"

Laureline felt her cheeks grow hot. "Alex? Pick him up! On eighteen!"

She waited, biting her bottom lip. It felt like hours, but it was only about ten seconds before she heard a breathless, irritated Valerian gasp, "Thanks, Alex! Bring on the beach!"

Laureline allowed herself a relieved smile.

Valerian switched his suit to normal mode and clambered into the cockpit. Energy returned to him in the form of adrenaline as the ship filled his screen and he realized that this was definitely the right place. The vessel docked in bay eighteen-not-eighty-one looked exactly like the sort of ships the pale, beautiful Pearls would build. It was huge, and its three sides came together in a shape like a star. The engines at its base were dozens of perfect white spheres, and its prominent surface wasn't any one single, bold color, but a soft, muted combination of delicate shades that seemed to undulate and shift.

Pretty though it was, it was gearing up to flee, and it had Commander Filitt on board. "I don't know where you come from," he muttered as he locked onto his target, "but I know where I'm going to send you."

The *XB982* opened fire on the ship. It swerved away and accelerated, with Valerian hot on its tail. It was fast, and it was smooth, and it led him on a merry chase. The two vessels sped in and out of the queue of tanker ships alongside the docking station, and Valerian was reluctantly impressed at the speed with which the much larger ship could maneuver. Even so, he managed to get a solid lock on the back of the vessel.

"I'm going to shoot out the engines," he announced to Laureline and Okto-Bar.

"Their protective shields are very sophisticated. You won't go through," Laureline warned him.

"Then let's try something bigger."

As he was about to fire, the unthinkable happened. Dozens of what looked like fissures appeared along the shell-hued sides of the vessel. For a second, Valerian thought it was going to explode. But instead, the "cracks" became deeper, and Valerian realized that the single enormous ship was splintering into several smaller, identical-looking ones that now peeled away in all directions.

"Shit! Laureline? The ship's just broken up into a bunch of little ones. Which one has the commander on board?" Valerian shouted.

"Nine o'clock! South!" Laureline answered.

"Nine o'clock?" Valerian repeated, furious and irritated. "You sure? Not six o'clock?"

"Nine o'clock!" Laureline snapped. "Hurry up!"

The vessels were flying above, ahead, behind, and below him now, and he spotted the vessel Laureline had pinpointed zipping along beneath him at, indeed, nine o'clock. The *Intruder* switched course to chase after the smaller spacecraft, which hurtled into the maze of the station's innards.

Valerian loved piloting the *Intruder*. He was very fond of Alex. But after he almost slammed into another vessel and Laureline had yelled, "Watch out!" in his ear, he reached a decision:

"I'm too big to follow them," he told her and Okto-Bar. "I'll take the Sky Jet!"

CHAPTER FIFTEEN

Oktobar frowned. "That's odd. It looks like they're not trying to escape into open space—they're heading right back..." His voice trailed off.

The two red dots were approaching the radioactive area at the heart of the station.

"You're near the dead zone," warned Laureline. "Reel them in before I lose you!"

Valerian, frenzied, shot back, "I'm working on it!"

Laureline kept her eyes glued to the map, watching with increasing agitation as the red dots that signified Commander Filitt and Valerian drew closer together even as they edged toward the zone that was bombarded with radiation.

"Valerian?" she said. "I'm going to lose you in ten seconds."

"I can't slow them down!" Valerian snapped.

"Five seconds..."

"Oh, shit!" Valerian shouted.

Then, silence.

The red dots had disappeared off the map. Laureline's heart contracted. "Valerian? Valerian, do you read me?"

There was no answer. No sign of life.

Laureline whirled to Okto-Bar. "I need a Sky Jet!"

"Sergeant Laureline, you can't go after him." Okto-Bar's voice was harsh.

"Why not?" she demanded.

He stabbed a finger at the map. "That zone is too dangerous and it's under enemy control."

"An enemy you don't even know!" she retorted.

"An enemy that just *attacked* us!"

"By putting us to sleep and not killing a single one of us?" she cried. "Why would they spare our lives? Why?"

He stared at her, and for a moment, his commanding, certain expression wavered. "I… don't know."

"Valerian has seen these creatures before. They are coming from planet Mül."

Okto-Bar frowned. "Ridiculous. Planet Mül exploded thirty years ago!"

She was running out of time. Valerian could already— no, she wouldn't let herself even think it. She turned to leave, done with trying to convince him. Okto-Bar grabbed her arm.

"I can't let you leave! What you're saying—it doesn't make any sense!"

"It's our *mission* that doesn't make any sense, sir!" Laureline shouted. She didn't care who heard her. "Somebody's lying to us. While you find out who, *I'm* going to find my partner!"

She wrested her arm away from him and stormed toward the door. The general nodded to two sentries to block the exit.

Laureline whirled. "General, Valerian's an invaluable agent. You can't afford to lose him."

"I most certainly can't afford to lose *two* in one day!"

He sighed. "I'm sorry, Sergeant." To the sentries, he said, "Confine her until backup arrives. Trigger the highest alert level, and *find me the commander!*"

One of the sentries took Laureline's gun. "Please follow us, Agent," he said.

She felt her face grow hot with anger, and bit back a retort. Okto-Bar wasn't about to listen to her. He was convinced the Pearls weren't real, and nothing she could do was going to change his mind.

She walked down the hallway, flanked by the two soldiers, her stride brisk and angry. At a junction with another hallway, though, she spied three very familiar squat, long-nosed, winged figures wandering away. An idea flashed into her mind and she came to a halt.

"Hey, guys!" she said to the soldiers. "I think you should cuff me."

They looked askance at her. "No, I'm serious. Cuff me. First, because it's procedure. And second, because I'm sorely tempted to escape!"

The two soldiers shared a glance, puzzled. One of them shrugged. "Whatever," he said.

He pulled out a pair of magnetic handcuffs. As he stepped forward and started to fasten them around Laureline's slender wrists, she seized his companion's arm and thrust it forward before the first sentry could halt his motion.

Snap.

The two men, one of them now partially handcuffed, stared at each other for just an instant in mutual shock.

It was long enough. Laureline's long leg shot out, impacting one sentry's knee with an ugly crunch. He dropped like the proverbial stone. She seized the other one's arm, twisted it, and before either one knew what was happening, there was a manacle around one man's wrist and another about the second's probably broken leg. He was white as a ghost. Deftly, she plucked her gun from his waist and gave them a shrug.

"Good job, boys."

She sprinted back to the intersection. The three Doghan Daguis were already partway down it, but she hurried after them. When they turned at the sound of footfalls, she drew her gun. For the second time in less than an hour, their short arms were reaching for the ceiling. Keeping her weapon trained on the trio, Laureline glanced around for a more private place to have this conversation. The door was ajar to a room that appeared to be for storage of some sort, and she gestured toward it with her gun.

"This way. I need a word."

They obeyed. She followed them in and closed the door behind them. "Newsflash!" she said with fake cheer. "If you don't help me find Valerian, you're all going to die."

She placed her gun against the side of Blue's wrinkled head. "And you're the first up."

Surprisingly, they did not look nearly as afraid as they ought to have been. In fact, Laureline thought they were smirking at a secret joke.

The first one said, "It's to avoid such situations—"

"—that all our information—"

"—is divided three ways," said the third, Yellow, rather smugly.

"Kill one of us," said the first, and Burgundy piped up, "and you kill the information."

"What a pity that would be!" Yellow said. He seemed to have the pithiest comments.

Laureline sighed, and lowered her gun. "Okay, you win," she admitted. "But you're going to have to give me credit. I don't have much on me."

In unison, the three Doghan Daguis shook their heads. "How tiresome," said Blue.

"If the commander were here—" said Burgundy.

"—he could use the converter to pay us," Yellow lamented.

"But he's been abducted—"

"—precisely because he had the converter on him," Burgundy finished.

"Unless, for security reasons," mused Yellow, and Blue chimed in, looking inordinately pleased with itself, "somebody else was carrying it for him."

Laureline stared at them, simultaneously appalled and impressed. "How the hell did you get that info?"

"It's not info," replied Burgundy.

"Just deduction," supplied Yellow.

"We know how humans work," Blue said, smugly.

"They're all *so* predictable," said Burgundy, with an undercurrent of arrogance and contempt.

Fury surged through Laureline. No doubt General Okto-Bar was tracking her down right this moment. Commander Filitt was still imprisoned, and who knew what had happened to Valerian. The last, the absolute last, thing she wanted to be doing was standing here listening to three stubby little informants disrespect her species. She lifted her gun again, bent over, and shouted into the sensitive earhole of Blue, "All except women!

Especially when they're in a bad mood."

Blue cringed and clapped his hands to his earholes. His wings flapped in agitation, striking a pile of boxes. "Ow! Okay, okay!"

"Calm down!" urged Burgundy.

"What do you want to know?" asked Yellow.

"Where Valerian is!" said Laureline.

"Hard to tell," began Blue, still covering his ears.

"But we know a way to track him down—"

"—with complete precision," Yellow finished.

"How much?" Laureline asked.

"A hundred baduls," said Blue.

"Each," clarified Burgundy.

"Cash up front," Yellow supplied.

Laureline wondered if they fully appreciated just how close she was to almost literally exploding. Through gritted teeth, she said, "I don't *have* baduls."

The first Doghan Daguis said, "You have a converter."

Laureline fished in a pouch at her waist and tossed a small sack at them. "Forget about it. Here's all I got."

The small sack contained a few dozen of the diamonds the converter had produced for her earlier. The Doghan Daguis peered in, then one by one they turned their heads to her. They were not happy.

"Diamonds are less valuable than baduls," Blue said.

That. Was. *It.*

"End of negotiation!" Laureline pointed her gun at his other earhole and his weaselly eyes widened.

"Okay, okay," Burgundy said, holding up his hands placatingly. "Under the circumstances—"

"—we accept the deal."

"Good," said Laureline. "Now. *Where's Valerian*?"

"Follow us," Blue said, and rubbed his ear.

General Okto-Bar had been a man of battle, but had found his true calling at Alpha Station. He had found a fascination and an odd sort of peace in managing the goings-on of the vast station, and he done so ably for the last four years. He'd grown fond of the aliens who, like him, called this place "home," and had made friendships among their number that would last a lifetime. The thought of peril to them, to his fellow humans, to this station that for centuries had stood as a beacon of harmonious interaction and interspecies goodwill and cooperation—it was unacceptable.

He had anticipated, with good reason, that if he continued to smoothly manage the day-to-day troubles of so enormous a collection of beings, he would be rewarded with a promotion to commander of the place he loved. But Commander Arun Filitt had always been a more immediately arresting figure, and when it was time for Filitt's superiors to give him something to do, Filitt had been given the command of Alpha Station instead of the man who'd actually been running it well with quiet, unappreciated passion for several years. And so Okto-Bar had continued his work in the shadow of the colorful, popular figure.

But now, the commander had vanished, and Okto-Bar was fully aware that Filitt's likely survival—and that of Okto-Bar's beloved station—was now his responsibility.

The news that Agent Laureline had escaped was especially irritating. He did not need rogue agents, decorated or not, dashing about. He stood, staring at the map of this place that was both his charge and his joy.

His soldiers, his finest commandos, stood beside him awaiting orders. "Phillips, you head straight for the spot where the major disappeared. Milo, you go after Agent Laureline. When you track her down, bring her in peacefully. No violence! Fall out!"

The commandos hurried on their way. The general gazed pensively at the map.

He was not a man of extreme emotions, nor one given to flights of fancy. Some who knew him would go so far as to accuse him of lacking an imagination entirely, which bothered him not at all. Agent Laureline's peculiar assertion that Mül inhabitants were on this station and that Agent Valerian had somehow known them was rubbish, of course.

And yet... he knew her as being someone who was solid and forthright, unlike her impulsive partner. She had been so very insistent.

He was running out of options, and it would do no harm to investigate.

Okto-Bar put his hand on a glass scanner. "Declassified. I want all available information on planet Mül."

After a moment, the scanner began to glow red. A message flashed up: ACCESS REFUSED.

What? The general's eyebrows rose in astonishment. "Who has authority over this file?" he asked.

The answer flashed up: COMMANDER ARUN FILITT.

Okto-Bar stared at the blinking name. He apparently *did* have an imagination, because right now, it was running wild.

CHAPTER
SIXTEEN

At first, Laureline suspected the Doghan Daguis were leading her on a merry chase. Her impatience rose with every step as they led her south, the part of the station designed to accommodate aquatic species. She realized they were in an area called Galana. Its underwater plains were supposed to be magnificent, but she had not come here to play tourist.

"You'd better not be trying to send me on a wild goose chase," she muttered at one point.

"What is—"

"—a wild goose?" asked Burgundy.

"And why would you chase it?" Yellow finished.

Laureline rubbed her temples. Adrenaline was still surging through her and it did not make patience any easier. "Never mind," she said. "Just remember my weapon is fully loaded and I'll be happy to use it if this starts to go south."

"We are—" said Blue.

"—already going—"

"—south."

Laureline did not reply. She knew if she opened her mouth it would be to emit a shriek of outrage, and that would not help Valerian at all. Though it would make her feel better.

At last, followed by Laureline, the Doghan Daguis reached a concrete dock on the banks of a murky green inland sea. There was a smell of brine mixed with rot, and Laureline tried not to wrinkle her nose at the stale stench. The area was derelict and deserted, and various odd sounds echoed in a weird and sinister fashion.

No, Laureline thought, *not quite deserted*. She could see the conning tower of a very small submarine, which appeared to be moored to the dock. Not that much of it was visible, but what she could see did not inspire confidence. The metal looked ancient and likely to spring a leak any second.

The Doghan Daguis seemed to know exactly what they were doing. They marched toward a red mechanism perched on the end of the dock, which, like the submarine, appeared to have seen better days. Laureline's best guests was that it was a crane of some sort. Blue pulled a lever and a small hook descended. Burgundy produced a bottle from one of the myriad pouches around his waist and attached it carefully to the hook. Blue pulled another lever and the crane swung around, then lowered the bottle so that it clanked against the side of the submarine without breaking.

There was a grinding noise and the conning tower lid flipped back.

One of the strangest-looking men Laureline had ever seen poked his head out. He squinted, seized the offering, opened it with his teeth, chugged the contents in a single gulp, and threw the empty bottle overboard into the murky green water.

He had long, wild, curly gray hair and a thick beard to match, and his face was as weathered as old leather. His nose looked like it had been broken about eight too many times, and the eyes that turned to regard them were mismatched. One was deep, dark and brown, the other an unnaturally pale blue Laureline suspected was artificial. Some sort of implant was affixed to his upper left brow, and his oddly shaped ears had earrings.

"I've got a sinking feeling about this plan of yours," Laureline muttered.

The pirate—or so she assumed him to be—leered at her with his strange eyes. Gruffly, he growled, "Whaddya want?"

The first Doghan Daguis spoke. "We'd like to go fishing—"

"—for cortex jellyfish," said Burgundy.

Yellow added, "Male, if possible."

Blue lobbed one of Laureline's diamonds toward the pirate. His left hand shot up and caught it more deftly than Laureline would have thought possible—until she realized the arm was completely cybernetic.

The pirate examined the gem and grunted. Peering up, but keeping the diamond, he called, "It's not the season."

Burgundy tossed him another gem. Again, he plucked the tiny item out of the air. This time, he said, "Males are harder to catch." He was clearly wondering how far he could press his luck.

Yellow sighed and tossed him a third jewel.

The pirate graced them all with his golden smile. "Welcome aboard," he declared.

* * *

Laureline wasn't having second thoughts; she was onto fifth, sixth, and seventh thoughts by this point. The sub was as small as she had guessed and even more rickety than she had feared. It could accommodate two humanoids, but only just, and the pirate with whom she'd just decided to ally herself took up a lot of the room. About a third of the ship was the cockpit, with a large viewing bubble. The rest was where the pirate slept and supposedly ate, though Laureline suspected he drank most of his calories, and the tail end was a surprisingly brisk engine. A small claw crane was affixed to the base of the sub, presumably for the previously mentioned purpose of fishing.

The small submarine scooted across the underwater plains of Galana. Laureline's anxiety about Valerian contrasted with the serene beauty on display all around her. She had to admit, what she was seeing was pretty amazing. Any other time, she might actually have enjoyed herself.

They passed through the famous cobalt fields of song and story; a cool, green-blue depth where dark blue flowers grew, gently waving in the water. Their edges were lined with a pale blue light. As Laureline watched, a Poulong farmer swam over the field. They were one of the first aquatic species to settle on Alpha, and they were a gentle people. On land, he would have seemed skeletal and awkward, his body hunched and unattractively angular. But here, he belonged. His skin was blue, mottled so that it looked like light from the surface was always dappling it. A light was affixed to a helmet that covered the top of his skull, with a tether back to a main hub. Laureline realized she was seeing the Krikbang, an advanced computer that linked all the Poulongs and controlled the activity of the field workers. She allowed her gaze to linger on the scene of the tranquil farmer gathering aquatic blossoms; the long, delicate fingers reaching around the slender stalk and plucking it from the seabed. As the stalk snapped, the luminescence that outlined the flower flared, blue-white and very bright, for a moment. The bloom floated helpless as the farmer tucked it into the gathering sack on his back and moved on to another. The glow was beautiful, but Laureline couldn't help but wonder if it was the plant crying out in pain.

She did not like that thought, so she turned to look ahead. The pirate had turned out to be taciturn, which suited her just fine. She sat in the seat beside him as the submarine passed through tall, half-crumbled columns, as if they were traveling through a gate into a lost world. It was all lulling and hypnotic, but soon enough, something jarred Laureline to full attention.

Something large was moving, a dark green smudge against the lighter background of the water. A few heartbeats later, she reclassified the motion from "large" to "gigantic," with a bit of "monstrous" thrown in for good measure.

The pirate stabbed a finger in its direction. "There!" he said triumphantly. "Bromosaurs."

They were drawing closer to the massive beasts, who were swimming about placidly enough. To her inexpert eye, a bromosaur looked like a cross between a reptile and an insect, with large plates layered along its back and down its tail and eight comparatively tiny legs dangling below its great bulk. It looked to her like it could curl in on itself nose to tail, with the plates providing protection. Laureline didn't want to know what was in the water that could threaten a creature that was seventy yards long if it was an inch.

"Are they dangerous?" she asked.

"Not really," the pirate answered. "You just have to be careful they don't inhale you."

Laureline relaxed, ever so slightly, watching now with more curiosity than concern as one of the Bromosaurs slowly sucked up the mud from the sea floor and everything it contained.

"We're lucky," he said. "That one's a male."

"How can you tell?" Laureline asked.

"They're much smaller than the females," the pirate explained.

Laureline raised her eyebrows. "That's good to hear."

The little sub drew closer. "Um… aren't we supposed to be looking for a cortex jellyfish?"

The pirate turned his disconcerting gaze on her. "You want to find the jellyfish, you find the Bromosaurs first!" He shook his grizzled head in a *what are they teaching kids in school these days?* gesture.

Laureline inquired, "Okay, so… how can you be sure that this one has a jellyfish in it?"

"They all do," said the pirate. "Y'see… the Bromosaur blows out pure water, an' cortex jellyfish can't survive without it. That's why jellyfish live on it all year round, and it's where they get their hypersensitivity from."

Laureline stared at him for a moment, almost more impressed by the hitherto-silent pirate's eloquence and ecological understanding than the giant being in front of them.

They were close enough now that she could see that the

Bromosaur had a single, huge nostril. And sure enough, a jellyfish clung on to its nose, just above the enormous hole currently expelling water.

The tiny submarine came to a halt facing the animal. Laureline was acutely aware that the Bromosaur was at least a hundred times larger than their vessel.

"Why are we stop—"

Her fingers tightened on the arm of the chair as the little ship was pulled forward. "We're being sucked in!" she yelped.

The pirate looked completely calm. "You have to approach it head on," he told her, in the same casual, knowledgeable tone with which he had explained the relationship between the jellyfish and the Bromosaur. He leaned over and said, almost conspiratorially, "It's the blind spot in its vision."

She gaped at him. She'd thought him crazy, then surprisingly knowledgeable, but now she was right back to "insane" again. The submarine was moving faster and faster. Her gaze was inexorably drawn toward the viewing bubble as she watched the talons of the claw crane on the sub's front unfurl.

"Now," the pirate purred, leaning forward as he maneuvered the crane, "here we go… as soft as silk…"

Laureline watched him, understanding now what he was going to attempt. "Can I help?" she offered. "I'm a good driver."

The pirate kept staring raptly, his entire body focused on what he was doing. "Oh, it's not about driving," he murmured. "It's all about… *feeling*."

"I'm not bad at that either," Laureline said helpfully.

"Shhh," the pirate hissed, his face turning dark with a thunderous frown. She sank back in her chair, chastised, and let the pirate do what he'd been given three diamonds to do.

They were still being pulled in at an astonishingly swift pace. Laureline swallowed, hoping the pirate was secretly brilliant at his job.

Sure enough, at the very last possible second, the pirate steered up, the little sub managing to break free of the Bromosaur's vacuum, and surged up and over the monster's head. He moved the controls swiftly, and the claw crane latched onto the jellyfish on the way past.

"That's the way to do it!" her companion roared, gleefully.

Laureline, relieved, was about to cheer as well when behind and below them, the Bromosaur abruptly reared up. With surprising speed for an animal that had been so slow and languid, it spun around. One moment she was looking at the creature's broad back and tail, the next into a *really big* mouth with teeth that were as long as the man sitting beside her was tall.

"I thought you said they weren't dangerous!" cried Laureline.

"Oh, they're not," the pirate said nonchalantly, adding, "except when you take their little buddy."

"Great!"

The chase was on. Completely unruffled, the pirate kicked the vessel into high gear and it zipped over the creature's back... and managed to dodge a second Bromosaur, who was apparently as outraged as its fellow that the little jellyfish "buddy" had been snatched away.

"We can't possibly outrun them!" Laureline shouted.

"We don't have to," the pirate replied calmly. Laureline hated sitting by while others acted, but there wasn't a lot she could do at this point other than hang on tight and hope the ship held together.

A massive tail lashed out, and the resulting surge of water sent the submarine hurtling forward. Laureline, though, now finally understood what the pirate's strategy was. Up ahead, two of the giant, now-crumbling columns loomed like stone sentinels. The pirate was heading straight for the gap between them.

Laureline's hands tightened on the chair's arms. *Come on, come on...*

The sub zipped between the twin pillars.

The Bromosaurs didn't; they slammed into the columns, their heads the only part of them small enough to get through, their shoulders smashing into the ancient stone so hard that a huge crack zigzagged along the length of one. Confused and angry, the two enormous denizens of the Galana Plains simply tried harder and harder. And by then, their tiny prey, and their even tinier little friend, had disappeared into the depths.

From behind, Laureline heard a loud, mournful bellow. She collapsed back into the seat and closed her eyes for the rest of the trip.

Laureline felt absolutely drained as she climbed out of the submarine, and she didn't want to admit that she was pleased to find the three Doghan Daguis still waiting there. She'd half-expected them to vamoose.

Once Laureline was on the dock, the lid of the conning

tower slammed shut and she heard the lock grind closed. That was fine with her. She wasn't sure she'd have any civil words of farewell for the peculiar pirate after that last adventure.

"Well?" asked Blue.

"Were they biting?" queried Burgundy.

"Did you catch one?" Yellow looked excited.

"Yes," Laureline replied.

They all turned to watch as the submarine's pincers slowly rose out of the water, brandishing its gooey catch.

"There's no time to lose," said Blue.

"The cortex jellyfish is extremely fragile," Burgundy explained.

"Show it images of Valerian—" said Yellow, and Blue finished, "—and it will show you what he has seen."

"Sure, but…" Laureline looked askance at the jellyfish still hovering in the pincers' clutches. "How?"

"You have to put it—"

"—on your head—"

"—down to the shoulders."

Laureline grimaced in disgust. "You're kidding."

They regarded her with serious expressions. "Never when we're working," Blue assured her.

"Through a kind of osmosis—" explained Burgundy.

"—you will be able to communicate," finished Yellow.

Laureline eyed the dripping, slimy mass with distaste. Part of her wondered if the Doghan Daguis were simply having a good joke at her expense. But she believed Blue when he denied it. They were slimy little information brokers, true, but toying with clients was bad for business. Speaking of slimy…

Gingerly, Laureline forced herself to pick up the slippery jellyfish, trying not to recoil as her fingers touched it.

On her head, down to her shoulders. *Ugh.*

She took a deep breath and steeled herself, then lifted the cool, clammy invertebrate. She paused when Blue spoke in a cautionary tone. "But be very careful—"

"—not to stay under there longer—" Burgundy continued.

"—than one minute—"

"—because then it starts to feed—"

"—on your memory," Burgundy finished.

Laureline stared at them, aghast. She let out a harsh, short bark of utterly false laughter.

"Anything *else* I should know before I let it swallow me up? Do I put my head straight up his ass?"

They blinked at her in perfect unison.

"Not as far as we know," said Blue, hedging his bet.

"You can begin."

"Good luck," added Yellow.

Laureline raised the jellyfish over her head.

"Don't forget!" Blue looked genuinely concerned.

"One minute!"

"Not a second more!"

"Got it," Laureline replied. And she pulled the jellyfish onto her head.

CHAPTER SEVENTEEN

The slimy body of the jellyfish oozed down, plastering itself to Laureline's face and swallowing her slender form down to her waist. It was even more disgusting than she had anticipated, and for a second she had to fight a quick frisson of fear as it pressed its gelatinous body over her mouth and nose. Yet she realized that, somehow, she could still breathe.

She placed aside all thought of queasiness and revulsion, and focused on Valerian.

In her mind's eye, she visualized him as clearly as she possibly could. She tried to remember everything: his face, his laughter, and his smart-assed, playful superiority. His voice, his scent, the feel of his touch. The pressure of his lips against hers. How he had looked when he was holding her, right before their arrival at the station. His eyes wide and soft, listening to her as she poured out some of her most private thoughts, which she had never shared with anyone. Her realization that, before he had answered and been interrupted, he had been trembling.

And so had she.

Valerian...

And then all at once, even though her eyes were closed, Laureline could see.

She was struggling out of the gel-like cocoon that the Pearls had—

No. She wasn't.

Valerian was.

The Doghan Daguis had been right. She was seeing everything through his eyes.

Laureline's heart sped up as she experienced everything with him: the startling, oddly euphoric sensation of running clear through walls with no fear of harm; leaping into space while creating your own stepping stones of translucent blue; running through nuclei fields, and being telepathically yelled at by furious Omelites; chasing the impossibly beautiful Pearl vessel, the shock of watching it splinter into several smaller ones; the decision to chase them down with the Sky Jet.

"Fifteen seconds!" The voice was jarring and almost pulled Laureline out of her focus. It took a heartbeat for her to realize it was one of the Doghan Daguis yelling a warning.

She dipped back down into Valerian's viewpoint, watching as he fired a harpoon that connected with the pretty, swift little vessel. She could feel her heart slamming against her ribcage now, faster than it had ever beaten before. Faster than it ought to beat.

Valerian was towed along as the ship tried to break free. It was hurtling him back and forth, like a child's plaything—

Sweat began to sheet down Laureline's body.

Back and forth Valerian swung, until at last—the hull of a cargo ship approaching, fast, too fast, and the Sky Jet slammed—

Laureline screamed.

The wreckage lay there, illuminated by erratic, faint, purple-blue light. Laureline was making bargains with the universe when, *thank goodness*, Valerian pulled himself out of the smoking wreckage of the Sky Jet, swayed, then slumped to the ground.

Everything went black. Then, suddenly, Laureline was out of his point of view, staring down into the precipice at his too-limp form. *Valerian!* His image suddenly became blurry. For an awful second, she thought she was losing contact with him, but then she realized that it was only her own tears that obscured her vision.

The voice of Burgundy penetrated her fear, shouting, "Thirty seconds!"

Laureline stared at Valerian an instant longer, then set her jaw. Crying over him wasn't going to save him. Figuring out where he had crashed would. She tore her gaze from his sprawled body and looked around the precipice where her vision-self stood.

"Fifty seconds!" yelled Yellow.

"Get out!"

"Now!" shrieked Burgundy.

Laureline couldn't.

Not yet. Not before she had located the man she—

The image blurred a second time, but not from tears. Laureline suddenly felt exhausted, as if she had run a hundred miles without stopping, and realized it wasn't her body, but her mind that was growing exhausted from the strain.

Come on, Laureline—

And there. Her frantically seeking gaze fell on a pipe

with words painted on it. Her head was starting to spin. She fought against it, but her legs quivered and abruptly gave way. She landed hard on her knees, but she had seen and memorized the information.

L.630.E.SUL-DEACTIVATED.

The image faded away.

Laureline could barely lift her arms, but she forced herself to do so. Shaking, numb fingers fumbled to grip the slippery creature that covered her head and torso. With her last ounce of energy, she wrenched the clinging creature off her. It landed on the deck with a soggy splat and she stared at it, trembling, drenched with sweat and seawater, exhausted to near-unconsciousness.

The jellyfish had turned completely black.

"Incredible!" Blue exclaimed.

"One minute—"

"—and ten seconds!" crowed Yellow, excited.

"A record!" announced Blue.

The jellyfish quivered, and as Laureline watched, her lip curling in disgust, it pulled itself to the edge of the dock and slipped back into its element with a soft splash.

"Are you all right?" Burgundy asked, worried.

"Did you find him?" Yellow inquired.

Panting, Laureline blurted, "L.630.E.SUL... DEACTIVATED." Still on hands and knees, she glanced up at her companions. "Any idea what that means?"

They looked at one another meaningfully, then Blue spoke. "Level six hundred thirty East."

"Most likely a sulfate pipe," added Burgundy.

"Deactivated, apparently," Yellow said, seemingly annoyed at being stuck with stating the obvious.

These three had been the source of many an irritation in the past. But today, they'd done everything they said they would do, though, admittedly, for a fee. Because of them, she was going to be able to find Valerian.

"Thanks," Laureline said sincerely, and gave them all a smile.

"Our pleasure, Sergeant," Blue said. He put a stubby hand to the center of his narrow chest and bowed slightly.

"You want a detailed map?" offered Burgundy.

And, naturally, Yellow added, "For an absolute bargain."

Sergeant Neza, at least, had some good news for Okto-Bar: they had located Agent Laureline.

Tall, slim, ramrod-straight, Neza pointed to the station's map. "We biologically traced Sergeant Laureline to here."

"What was she doing out by the Galana Sea?" Okto-Bar asked, surprised. This whole thing was becoming stranger by the minute.

"We don't yet know, sir," Neza replied. "What we do know is that afterwards she stole a vehicle and headed into the red zone." His assuredness faltered slightly as he added, "We lost track of her at that point."

Okto-Bar's eyebrows rose. *The red zone…* A slight smile touched his face. "No idea how, but she must have located the major!" A little more good news, if it was true.

Another sergeant poked her head in and asked, timidly, "General? There ah… there are three Doghan Daguis who claim to have information that might interest us."

No one liked Doghan Daguis. They lived by selling

information, not volunteering it. The young sergeant had been right to be hesitant to mention them. But at this point, two of the spatio-temporal agency's best were missing, and Okto-Bar was not about to let any lead—even one brought to him by a trio of Doghan Daguis—pass by unexamined.

"Let them in."

Okto-Bar turned as the three shuffled in obsequiously. He eyed them each in turn, sternly.

"Our humble respects, General," Blue began.

"May you be healthy—"

"—and prosperous," Yellow finished, and gave Okto-Bar what passed among his species for a smile.

"Shoot," said the general, brusquely. He folded his arms.

They spoke, and the more they said, the grayer Okto-Bar's face grew. When they were done, he had a knot of cold fury in his stomach. To Neza, who also looked stunned and slightly sick, he said, "Follow me."

General Okto-Bar marched into the interrogation room with four of his best people at his heels. Trundling along behind them, as fast as their short legs would carry them, came the three Doghan Daguis. The guards who had been standing at the door stood at attention, looking confused, a little scared, and as if they wished they were anywhere but here.

"Sir, we—" one of them began.

"Open that door, Lieutenant," Okto-Bar said in a chillingly soft voice, "or you'll be very sorry you didn't."

She did.

Okto-Bar truly hoped that the information purchased from the Doghan Daguis had been wrong. But, sickeningly, it wasn't.

The slender, pale alien was tied to the chair. He had obviously been beaten, and when that hadn't produced the desired results, well—the general suspected that the dozen or so tubes that perforated his body were not supplying anything wholesome. The three small aliens who had led him here were now peering cautiously in the door.

Okto-Bar whirled on the poor creature's tormentor and demanded, simmering with anger, "Captain! What's going on here?"

The captain stared at him, obviously panic-stricken. His eyes flitted about as if searching for an escape route and his voice quivered as he replied. "I report directly to the Commander Arun Filitt! I don't have to—"

"I am General Okto-Bar!" he roared, stepping in to close the distance between him and the captain. He had lost whatever shred had remained of his patience. Patience had no place in the face of torture. "In the commander's absence, I am in command on Alpha Station. Sergeant Neza—arrest these men! And release that poor fellow immediately."

Sergeant Neza and another soldier eagerly hastened to obey the general's order. The Doghan Daguis lingered at the door. They looked like they were lapping this up.

The pale alien had been liberated from his bonds, and two of the men were removing the drips. His head lolled back and his thin chest heaved. Okto-Bar stood beside him and said, his voice gentle yet still filled with righteous anger, "I deeply apologize for your mistreatment. We're going to take you to our jail now, because your people attacked us, but I promise, our doctors will take care of you. You won't be harmed anymore."

Even as he spoke, Okto-Bar wondered if the creature would survive long enough to be treated. What had been done to him...

The being opened impossibly blue eyes and smiled feebly at the general. With an effort, he reached up a hand and grasped Okto-Bar's.

"Help us..." he pleaded.

It was a curious request from someone whose species had attacked the station, but Okto-Bar said, "If you want me to help you, tell me all you know and, first of all, why you're attacking us."

Faintly, the battered prisoner replied, "Because... you have... what we need."

He closed his eyes. For a moment, Okto-Bar thought he was gone. Then, unexpectedly, the wounded being stretched his arms out wide and arched his back, as if he were trying to embrace the whole universe.

A blue wave seemed to surge from his body, pulsing as it rippled across the room, *through* the room and everyone in it, while they stood, eyes wide and mouths open in wonder.

CHAPTER
EIGHTEEN

Laureline emerged from the deactivated sulfate pipe in Level 630 East, leading with her gun, to find herself in a gully alongside a precipice. She approached the edge quickly but carefully and peered down into a bottomless blackness intermittently illuminated by a few skittering, phosphorescent butterflies lighting up the stretch of wall. They were beautiful and magical-looking, their fluttering wings painted in softly glowing shades of magenta, violet, and midnight blue.

"Valerian?" Laureline called. Her voice echoed and suddenly she wondered if yelling had been the smartest thing to do. But if he could answer her…

She heard only the dying echo of her own voice, and then silence in response.

This was the right place, she was sure of it. She hadn't noticed the butterflies specifically, but she'd seen Valerian's form and the wreckage of the Sky Jet lit up by their luminescence. And she'd had the converter reproduce enough diamonds to be sure that the map the Doghan Daguis had provided her was accurate. Valerian had been in pretty bad shape in her vision. She could only hope he would hang on until she could reach him.

She fished in her kit until she found a slender but strong line of cable attached to a piton. With a firm shove, Laureline autoset the piton into the rock, tugged to make sure it was secure, then carefully rappelled down the black, nearly vertical rock face. She kept going until her feet touched a ledge that jutted out about ten feet from the wall. With a flick of her wrist, the line detached, and she quickly wound it up and returned it to her kit. The stone beneath her feet was slick, and she moved carefully along the ledge in search of her partner. Now and then a butterfly would waft air against her cheek, a feather-light little kiss; it was a strange pleasantness in this moment of fear and worry.

The ledge curved and then deepened into a cave. Laureline shone a light ahead, gasped. She had found the Sky Jet—at least, what was left of it. She pressed her lips together in a grim line, chasing away the fear that would weaken her, and called out again. "Valerian?"

No answer. She hastened to the wreckage as swiftly as she dared. On the far side, she found him.

Valerian was sprawled on the ground, his suit torn and bloody. Laureline ran to him, dropping to her knees beside him.

"Valerian! I'm here!" She placed her gun on the ground and frantically searched in her kit. She pulled out a compact first aid system, eased her hand around the back of his head, and slipped it into his mouth. Its red light turned blue, as a mini cartridge pumped in the prescribed medication.

"Wake up, Valerian… please!"

Nothing. The seconds ticked by. Had she come too late? The kit was good, but—

His eyes flew open and he sat up, coughing and spitting. Relief washed through her, so powerful it made her weak. Her face hurt, and she realized it was because she couldn't stop smiling. She touched his cheek and impulsively leaned in, pressed her lips to his, and kissed him hard.

He sat there for a second, utterly taken by surprise, then returned the kiss. When she pulled back, though, he stared at her in confusion.

"Laureline! What are you doing here?"

"I came to get you," she said. "You totaled your Sky Jet. Remember?" She jerked her head in the direction of the wreckage.

Valerian blinked, still slightly dazed. "Yeah... I... I lost it in a curve."

"You nearly died, you mean," Laureline replied, unable to smother her grin. She couldn't take her hands or her eyes off him, and she didn't want to. This had hit her too hard. "It's lucky I found you!"

Memory seemed to be returning to him in fits and spurts. "What about the commander?" Valerian asked. "Do we know where he is?"

"No sign of him," Laureline answered. "Their spaceship disappeared in the red zone. We couldn't track it or him."

Valerian nodded. "Okay. Sounds like we have no time to waste. Let's go." He hauled himself stiffly to his feet.

Laureline remained kneeling on the hard rock, staring at him, utterly taken aback as he made his way to the wreckage to recover what he could. For a moment she couldn't even form words. Then, she said, "Is that all?"

He turned back to peer down at her. Damn him, he wasn't even extending a hand to help her up. "Why?"

"No 'thank you,' no 'you did great, Laureline?'"

Valerian's face melted into his old familiar, smartass grin. He strode over to her, pulled her to her feet, and kissed her on the lips. She was just melting into it when he pulled back, cupped her face with his hands, and said, very sincerely, "Thanks."

And then he added, "But I'd have done the same for you."

Laureline's eyes narrowed and she felt the heat of absolute fury rise in her cheeks. Valerian flashed a smile, and dodged the slap she aimed at him.

She thought about everything she'd endured—the smelly pirate, nearly getting gobbled by Bromosaurs, the clammy stickiness of the jellyfish enclosing half her body, the risk of nearly having her memories *eaten by it*—

Laureline wanted to tell him, in excruciating detail, but she couldn't even think that clearly right now, and so all that came out was, "You are such a jack ass!"

"Hey, chill," Valerian said, laughing a little. He was *enjoying* this! He reached down to pick up the gun she'd placed on the rocky surface and tucked it into his belt. "I trusted you, even more than I trust myself. Isn't that what you wanted?"

"No!"

Valerian ducked another swing, then wrapped his arms around her and pulled her to him. "You are an amazing woman, Laureline. Why do you think I want to marry you?"

"Why would I marry a conceited, ungrateful—"

"Oh, I don't know," he said, "probably because you can't live without him. I mean, look, whenever he wanders out of your sight, you chase after him!"

His ego and audacity left Laureline speechless. He leaned in for another kiss, but she was having none of it. She turned her head and stiff-armed him away. When he stepped back, she graced him with the coldness of her blue eyes. Icily, she said, "We have a mission to finish, Major. Remember?"

Valerian sighed and dropped his arms. Then he lifted them in a *you win* gesture as he returned to scavenge the Sky Jet. They would need weapons where they were going.

Laureline turned away, gazing out into the cavern that opened before them. One hand reached into the carrier attached to her belt to pat the converter, as much to comfort herself as him. He nibbled delicately on her fingers, and she smiled.

"Didn't you say the girl in your dreams had a converter like this little fellow?" Laureline asked. She gave the converter's scaly back a final stroke, then closed the container securely.

"That's right," Valerian answered, his back to her as he rummaged.

A butterfly landed on Laureline's hand. It was so beautiful—so delicate, and fragile, and the colors so vivid. It had a sort of tail, too; a long, wavy tendril that swayed and undulated behind it. She watched it as it slowly closed and opened its wings, keeping her hand still so as not to frighten it.

"So, if the converter is native to their planet," she continued, "it's fairly understandable that they want to retrieve the last living specimen, isn't it?"

"Yes," agreed Valerian, "and they probably kidnapped the commander because they thought he was carrying it on him."

"And when they found out he wasn't, I'll be the next one on their list," Laureline said. The butterfly stayed where it was, and despite her annoyance with Valerian's most recent display of reliably boorish behavior, she smiled. There was still beauty in the universe.

"Don't worry," Valerian reassured her. "I'm not letting you go anywhere!"

She sighed, and let her resentment go. "I'm not letting *you* go anywhere!"

She heard him chuckle. All was well between them again. "I think I'll quit while I'm ahead and not comment on that," he said.

"O-ho, you're learning wisdom to go along with those gray hairs," Laureline teased.

"One," he retorted. "You found *one*."

Laureline continued to regard the beautiful insect that had graced her with its presence. She smiled at it. "Pretty butterflies here," she said.

"Sure," he said absently, "but don't let them touch you, whatever you do."

Laureline's smile bled from her face. "Why not?" Her voice was strained.

The butterfly closed and opened its wings.

She stood perfectly still.

"Because," he said, turning to address her, "some of them are—" His eyes widened. "*No!*"

He lunged toward her, but it was too late. In a flash, the butterfly's deceptively delicate "tail" wrapped itself around Laureline's hand, and she was yanked over the edge of the precipice.

Valerian rushed over to see Laureline dangling by her

wrist on the end of long, glowing violet tendril, swinging over the seemingly infinite drop. His gaze followed the line about a hundred and fifty feet up to see an enormous, lumpy, only-vaguely humanoid creature sitting on the edge of another precipice, swinging its ugly legs and holding onto what looked terribly like a human fishing pole.

And now, it was reeling Laureline in, reaching out with a powerful hand to grab her like a doll and bellowing happily as it displayed her to its compatriots also fishing on the edge of the canyon, who made admiring little yelps.

Valerian drew his gun and took aim, then abruptly realized that if he killed the creature, it would likely let go of the pole… and Laureline. He swore softly and took a breath.

"Here goes nothing," he muttered. Valerian holstered his gun, took a running leap, and threw himself into the void to catch a butterfly.

His hands closed tight around one.

Please don't be real. Please don't be real.

It wasn't. It, too, was a lure, which meant that he wasn't about to plunge to his death after leaping to grab a damned butterfly.

The decoy wrapped its "tail" firmly around his waist and Valerian was yanked upwards so fast he could barely breathe. He was reeled in and brought within a few feet of a hideous, froglike face whose downturned mouth opened in an ear-shattering shriek of presumed joy. Red, glowing eyes with barely discernable slitted pupils blinked rapidly as the eight-foot-tall Boulan-Bathor hauled in what surely had to be the finest catch of the day.

He plunked Valerian down on the ledge and reached

out with a net. But Valerian gave him a lopsided grin and lifted his gun.

"Sorry," he shouted, "I'm inedible!"

He abandoned the very messy headless corpse of his giant would-be captor, and ran in the direction of where he'd seen Laureline disappear. Unfortunately, it looked as though Valerian's partner had been the last catch of the day. Her fisherman had placed a large circular basket that appeared to be fashioned of twisted metal bands on his back and was moving toward the large gate that marked Boulan-Bathor territory. Valerian caught a fleeting glimpse of Laureline in the basket. As expected, she was ranting at her alien captor while at the same time attempting to find a weakness in the curving cage that held her prisoner.

Valerian ran as fast as he could, his legs pumping, but the fisherman had a head start and those froggy legs could move pretty damn fast. The huge steel door was opened to admit the fisherman, and Valerian skidded to a halt when he saw a dozen guards bristling with spears and pikes.

Valerian veered sharply to the right, hiding behind a jutting piece of black rock and watched, sickened, as the fisherman—and Laureline—were admitted inside and the gate closed with a terrible finality.

His beloved was trapped inside the Boulan-Bathor palace. And there was nothing he could do.

CHAPTER
NINETEEN

Okto-Bar should not have grieved the death of the unusual alien as much as he did, but there it was. Something inside him was oddly sad, even though the emotion went against all rational thought. How could one mourn the death of a being one didn't even know—especially from a race that had shown itself to be aggressive?

Help us, it had begged.

And, strangely, Okto-Bar wanted to help. He would begin with finding out as much as he could about the delicate and beautiful alien, whose people, as Agent Laureline had pointed out, had managed to attack a roomful of beings without harming a single one of them.

Peculiar enemies. He sighed and asked Neza, "Did you run a DNA search?"

"Yes," replied the sergeant, "but it didn't match any of the millions of species in our database."

"How is that possible?" Okto-Bar couldn't believe it.

"There are a couple of possibilities," Neza explained. "Either he belonged to a completely unknown species or…" The soldier didn't finish.

"Or?" prompted Okto-Bar.

"Or his species was deliberately deleted from the database."

They stared at one another. It wasn't Neza's place to volunteer theories to his superior officer without being requested to do so, and Okto-Bar wasn't ready to give voice to any of the increasingly strange ones knocking about in his head. He returned to his chair, slumping into it, trying and largely failing to wrestle the known facts into something that didn't sound ludicrous. He stared at the myriad colored, flashing screens but didn't really see them.

Who were these peculiar aliens who had kidnapped Commander Filitt? Why was there no record of them?

Sergeant Neza spoke up, interrupting his brooding. "General, the major has resurfaced! On the edge of the red zone."

Okto-Bar was on his feet at once. "Excellent. Which district is he in?"

Color crept into the sergeant's cheeks as he replied, "Ah… that would be Paradise Alley, sir."

Paradise Alley? "What the *hell* is he doing there?" Okto-Bar demanded.

The sergeant's blush deepened. "I have no idea, sir."

"Well," the general said in a gruffer voice than normal to cover his surprise, "put a call out to all units in the sector."

Every night was a busy night in Paradise Alley for law enforcement. Tonight, it seemed, would be no different. A police officer glanced down at his forearm at a screen fastened around his wrist.

A picture of a young man with dark hair appeared on the screen. The officer nodded; someone was speaking in his ear. "Copy that," he said quietly and started to look around—only to feel a gun pressed to his temple by the self-same young man whose picture adorned his wrist.

"May I help you?" the officer said tightly.

"Yes, you sure can," Valerian said. "Move. Now! Slide your gun into my holster."

The officer did as he was told. "Thanks," said Valerian. "Now, hold still."

Valerian fired a streak of blue light into the officer's neck. The officer was frozen where he stood, turned into an apparent statue. He wouldn't be going anywhere, not unless someone came along to reverse the immobilizer within the next three hours. It would wear off on its own after that.

Valerian pressed a button on his gun. A small shield hummed over it, bending the light rays so the gun became invisible for all intents and purposes. He tucked it in the back of his pants and steeled himself for the ordeal that was about to unfold.

Squaring his shoulders, he stepped out into the main street, into the throng of a staggering variety of races displaying their charms beneath garish, brightly colored lights in a place where it was always night.

"Hey, handsome. Want to walk on the wild side?" The speaker's voice was deep and husky, but feminine, and the fur on her face was very light and looked soft. But the teeth she bared were sharp, and Valerian stammered a polite, "Uh, no thank you."

Backing away from her, he collided with a pair of twins with long legs, long blond hair, and long white dresses. "Hello there," they said in perfect unison. "Two-for-one deal. Tonight only."

A scantily clad girl in a swing soared over Valerian,

smiling sweetly and providing him a chance to break away from the unnaturally gorgeous twins. She looked perfectly human until the light caught the gossamer wings attached to her shoulders on the second pass. She waved cheerfully and inquired, "Want a ride?"

A buxom woman clad in pointed shoes, white stockings, garters, a full but very short skirt, and a tightly cinched bodice waved a handkerchief and smiled at him. Her round face was heavily powdered and her hair—which might or might not have been a wig—seemed to stretch two feet upwards. She called out in archaic French, "*Par ici, mon chéri!*"

Valerian covered his eyes with his hand. "No, thanks!"

Another pretty creature moved to block his path. She had a firm, taut body covered with beautiful, iridescent blue and green feathers. Her fingers ended in sharp claws, but she was delicate and playful as she cupped his chin in her hands and spread her tail feathers like a peacock. "Come fly with me!" she whispered.

"Sorry," apologized Valerian, "I'm allergic to feathers."

He backed away from her, looking around for an escape. His eyes fell on a sign: "All U Like. Humans Only."

"Get out of here, pervert!" came a male voice. "You've made the right choice, soldier! Jolly will see to it that you spend time with only the finest company Paradise Alley has to offer."

Valerian turned to behold a man, presumably Jolly, who was undeniably human, but also undeniably ridiculous-looking. He had military-issue boots and gray camouflage pants. His jacket, too, looked like it was of a historical military design. And his hat looked like it could have once adorned someone from the era called the Old West. But the coat was an astonishing rainbow of colors from its blue sleeves to teal stripes to red epaulettes, and it covered a black and yellow shirt. Dark glasses, a gun belt loaded with bullets, and a close-trimmed goatee completed the bizarre ensemble.

The pimp grinned, revealing even white teeth as he slipped his arm around Valerian's shoulder in a fraternal manner, casually but deliberately propelling the agent into his establishment.

"I'm telling ya, this club is the best you'll find in the whole damn space station!" He clapped Valerian on the shoulder. "Stay right there. I'll be with you in a second."

But now that he had found the establishment he'd been looking for, Valerian was anxious to get what he was after. "I'm looking for something a bit special—"

Jolly held up his arms in an expansive gesture. "No matter what you want, I got it! Trust me. Come on in!"

Valerian hesitated. "I'm, uh… not entirely sure about that."

I cannot believe I'm here. Laureline will kill me if she ever finds out. She certainly won't accept a marriage proposal.

But it was for her that Valerian had sought out this place. If she ever did find out, he hoped she'd allow him the chance to explain that before she knocked him on his ass.

"So!" Jolly exclaimed. "What are you looking for? Tell me."

"A glamopod," Valerian replied.

"Ah! You, sir, are about to be a very lucky man! Not only do I have one, I've got the *best* one in the whole universe."

Valerian let Jolly lead him inside, watched beadily by

the two bouncers on either side of the door.

He really, really hoped he was doing the right thing—and that Laureline was staying alive long enough for him to rescue her.

Laureline hoped that Valerian was all right.

The last she had seen of him, she'd been pulled upward and at a high speed and he had performed a literal leap of faith, trying to grab onto a decoy and follow her up. But they had gotten separated, and she had been plopped into a basket and brought into what looked like a magnificent palace—albeit one inhabited by frogs.

The palace was built by Boulan-Bathors for Boulan-Bathors, and consequently everything was oversized from a human female's perspective. The fisherman, immune to her pleas, rants, and threats, brought Laureline to an enormous room off the side of the enormous stone hallway. The basket that contained her was opened and then upended, depositing her unceremoniously on a thick, soft carpet. Laureline got to her feet, but by then the door was closing and she was left in the room.

It was comfortable enough, she supposed. The high ceilings were painted with geometrical designs that were only faintly glimpsed in the dim light, and the walls were covered with hangings. In the center of the room, fragrant smoke wisped out of a huge amphora.

She had company. Several female Boulan-Bathors also occupied the large room, busy cutting fabric and stitching it together. Laureline looked around at them nervously, but the Boulan-Bathor seamstresses chatted amongst themselves and appeared to be fairly relaxed. The curtains at the end of the room parted, and another female, this one carrying a large basket, trundled inside. Laureline thought she must be the supervisor or someone important, because her appearance sent off a flurry of nods and bows and increased activity.

She had the same build as the males—large and rotund, with a long spindly neck and small head—and like them, she wore a loincloth. But she also had two sets of metal cups modestly covering four large breasts, and a hat of bright red plumes that jutted upward from her head in creative disarray. She wore jewelry as well, in the form of huge circlets around her scrawny throat and rings on two fingers. She came over to Laureline and twisted her lips in what appeared to be a smile, which didn't necessarily improve her looks.

Laureline straightened to her full height of five foot nine, craning her neck to look up at the towering female. Valerian, *curse him*, had taken her gun, but she still had her ID, and she held up her credentials now.

"Hey, I'm Agent Laureline and I'm working for the government," she said briskly. "If you want to avoid a diplomatic incident, I suggest you release me immediately."

The female Boulan-Bathor gazed at her, blinked her bulging eyes, nodded, and proceeded to empty the bin she had been carrying at Laureline's feet.

The spatio-temporal agent looked at the heap of fabric and realized the female had just put a pile of human-sized clothing on the floor.

"No, thanks," she said, "I don't plan on getting a makeover. I have to go. Do you understand?"

The female gave her another ghastly smile and nodded again, the feathers atop her head fluttering with the movement. She stooped, grabbed one of the dresses with a thick-fingered hand, and presented it to Laureline.

Laureline pressed her lips together. "I'm not going to wear your stupid dress! Call your chief, or translator, so we can at least communicate."

The female smiled a third time, and Laureline tried not to grimace at that mouthful of ugly, odd-sized teeth. The female selected another dress and presented it, cocking her head in a position of inquiry. Perhaps Laureline would like this one?

Laureline had had enough. She took a deep breath, stood on her tiptoes, and she screamed as loud as she possibly could in the Boulan-Bathor's amphibian face.

The female recoiled, startled, her arms flailing. *Now maybe you'll go get someone I can talk to,* Laureline thought. But the female only blinked and seemed to be considering something. Then she stooped so that she was face to face with Laureline, opened that enormous mouth, and emitted an inhuman bellow that made the agent's shriek sound like a kitten's mew.

Her ears ringing, soaked in Boulan-Bathor spittle from head to foot, Laureline blinked.

"Okay, I… I'll put your dress on."

The inside of the club was a lot nicer than Valerian had expected. Then again, he'd really had no idea what to expect.

There were large, overstuffed pieces of furniture covered in warm, dark shades of velvet. Paintings hung on the wall depicting—well, certain activities Valerian really didn't want to see right now. Several doors lined the long central room. Some of them were open, some of them were closed.

There was a small counter just inside the main door and Jolly stepped beside it, smiling his wide, cheerful, artificial smile. "This is where you leave your hardware, cowboy," he told Valerian.

"I'd rather hold onto it. I'm on duty," Valerian explained.

Jolly's smile became fixed and markedly less cheerful. "Rules are rules, soldier! We make *love* here, not war."

Valerian debated in his mind, then made a show of placing the gun he'd acquired from the police officer on the counter with great reluctance.

"There, that's better! One less thing to worry about removing, if you catch my meaning."

"Um," said Valerian.

Jolly took him by the elbow and Valerian had to deliberately resist yanking his arm away. The pimp steered him through one of the doorways and into a small, cozy, old-fashioned theater with only a handful of seats. Thick black velvet curtains were drawn over the stage, which was lit up by small running lights. An antiquated piano was situated on another platform, off to the side. Jolly escorted Valerian to a seat and pressed him down into it.

"Listen," Valerian began, instantly hopping back to his feet, "let's make a deal—"

"Now, now, we'll talk money later, soldier. For now, let's talk pleasure." He pushed Valerian back down and waggled his eyebrows. "What kind of music do you like? Techno? Macro? Bio? Nano?"

"Uh," Valerian said, "I'm more retro."

Jolly looked delighted. "You're so right, my friend! Oldies but goodies! Now relax… and enjoy the show!"

He went to the piano and seated himself in front of it, cracked knuckles, and began to play. Valerian was surprised and impressed. Usually, pimps didn't have any useful skills or talents other than knowing how to bully people, but Jolly appeared to be an exception.

The lights dimmed, and the curtain parted to reveal the silhouette of a stunningly shapely female. She stood, legs crossed at the ankles, one hand on a cane, the other on the brim of a small round-topped hat perched on her head. From perfect stillness, she began to dance, her feet flying in rapid taps, the cane tossed from one hand to the other, a gorgeous form in beautiful, flowing motion.

And then the spotlight came up, and Valerian gasped.

CHAPTER TWENTY

The dancer had smooth, dark skin and wore a black sparkling vest over a see-through body stocking. Her legs were long and sleekly muscled, and her face had wide, mesmerizing brown eyes that looked as though they knew the darkest secrets of his soul.

The cane vanished, dissolving into her hand, and that hand reached up to remove the small hat. Her black hair melted into a pale yellow, cascading down her shoulders and the black vest morphed into a form-fitting white sequined dress as she strode downstage toward Valerian, licking her lips.

He couldn't tear his eyes off her and shifted uncomfortably in his seat. She strutted across the stage as if she owned it, tossing back that lustrous, pale yellow hair as the sequins on her gown glittered and gleamed.

A pole rose from the floor, and the dancer leaped onto it, her strong arms and long legs propelling her through an acrobatic and almost aerial routine. The sultry blonde was gone, and suddenly she was clad in black leather from head to toe—with pointed feline ears and a lashing tail. Then in the blink of an eye she had pigtails and was wearing a schoolgirl uniform on a decidedly adult female form.

The giggly "schoolgirl" was replaced by a dynamic dancer, with strong muscles and dark skin that gleamed as she moved with powerful, strong steps, throwing back her head, lost in the ecstasy of an ancient rhythm. Bare feet stamped the stage—then were abruptly encased in roller skates. Valerian blinked, stunned to think that anyone could dance on roller skates—but dance she did, zooming around in tight shorts, a tube top, and long striped socks.

His heart jumped into his throat as she leaped upward, turning a somersault, then transformed in mid-air into a maid with a short black skirt, white apron, and a feather duster. With a wink of one dark eye, the maid used the feather duster like a wand, waving it about playfully in Valerian's direction before leaping into the air, rolling, and coming up as, again, the tawny-skinned cabaret girl with the hat and cane.

She tipped her bowler hat to him and smiled. She was not even out of breath. Jolly the Pimp winked, closed the piano, and left the auditorium discreetly.

"So," purred the dancer, walking toward him slowly and putting a foot on the chair next to Valerian's thigh, "what'll it be, soldier?"

"Look," stammered Valerian, trying desperately to drag this whole debacle back on track, "that's pretty cool, but not exactly what I'm looking for right now."

She extended a finger and tilted his chin up. "I have a *whole* lot more in stock. Just tell me what you have in mind."

He leaned back in his chair, trying to put some distance between the two of them. "I have a lot in mind. And no time for this. I'll pass."

Her eyes widened and she withdrew her leg, standing

in front of him. The cane and hat melted back into her hands and her breath came quickly. Tears sprang to her large eyes and she started to tremble. "You—didn't like my performance?"

"No!" He got to his feet, distressed that she was so upset. He hadn't meant that at all. Unfortunately, the word only seemed to devastate her more. "I mean, yes!" Valerian amended desperately, frantic to placate her. "I mean I loved it, absolutely! You were amazing!" It was, in fact, absolutely true. He'd never seen a glamopod performance before.

His chest eased as a proud yet shy smile touched her full lips and she beamed up at him. "I started very young, and learned my trade at the top schools. I can play anyone or anything."

A variety of extremely awkward scenarios marched unbidden into Valerian's mind. "I, ah… I'm sure you can."

"Well," she amended, either not seeing or not acknowledging his discomfiture, "except Nefertiti. I'm still honing that performance. It's not ready to show anyone yet. I'll master it though!"

She looked up at him searchingly. "Let me guess. You're a classical kind of guy, aren't you? I know all of Shakespeare by heart, if you want. Or I can quote the complete works of Molière. Or poetry, maybe? You like poetry?" She closed the already short distance between them and came and draped her soft arms around Valerian's neck.

"Uh, sure," Valerian stammered.

"Rimbaud? Keats? Verlaine?" she continued.

Valerian was lost. He knew not a thing about poetry. "Difficult choice," he managed. His mouth was desert dry and he couldn't seem to stop looking into the dark pools of her eyes.

One hand played with the nape of his neck, then she dug her fingers into it slightly, the lacquered nails pressing against his skin. "'I'm afraid of a kiss, like the kiss of the bee,'" she whispered, quoting, "'I suffer like this, and wake endlessly…'"

And then, kicking off a cascade of emotions in Valerian, she morphed into Laureline.

"I'm afraid of a kiss," she whispered.

Valerian stared at her, stunned. How had she known? It was Laureline, down to the last dark blonde strand of hair, to the curve of her mouth, even to the scent that was unmistakably and uniquely her.

And she was in his arms. Willing, wanting him, her lips slightly parted, her blue eyes wide. All he had to do was lower his head, put his arms around her, and pull her against him.

He lifted one hand and reached down toward his waist. Then in one smooth movement, he pressed the button on the gun to render it visible and held it against "Laureline's" temple. The blue eyes widened in shock.

"How about I tell you what I really have in mind?" Valerian said in a cold, almost cruel voice.

The false Laureline recoiled in fear and began to scream. Her form shifted yet again, but this time not into the shape of a beautiful woman. The cabaret performer melted into a pale blue, gelatinous, transparent mass. Three boneless arms with three fingers each undulated and waved about, and two large eyes, slightly bluer than the rest of the creature's body, blinked rapidly. In its fear, the glamopod had reverted to its true form.

"Hey!" exclaimed Valerian. "Quit screaming!"

But it was too late. Jolly burst in and assessed the situation instantly, his eyes going straight to Valerian's hand and the gun in it.

"I said no weapons, pal!" he snapped. He reached for his own and brought it up, but Valerian got two shots off before the pimp could open fire. Valerian whirled back to the glamopod and found himself staring straight into the angry face of the minister of defense.

"Major Valerian," the "minister" demanded, "I advise you to put that gun down!"

But Valerian was done with its games. The performance was over. It had been over the minute the creature had chosen to assume the shape of Laureline.

He leveled the gun at the glamopod. "And I advise *you* to sit down."

It obeyed, plopping into one of the auditorium seats, and immediately morphed into the form of a ten-year-old boy with dark hair and wide, tear-filled blue eyes. "Please!" sobbed the boy. "No! Don't hurt me!"

Valerian stared, appalled and slightly sick. He felt like he'd been punched in the gut. "What the hell is this?"

But he knew. He knew.

The boy looked up at him with eyes that Valerian recognized. "This is you, when you were ten. You're not going to shoot yourself, are you?"

Emotions flooded Valerian. *Five.* When he'd lost his mother and, along with her, his innocence about so very much. When ugly revelations and brutal realities had come crashing in on him, which kicked off his own sort of transformation—from Valentin Twain into

Valerian into a devil-may-care agent.

"Cut it out!" he snarled. The form the glamopod wore shrank back, terrified, and Valerian took a deep breath. "Go back to normal, please."

"Okay," the child said in a small, frightened voice. The boy who wore Valerian's face was absorbed into the jelly-like quivering mass.

Valerian winced. "Not that normal! The other one. The first one. With the hat."

Anxious to please, the glamopod obeyed, and turned back into the cabaret dancer with the sexy vest-and-fishnet outfit and bowler.

That was not going to work either. Valerian forced himself to be patient. She—it?—was trying to cooperate. "Can you put on something a little more casual? We need to talk."

The vest and stockings became solid fabric and spread out to cover her whole body. She tweaked it slightly, and the outfit rippled and changed into an austere men's suit.

Valerian sighed a little in relief. "Thank you," he said. "Okay. So, what's your name?"

She smiled at him. "Whatever you want it to be, sweetie." Valerian still had the gun trained on her, and now he waggled it in annoyance.

"I have no time for games… sweetie. Come on, what's your name?"

"They call me Bubble," she replied.

Valerian felt a sudden quick, guilty pang. He wondered if she even knew her name, or if her species had such things. He wondered how long she had been in this place.

"Look," he told her, "I lost my partner, Bubble. You help me out for an hour, and in return, I'll set you free."

He thought she'd be pleased. Instead, she looked even sadder at the words. "What good is freedom when you're an illegal immigrant far from home?"

"I work for the government," Valerian persisted. "You'll be doing something very helpful for me and for them. I can get you an ID pass. You have my word."

Bubble squirmed in her seat, seemingly uncertain as to what to do. Part of her face and a leg reverted to the blue jelly of her original form, and a third arm tried to form before she refocused and looked up at him.

"You don't understand," she said. "If I leave here, Jolly will kill me."

Valerian glanced over toward the door. A red pool had spread out from it, and he could just glimpse a pair of boots with their toes pointing toward the ceiling. "Jolly won't kill anyone ever again."

Bubble followed his gaze and her eyes widened. She did not strike him as malicious, but a hint of joy and relief commingled on her gorgeous features. Then she looked back up at him.

"...You really liked my performance?" she asked, hesitantly, almost shyly.

His anger at her melting away, Valerian gave her a genuine smile. "Best I ever saw," he said, and meant every word.

Bubble smiled like an angel. She again glanced toward the door and seemed to reach a decision.

"So," she asked, "what do you need me to do?"

It had been a comparatively quiet evening, and the pair of bouncers flanking Jolly's club hadn't seen much action, which was okay with them. There had been a bit of a ruckus earlier, when someone had spotted a cop who seemingly had been turned into stone. Or maybe it was just a statue someone had snuck onto the street for a laugh. Regardless, the policeman/statue was now wearing a huge floppy hat, sunglasses, a fake beard, three scarves, and a garland of flowers, and had lewd messages painted on him in at least four different languages. That had been more entertaining than bashing heads.

Both of them, though, straightened up to look imposing and scary as their boss sauntered outside and looked at them each in turn. "So, ahhh," he said to them, "I'm gonna take ten!" He smiled, almost baring his teeth. "You two, keep an eye on old soldier boy in there... He seems like a real freak to me..."

"Okay, boss," one of the bouncers replied. His eyes widened in confusion as Jolly patted him on the cheek and walked away down the street.

"You think he's been smoking some of that stuff that's been floating around the clubs?" one of them muttered.

"No idea," the other replied, "but that was weird."

"Okay, Bubble," Valerian said. "Get us out of sight. That's the place, right there." His voice felt muffled to him, but she heard him.

"Wow, those are some gates," she said in awe. Her voice floated to him thickly.

"Yes, they're big. Get off me!"

"All right, all right, I'm doing this," the glamopod replied. He felt the warm, gelatinous flesh—could you even call it flesh?—peel back from his face and body as she climbed off him. Valerian shook himself and took a gulp of the not very fresh but still welcome air.

The plan had, it seemed, worked. Bubble had expanded her form to engulf him and had adopted the guise of her hated late employer. Wearing Jolly's face and body, they had made it from Paradise Alley back to the Boulan-Bathor palace. Bubble resumed her suited cabaret dancer form. She'd located a sheltered area across the plaza, and was now gazing at the huge gates—and the guards who patrolled in front of them.

The entrance to the palace was hewn out of the same black rock that composed the deep canyon from which Valerian and Laureline had been fished. The Boulan-Bathor species was a contradiction in terms—hideously ugly, at least to human eyes, but capable of designing things of great beauty. The palace was justifiably named, row after row of exquisitely carved pillars covered in gold leaf that towered into the air.

Huge braziers made the gold pillars glow warmly, and gave off intense heat even from a distance. Black carved steps led up to the gate, and more pillars receded into the heart of the palace. It was almost overwhelming… and clearly Bubble was indeed almost overwhelmed.

"You want to go in *there*?"

"Yes," Valerian replied, "but no foreigners are admitted. The only way to get inside is to look like one of them."

"Sure, but…" she hesitated, then said, "I've never played a Boulan-Bathor."

Valerian debated telling her how profoundly glad he was that she'd never had an audience wanting her to assume the form of one of these hulking creatures, but decided not to go down that path right now.

Instead, he appealed to her justifiable pride in her skill. "Hey," he challenged, "are you an artist or not?"

"Yes, but I need time to get into a role," she said, "to capture behavior and movements and understand the character's arc. What are their motivations, their backstory? That sort of thing. Then we do a couple rehearsals, you give me some notes—"

Valerian knew the Boulan-Bathors better than most, but he didn't think that sharing that information with Bubble would boost her confidence about playing the role. More than likely it would send her running in the opposite direction—which, honestly, would be a pretty sane response. What they were about to do wasn't. But Laureline was in there, and he knew what she was up against, and he had to get her out.

"A little improv won't do you any harm," Valerian interrupted. He wasn't particularly eager to once again be engulfed by the glamopod, but time was racing past. Laureline was still in that palace, and the commander was still missing. He thought about her recent performance of Laureline and his younger self; now that his anger had faded, he had to admit Bubble had done an amazing job. "Come on!"

Bubble sighed. "All right," she said reluctantly. "Turn around!" She stepped behind Valerian and extended her arm, slipping them around him. For a second, she rested her head on his shoulder, but then she swiftly shifted.

Valerian moved awkwardly, wearing the alien like some kind of weird cloak, checking out his new body while Bubble lamented, "This is not right! Those claws—I should get a manicure!"

"Let's go," Valerian insisted, and they emerged from their hiding place and headed for the palace gates.

CHAPTER
TWENTY-ONE

This felt very different from walking in tandem with Bubble to portray Jolly the pimp. From within the disguise, Valerian noticed that they were lurching from side to side. The effect must be that the creature they were impersonating had had a bit too much to drink. He wondered if Boulan-Bathors even *got* drunk.

"Hey, what are you doing?" Valerian asked.

"Give me a second to get the hang of it," Bubble replied crossly.

"Hurry," Valerian hissed, looking through her, "people are staring at us!"

"I *told* you I needed rehearsals!"

Valerian watched anxiously as they approached the gate. One of the guards nudged his buddy, but by now Bubble had gotten the awkward, lurching gait under control and was lumbering in a more appropriate manner. The huge metal gate swung open, allowing them admittance. The guards were watching suspiciously as they passed by, but they did nothing.

Valerian dared to hope they might pull this off. "Much better," he said to Bubble. "You're doing great!"

"It's harder than playing femme fatales, believe me!" Bubble murmured.

Despite himself, Valerian's thoughts went back to the cabaret dancer, the maid, the grown-up "schoolgirl."

And Laureline.

Laureline. Please be okay.

"General," said Neza, turning to his commanding officer, "we picked up the major's trail again."

"Ah, excellent," Okto-Bar said. "Where is he?"

Neza's brow furrowed in concern. "In Boulan-Bathor territory," he said.

Okto-Bar raised his eyebrows and stepped to the map, looking for himself. "Are you sure there's not an error?"

"Negative, sir. He's there, all right."

"How is that possible?" demanded Okto-Bar. "*Nobody* gets in there!"

"And definitely not out of there." Neza looked as troubled as Okto-Bar felt. At the moment, the political situation was tense between the station and the Boulan-Bathors. The current emperor, Boulan III, had forbidden any other species to enter the sector. It was rumored that his wife, Nopa the Beautiful, was the real power behind the throne, and that all that Boulan cared about was the cult of personality that had sprung up around him and his next excessive, gluttonous meal.

"We're going to need backup," the general decided. "Call the minister."

"Aye, sir."

* * *

The Creation, as Valerian finally decided to mentally title the compilation of himself, Bubble, and the Boulan-Bathor they were both pretending to be, made its ponderous way through a large kitchen. It was a veritable chamber of horrors, Valerian thought.

On the wall hung items that would have looked more at home in an ancient armory—or a torture chamber: knives, filleting tools, hooks, small axes, saws—everything to prepare large and potentially resistant meat into meals. Strings of dried herbs, fruits, and whole peppers of some sort hung from the ceiling. So did haunches of meat, whole crustaceans and fish, and severed tentacles. While bright lights blazed over the tables, the "supplies" were kept in corners until the moment of preparation. Housed in tanks, cages, or suspended from the ceiling was a staggering variety of creatures.

The tables were covered with blood, ichor, and other fluids. Dozens of Boulan-Bathors, their white aprons looking like the grisly canvases of a mad artist, tirelessly plucked future food from tank or cage and brought it, often writhing in protest, to the table where the huge blades thunked down ominously, killing, chopping, slicing, dicing, and filleting. For the first time since he'd teamed up with Bubble, Valerian was grateful for the fact that she covered his nose so completely he couldn't smell. He didn't want to know what the kitchen reek was like. His stomach was skittish enough.

"Boy, these guys are all about food, huh?" Bubble observed.

"Yeah," Valerian said. "It's a cultural thing for them. The most powerful among them is entitled to the most food. Eating pretty much everything is a status symbol."

"Can I ask what we're looking for?" Bubble murmured.

"My wife," Valerian answered.

"Oh, you're married?" She sounded happy for him.

"Well," Valerian amended, "I will be, as soon as I find her."

"I see," Bubble said sagely. "Just before the wedding, right? Scared of commitment?"

"Something like that," Valerian replied.

"Maybe she doesn't love you," Bubble commented as they edged past a Boulan-Bathor chef as he cleaved a frantically wriggling octopod into several still-wriggling sections.

"Oh, actually, she's crazy about me," Valerian said, with more certainty than he felt.

"How do you know?" Bubble said.

One of the chefs bellowed to another. He tossed her a sack canister of something that, when opened, looked at first to be some sort of berry for garnishing, but upon closer inspection was revealed to be eyeballs.

"She's fighting it," Valerian said. *And I'm fighting my impulse to puke. What kind of situation has Laureline gotten herself into?* "What more proof do you need?" And, as they maneuvered through the ghoulish kitchen, he hissed, "Don't touch anything!"

"What about you?" Bubble asked. "Do you love her?"

Valerian hesitated. He thought about his momentary shock as Bubble had transformed herself into Laureline. How he hadn't even been tempted to seduce the illusion. Not that the fantasy wouldn't have been nice, but his heart had rejected it instantly. He didn't want to just make love to her. He wanted to…

"Yes," he said. "I do love her."

"And you let her go?"

He opened his mouth to deny it vigorously. After all, he hadn't exactly walked away from her—she'd been fished up by a Boulan-Bathor lure, whisked away from him in a matter of seconds. But in a very real sense, he had "let her go." He'd done it every time he had a fling with a "coworker." Every time he laughed when he reached for her, he had downplayed the seriousness behind their flirtation.

He'd let her go, instead of holding on with all his heart.

And so, he said, almost more to himself than to the glamopod, "Sometimes, you have to lose something to realize how much it meant to you."

A form abruptly loomed up in front of him, pulling his attention firmly into the present. It was a guard, and he was yelling at The Creation. Bravely, Bubble did her best to pretend to reply. The guard said something back, then grabbed her arm and shoved them toward a line of Boulan-Bathors.

"I think he wants us to join the group," Valerian said as Bubbles, slightly off balance, lurched forward.

"I'm not sure that's a good idea," Bubble replied.

"Doesn't look like he's giving us much choice."

"Well, here goes nothing," Bubble muttered, and joined the line. Each Boulan-Bathor was presented with an enormous plate upon which were piled a variety of delicacies: pieces of what appeared to be fruit and vegetables, though none that Valerian recognized, cut up and arranged in small towers intended to be Boulan-Bathor-sized finger foods. Slices of... something... wrapped up in jellyfish skins and covered with a sauce so spicy it stung Valerian's eyes even through Bubble's draping. Disemboweled aquatic creatures, part fish and part really bad dream, sprawled on plates while the eyes with which they had seen in life adorned them in death, impaled on small skewers.

There was an astoundingly long line of servers stretching far ahead and behind The Creation. Initially Valerian assumed they were attending to a large, hungry crowd. The doors opened and they, along with the small army of waiters, bore their delicacies into a room that made the vast kitchens look like a cupboard.

The Boulan-Bathors might eat grotesqueries, but as their main gate and now this hall indicated, they must have had a word in their language for "lavish." The hall was enormous, easily a hundred yards long and at least half as tall and wide. The flooring was intricately decorated—warm brown tiles covered by a long red and yellow carpet that stretched too far ahead for Valerian to see. The walls were made of a clear material, curved and reinforced with thick metal bands, which opened up to a grand vista of stars and ships. Huge pillars were spaced evenly along the room… as, Valerian noticed, were guards. Quite a lot of them.

"What's going on?" asked Bubble, sounding worried.

"I guess it's lunchtime," Valerian replied.

Bubble's voice was just a step below a sob. "*Bussing tables!* Every artiste's worst nightmare! Never mention this to anybody, okay?"

"You should be thanking your lucky stars we're not the main course!" Valerian hissed back. "Think of it as a role, not a job. You're a down-on-your-luck girl trying to make the big time."

Bubble sniffled. "Am I plucky?" she asked.

"Sure," he said. "You can be plucky."

They had moved down far enough so that Valerian could glimpse the diners. Well... the *diner*. At the far end of the room, on a massive throne that appeared to have been hewed from a single chunk of gray stone and then adorned with intricate carvings in gold leaf, slumped a Boulan-Bathor wearing a golden crown. His Majesty nibbled every dish presented to him. Behind him was a circular window that opened onto an incongruously beautiful space-scape, and beside him towered a pair of statues.

Valerian identified him as the species emperor, Boulan III. His eyes were large and glowing red, and scarlet markings had been painted or tattooed all over his body. It was both mesmerizing and horrible to watch that mouth drop open and food disappear into the yawning gullet. What he didn't eat off the plate, which usually wasn't much, the server emptied into a grate beside the throne.

Next to him, his wife, a strange crown of her own topped with jutting red feathers, watched keenly for the tiniest flicker of satisfaction on her husband's face.

Valerian felt Bubble trembling around him as they drew closer. "It's okay," he reassured her. "He'll eat the food, then we go right back to the kitchen. You got this."

Nonetheless, even he felt uneasy as The Creation stood before the bored Boulan III while the emperor reached out one giant hand, grabbed the head of some unfortunate creature from an offered plate, brought it to his mouth and devoured it in two bloody chomps.

"I'm going to be sick!" Bubble whispered.

"No, no," Valerian pleaded desperately, "you're going to

wait and be sick later! Just follow the line."

The Creation merged with the long line headed back to the kitchen with their empty plates. The food kept coming, and as he looked about, Valerian's heart surged in his chest.

Laureline! She's alive! And, apparently, enlisted as a serving girl.

They had dressed her in a long, trailing white dress, which was really quite pretty, and plopped an enormous white hat on her head, which was not. The hat was, essentially, nothing more than a large brim, and her blonde hair poked out of a hole in the center. Boulan-Bathor fashion was never going to set the galaxy on fire.

In her arms Laureline bore a large platter of fruits of all shapes, colors and sizes, which were likely intended as a light dessert after a heavy meal, given her position as the last one in line. It was the only dish of all that Valerian had glimpsed that looked even remotely appetizing.

Valerian suddenly felt a little light-headed with relief. "There she is!" he said to Bubble.

"Wow," approved Bubble. "You're right, she's a ten."

"You already knew what she looked like." Valerian was still bothered that Bubble had assumed Laureline's appearance earlier.

"Yes, but there's a lot more to being a ten than appearances," Bubble said.

The glamopod confounded Valerian. She was so innocent and, well, ditzy sometimes, and so strangely wise at others. And of course she was right. He thought about what he most loved about Laureline, and to his surprise it wasn't her lithe, fit body or gorgeous features. It was *her*. And that was why Bubble hadn't been able to tempt him.

He *was* going to get them both out of here. And, hopefully, she *was* going to say yes to his proposal.

Laureline's line advanced inexorably towards the emperor, whose wife was bouncing a little in her seat as the human girl approached.

Valerian frowned slightly. "Something's wrong," he said as he watched the empress, whose yellow, froggy eyes were fastened on Laureline. The emperor followed her gaze and now he, too, sat up, abruptly interested in the girl in white carrying the platter of fruit.

He'd dealt with humans before. Why so interested in Laureline? What could be special about her to a Boulan-Bathor? Frantically Valerian tried to recall everything he knew about the species and Boulan III in particular. He'd grown up traveling. He loved food—unique, different, perfect food...

"How about I do a little dance to create a diversion?" Bubble offered.

"No, thanks," Valerian said quickly.

Laureline now stood before the salivating emperor. His wife applauded ecstatically. Boulan III plucked a huge slice of juicy fruit from Laureline's platter. But instead of popping it into his mouth, he squeezed it over the top of her head that protruded from the hat.

Comprehension slammed into Valerian.

She's not carrying the dessert. She is the dessert—and the hat's a plate!

The emperor reached for a sharp set of tongs. An enormous drop of saliva splattered on the floor.

CHAPTER TWENTY-TWO

Just as Valerian drew breath to shout out a warning, Laureline herself realized what was going on. She hurled the platter at the emperor and bolted, but was caught by two of the guards. Shrieking and kicking, she tried to struggle free, but they were too strong and too big. The emperor grunted his approval as his wayward dessert was returned to him.

"I think we should go!" Bubble squeaked.

"*I* think you should let me handle this!" Valerian shot back.

"Okay!" Bubble readily agreed.

"Valerian!" Laureline cried out, still twisting in the grip of the two guards.

Even in the direness of the moment, Valerian's breath caught and his heart swelled. Here she was, facing certain death, and Laureline still had faith that somehow, some way, Valerian would find her.

And, dammit, he had.

"I'm here, Laureline!" he shouted past the lump in his throat. "It's me, Valerian!"

Bubble had indeed given all motor control to Valerian now. He broke into a run and headed for the gap between two guards. The first guard took a swing at Valerian with a massive sword. Valerian dodged the sweeping strike, ducked in, and seized the second guard's sword. Before the stunned guards could react, he had stabbed the second one with his own weapon, whirled, and brought the bloodied blade sweeping across the vastness of the first guard's belly. Both of them fell, and Laureline was free.

Valerian was hoping to draw the emperor's attention away from his dessert, and he succeeded. The emperor's red eyes were firmly on him now. *Good*, Valerian thought. *Watch this*.

Thanks to Bubble's talent, Valerian had the form and strength of a Boulan-Bathor, but his own speed and agility. The result was, he was sure, going to go down in the species' history. He bellowed with the voice of one of their own as he raced toward more oncoming guards, sword flashing as it lopped off arms, severed heads from their long necks, and pierced bulging bellies. The fact that the guards didn't appear to have much in the way of armor—well, much in the way of any kind of clothing, really—made it that much easier. They did know how to use their weapons, but he seemed to be quick enough to dodge them without any harm.

More guards surged into Valerian's path, trying to protect their emperor. Valerian cut and ducked and pressed on, leaping over the bodies that were starting to pile up. The empress was quailing off to the side, but the emperor was bellowing and pointing, his red eyes glaring at Valerian.

Valerian yelled, sprang the last few feet, and brought his sword slashing down.

The emperor stayed seated and still. The only thing that moved was the top of his head, right below the crown. It slid to one side, then toppled off.

The crowd gasped. Emperor Boulan III was dead.

Laureline had plastered herself to the floor to the side of the throne, staying safe amidst the flashing blades and toppling bodies. Panting from exertion, Valerian cried out to her.

"Laureline!"

Startled, she glanced up at him. He reached down to her, grabbing her arm with one hand and trying to pull off the awful hat-plate with the other. She thrashed fiercely and abruptly, and Valerian realized that, to her, he looked like just another Boulan-Bathor—one crazy enough to attack a room full of guards and kill the emperor.

"Bubble!" he shouted, "Get off of me!"

Bubble obliged, slipping from around Valerian and returning to her original gelatinous form. Laureline's eyes went from the blue blobby alien to her partner.

Valerian couldn't resist. "Let's get married," he quipped, "You're already all in white."

Those beautiful eyes narrowed and those perfect lips drew back from white teeth in a snarl, and the next thing he knew, she'd landed a solid punch to his jaw.

Blinking, dazed, he peered at her incredulously, and then suddenly she had thrown her arms around him. When she pulled back, she was beaming at him, her eyes shining. He leaned in to kiss her, but as she had done earlier, she lifted a ringed finger and blocked their lips from touching. He frowned, questioning. With the same finger, she pointed behind him.

He followed her gaze.

Every single remaining guard in the room—and there were a lot—was charging toward them, screaming at the top of their lungs and brandishing weapons.

Valerian grabbed Laureline's hand and shouted, "Bubble! Come on!"

The three started running back toward the kitchens. A dozen snarling warriors, gripping pikes and spears, hastened to block their path. The trio skidded to a halt. Valerian looked around wildly and saw only space surrounding him. There was no other way out. Or was there?

"Back to the throne!" he yelled.

"Are you crazy?" shouted Laureline.

He didn't answer, but it was the only shot they had. He tightened his grip on her hand and they hurried back the way they had come, Bubble hard on their heels. The move was so suicidal that it took the guards completely by surprise and the path was clear.

Valerian headed straight for one side of the throne. The empress was nowhere to be seen, and there was no need for guards to stay and protect a dead emperor. And there it was, as he had hoped.

A grate.

He dropped to his knees and, with the help of Laureline and Bubbles, managed to move the grate to the side.

The howling guards were approaching. "Go, go!" shouted Valerian to the other two. They slid down into... whatever awaited them below. It had to be better than what was running toward them, mouths open in those awful screams, weapons flashing.

They were three strides away when Valerian hurled himself through the floor.

"Third Regiment approaching, sir," said Sergeant Neza.

Okto-Bar was pacing and glanced up at the screen in time to see three huge vessels materialize from exospace.

"No further news of our agents?" he inquired, although he knew the answer. Neza would have told him immediately.

"None," Neza replied nonetheless.

Okto-Bar's frown deepened. Two humans in the Boulan-Bathor area of the station, and no further news. It did not bode well for their survival.

He thought, too, of the dying words of the brutalized alien they had found in the interrogation room, when the general had questioned why they had attacked the station.

You have what we need.

If that were true, why were the aliens not communicating with them?

"And the commander? No ransom demands?" *How can we help you when we don't know what you want?* Okto-Bar thought helplessly.

"Negative," replied Neza. "Sir—I have the minister online."

"Put him on," Okto-Bar said, rising and straightening his jacket.

The minister of defense appeared on-screen. "My respects, Minister," said Okto-Bar.

"General, you have been authorized by the Council to assume command of this operation. Congratulations," the image of the minister said.

At any other time, this would have been a moment of quiet, joyful satisfaction to Okto-Bar. He had served steadfastly and without fanfare for years, striving steadily toward this goal.

But now, the long-anticipated promotion had lost some of its luster in the wake of the horror that surrounded it.

"Thank you, sir. But to fulfill my mission, I will need temporary access to all of Commander Filitt's data and passwords."

The minister looked troubled and didn't respond at once. Finally, he said, "According to regulations, that is impossible without his explicit agreement."

"I'm well aware of that, sir. But even as we speak, the commander may well be dead. If I am to succeed in my new assignment, I need to know *everything*. It's too dangerous for me to be operating in the dark about anything at this juncture."

Again, the minister hesitated. A military man born and bred, Okto-Bar understood and sympathized with the other man's dilemma. But he also knew he was in the right.

Then, finally, "Access granted," said the minister.

"Thank you, sir," said Okto-Bar, relieved.

The face of the minister disappeared from the screen. To his captain, Okto-Bar said, "Authorize docking."

"Yes, sir," the captain said, suiting word to action. Okto-Bar took a deep breath. He had learned over the years to trust his instincts, and right now they were telling him that dark things were at play—things that, perhaps, he would later wish he didn't know.

But he didn't have that luxury, and so he placed his hand on the scanner.

"Pull up the file on the Mül operation."

"Request authorized."

Documents flashed up on the screen. Okto-Bar skimmed the information as it scrolled by. It was a list of the names of hundreds of warships, their identification numbers and firepower.

This was the army humanity had fronted in one of the worst wars of its entire checkered history—the War against the Southern Territories. It was largely because of this war, with its years of violence and astronomical numbers of casualties on both sides, that humanity had firmly rededicated itself to pursuing peace if at all possible.

Peace bought with the bloodiest of prices, Okto-Bar remembered his father saying. He continued to read the list of ships and their captains.

But one piece of information was conspicuous by its absence. "Who was commanding the operation?" Okto-Bar asked the computer.

A message flashed up: *Information not available.*

The general frowned. He was not fond of mysteries or puzzles. He was particularly not fond of things that seemed to make no sense at all.

And this didn't smell good.

They had fallen some forty feet, but had landed safely, if malodorously. Valerian had noticed the Boulan-Bathor servers dumping the uneaten food beside the emperor's throne, and sure enough, it had been a room-sized trash can. Valerian didn't want to think about what might be composing—or decomposing—the orchestra of smells that were assaulting their nostrils.

Above, the guards were shouting in anger and frustration. "They're too big to get through," Valerian reassured his companions.

"They'll find a way to get to us, and we're trapped in here!" Laureline retorted.

"No, we're not," Valerian replied. "There's got to be a way to empty the trash, so that means there has to be a door."

They looked at each other, then down at the dead carcasses, rotting fruit, and other unsavory items that were doubtless piled layers thick beneath their feet.

Abruptly, they were falling again, this time along with all the trash surrounding them and tumbling over their heads. Gasping, they clawed their way desperately to where they could breathe. Valerian looked around triumphantly.

"I told you there was a door," Valerian said reasonably.

Laureline got up awkwardly, plucking a scale the size of her palm from her hair. "You didn't study the plans before you came rushing in. As usual."

As she finished extricating herself, she came face to face with a humanoid skeleton. She blinked, swallowed, checked out its clothing, and began to remove it. Valerian did think it was somewhat less filthy than what she was wearing.

"You'd rather I got here after the main event?" Valerian asked, indicating the skeleton.

Laureline sighed. "I'd rather you took me someplace other than a giant trash can!"

Valerian scowled. "If it weren't for me, you'd be brainless right now!"

Suddenly, unexpectedly, Laureline grinned. "That would make two of us."

"Oh yeah?" Valerian shot back. He was starting to get really pissed off now. "And who got it into her head to go butterfly hunting near canyons?"

"And who can't even drive a Sky Jet?" She glared at him.

"And who nearly got me killed because she can't read numbers the right way up?"

"Who would be one arm lighter if I hadn't been able to repair a transmitter in under thirty seconds?"

Valerian was almost purple with outrage. "I just saved your life and that's the thanks I get?"

"I saved yours, remember? And I nearly got my brain sucked by a jellyfish to find you!"

"What is it with you and almost losing your brain?" exclaimed Valerian.

"Hey… guys?" The soft voice belonged to Bubble.

The arguing pair turned and, as one, snapped, "What?"

"I don't feel so good…"

Valerian's anger vanished, to be replaced by concern. Bubble had almost, but not entirely, resumed a female human shape. And instead of the cool blue he remembered her natural color being, she was turning the ugly purple of a bruise. She lifted a featureless face up to him as he slogged through the trash over to where she had propped herself up.

"What's wrong?" he asked, worried now.

"I must've been injured during the fight." Her voice was faint, and as she spoke her body began to turn from purple to red. Bubble strained, wincing, and for an instant the features of the cabaret dancer flitted across the blank canvas of her face.

The fight… Valerian had fought like a madman,

certain that the blades wielded by the guards weren't even touching him because he was just that good. Of course the weapons hadn't struck him—Bubble had protected him with her own body, taking blows meant for him. He hadn't even thought about her—he was too busy being headstrong, impulsive Valerian. And now—

"Bubble!" he murmured. "No, no… I'm so sorry. Tell me what to do!"

The slit of her mouth turned upward in a lopsided attempt at a smile that broke his heart.

"There's not much you can do. It's all right. Where I come from, death is less painful than life."

The words were a knife. "Don't say that!"

Bubble gave him a faint smile. "Unfortunately, it's true. Life's a drag when you never have an identity to call your own."

Taken aback, Valerian suddenly smiled at Bubble. He cradled her in his arms, very tenderly. "But you do have an identity. You're a hero. And more than that—you're the greatest artiste I have ever seen."

Bubble's blank eyes filled with scarlet tears. "I thank you. It was a pleasure performing for you. Just… one last role…"

Her face screwed up with effort. Then, suddenly, her color shimmered, cutting through the red into white cloth, gold jewelry, smooth brown skin, and sleek black hair. Eyes decorated with exaggerated black lines crinkled in a smile.

Nefertiti.

"I leave you my kingdom," she said, her voice sonorous and strong, though her body was failing. "Take good care of it."

"I will," Valerian promised her solemnly

Through her pain, Bubble continued to struggle to speak. "Most importantly…"

"Yes?"

The Queen of Egypt—or more importantly to Valerian, a big-hearted glamopod—extended an arm in the direction of Laureline, who stood a few steps away, eyes wide and silent. "Take good care of *her*. Love her without measure." She smiled gently. "'There's beggary in the love that can be reckoned.'"

Bubble closed her eyes and sank back into Valerian's arms. As he held her and watched in grieving, respectful silence, her body began to solidify until it became rock hard—an ancient statue of Nefertiti. Then, in the space of a heartbeat, she crumbled into sand, trickling through Valerian's arms till nothing was there.

Valerian stared at the pile of sand, feeling lost and alone. Something brushed his shoulder, and he looked up to see Laureline gazing down at him, her eyes bright with unshed tears.

Valerian's own eyes filled as well as he reached up and took her hand.

CHAPTER
TWENTY-THREE

General Okto-Bar stood at the console. His eyes were on the ships gathering in preparation for… what? War? Evacuation of the station? The more facts that came to light, the murkier everything seemed to become.

Sergeant Neza stepped beside his commanding officer. "All the battleships have docked, General," Neza informed him.

Okto-Bar glanced at the map. He saw no signal from his agents. But he did see that the red spot in the center of the station had increased.

"I want Section One operative now," Okto-Bar ordered.

"Yes, sir."

"Good." His eyes flitted to the doorway—and the large, featureless, black metal robot that stood there. "What is this K-TRON doing here?"

"Commander Filitt's orders," Neza answered. "He personally programmed them, and he's therefore the only one who can deactivate them."

What the hell did he program them to do if he was killed? Okto-Bar wondered, but did not say. The general eyed them. They endured the scrutiny with their usual stoic silence. "So, we're stuck with them until we find their master?"

"No, sir, not at all. Once you choose the section to

execute the operation, the K-TRON will follow and assist them."

"Great," grumbled the general. "That's all we need."

Valerian and Laureline walked along a trail that became ever narrower and rockier, as if they were headed into the center of a planet. They moved steadily and briskly, but there was a somberness that dogged their steps. So much had happened in so short a time, and they were still no closer to finding out what had happened with Commander Filitt, or the identities of the mysterious aliens who had kidnapped him—including the one who Valerian knew he had seen before. They hadn't spoken much since… since Bubble.

At one point, they passed the wreck of a spaceship, and Laureline asked, "You know where you're going?"

"Sure. I mean, I guess…" Valerian replied. He frowned a little.

"You're sure, or you guess?" prodded Laureline.

He gave an exasperated little grunt and looked at her. "Don't ask how, but the princess, the one in my dream… she's guiding me."

"The princess is *guiding* you?"

Valerian made a face. "Yeah, I know it sounds weird, but… it's like she's been with me the whole time."

Laureline came to a halt. "Wait just a minute," she said. "You mean… you have a woman inside you? Since the beginning of this mission?"

Valerian sighed. The whole thing made him both uncomfortable and confident in ways he couldn't even begin to articulate. "Laureline, can we keep going and talk about this later?"

"Sure," she said, and then smothered an impish smile as she extended an arm, indicating that he should precede her. "Ladies first?"

"Hilarious," Valerian said flatly.

But he stepped forward.

Captain Kris was the leader of Section One. Forty years old, his scarred face was mute testimony to the fact that he had seen his share of battle. He was honored that his unit had been tapped to lead the mission to infiltrate the center of the station and recover the abducted Arun Filitt. The ship docked with the station, sealed, and then the steel door opened. On their captain's orders, dozens of heavily armed soldiers sprinted inside the station. Kris brought up the rear and moved to one side.

"Captain Kris, Section One operational, General Okto-Bar," he reported.

"Good," came Okto-Bar's voice. "You may proceed. Be advised that a unit of K-TRONs will join you."

Kris's lips thinned. He had no fondness for the silent, hulking robots. He had fought enough battles to know that while robots and androids had their uses, in the thick of battle, you wanted a sentient, thinking, feeling being beside you. He admired Okto-Bar's reputation, but wondered if the general had been away from active fighting too long to understand that sending in a unit of K-TRONs was an insult to an elite team like Section One. "That won't be necessary, sir. My people can handle this."

"It's an order, Captain."

"Copy that."

Even as he spoke, the promised unit of robots clattered up. They halted as one, weapons in hand, perfectly still, awaiting his orders. Kris swallowed his annoyance.

"Elite unit, with me."

They followed his team obediently as he led them into the heart of the station.

Guided by a mysterious, literal "dream girl," feeling the little tugs inside that said *this way* and *over here*, Valerian guided Laureline deeper into the heart of Alpha Station. The desolate landscape, looking as if it had been abandoned for years, did nothing to improve his mood.

He wondered if he should keep his conclusions to himself, but decided not to. Laureline was his partner. She deserved to know.

"We've been manipulated from the start." Valerian's face was grim.

"What do you mean?"

"Right now, we're in the middle of the so-called dead zone. And we can breathe normally."

Little rodents scurried past, pausing to look up at them curiously before scampering about on ratty business.

"We're that far in?"

He nodded somberly.

"You're right… and there's absolutely no trace of contamination," said Laureline, looking around.

"This whole mission is a set up," Valerian said, angrily. "We've been played, Laureline. Out and out lied to. Everyone has, including General Okto-Bar. The commander was fully aware of what was behind this so-called 'absolute evil.'

"What?" Laureline stared at him aghast. He was moving quickly now, following the prods in the back of his mind, and she was struggling to keep up.

Turn here, the inner guidance said.

Valerian obeyed—and the two agents found themselves at the foot of a huge wall. In contrast with the derelict nature of the rest of the surroundings, this barrier looked new and imposing, comprised of large plates of some kind of matter completely unfamiliar to Valerian. As he and Laureline stared at the wall, the plates moved, shifting and overlapping.

Then things grew even stranger when, without warning, a figure—tall, willowy, pale, and quite beautiful—stepped through the wall, to stand gracefully in front of them. Moments later, four others joined him, all beautiful, all luminous and apparently benevolent.

"Pearls!" gasped Valerian.

"Okay," Laureline said, in an admiring whisper, "that's not *at all* how I pictured absolute evil."

"My name is Tsûuri," said the first one who had stepped through. He was looking at Valerian with a strange expression—half-longing, half-eager. "I am the emperor's son."

"Great," said Valerian. *Two emperors in one day.* Emotions were churning inside him, and he knew that some of them weren't his emotions at all. He was struggling to stay in control of the wave. "How about you introduce us to Daddy?"

"He is expecting you," said Tsûuri. "Follow me."

He turned and vanished through the wall. Valerian hesitated, stepped closer, and reached out.

His hand went through the wall.

He squared his shoulders. "Try to contact the general and get everybody down here," he said to Laureline. "Meanwhile, I'll try to buy us some time."

"Uh-uh," Laureline said, tossing her head. "How about you run backup for a change?" And without another word she strode resolutely through the wall.

Valerian sighed. "Unbelievable," he muttered, and followed his partner.

He emerged to find Laureline and Tsûuri waiting for him. Inside, everything was completely different from the austere outside landscape and the moving wall. He tried to make sense of what he was seeing, but wasn't sure he could even find the words. The closest comparison Valerian could draw was that he stood inside an enormous zeppelin, but its curving, ribbed walls were made not of cold metal, but of organic matter. Large, woven baskets of some sort adorned the walls, looking like they had been crafted from twigs or grass. He wondered if they served the Pearls for sleeping containers, and thought of the beautiful shell houses of his dream.

There were several Pearls present, and it was clear the ship was modeled to be what its people were—simple, in touch with what came from nature, and at the same time highly advanced. Tsûuri led them through this ship that had become a village. All turned their pale, kind faces toward the pair and inclined their heads in welcome. Some bore weapons, deceptively primitive in design, that were surely much more than they seemed to be, but no one made a threatening movement toward the two humans.

Still others clung to the walls, strong and lithe, reweaving, mending, caretaking with a calm and pure focus. Tsûuri led the way to what seemed to be the center of this "village." Valerian noticed a few small vessels, like the ones he had chased. Nearby, what appeared to be extremely sophisticated machines were hooked up together to create another, even bigger one.

In the center of the village was something that both he and Laureline recognized from their history lessons.

It was the *Destiny* module, once a primary research lab that had been part of the International Space Station in the Earth year 2001. In many ways, it was the true and perfect center, and origin, of Alpha Space Station.

The Pearl emperor sat in the capsule's tailpipe as if it were a throne, but he was the most casual, accessible royalty Valerian could imagine. Even more handsome than his radiant son, he smiled gently in welcome. Beside him was a stunningly beautiful female Pearl. They clasped one another's hand, tenderly, familiarly, and Valerian knew instantly that whatever age these beings were, they had been in love a long, long time.

Then his eye fell to a straw mattress on the ship's floor.

Commander Arun Filitt was sprawled, unmoving, at the emperor's feet. From this distance, Valerian couldn't tell if he was alive or dead.

"I present to you my father, the emperor," Tsûuri said solemnly.

"My name is Haban-Limaï, and this is my wife, Aloi," the emperor said. His voice was as beautiful as he was, as everything here was, and Valerian shivered at the sound.

The empress's face lit up with joy. "*Melo hiné!* We are so pleased to welcome you here."

Valerian's gaze darted again to Tsûuri. The movement did not escape the emperor's notice. "You ran into my son this morning, I understand," Haban-Limaï observed.

"Briefly, between bullets," Valerian responded.

Haban-Limaï looked at Tsûuri with great affection. Then he said, "My son sensed the presence of his sister, Princess Lïho-Minaa."

He turned his mesmerizing, deep blue eyes upon Valerian. His cheeks suffused with a soft, luminous pink hue. "It seems she chose you."

"What do you mean?" Valerian asked.

Sorrow flitted across the elegant features. "We are a long-lived people, but not even a star can shine forever. Or a Pearl. At the moment of our passing, we release all the energy left in our body in the form of a wave, which travels through space and time. We cast our memories, our souls, all that is when the body is no more, out into the universe. Sometimes, the wave crests and dissipates alone in the cold darkness. But not always. Sometimes it finds a benevolent host."

He paused, and then said, "My Lïho-Minaa chose *you* to be the guardian of her soul."

"Ah," Valerian said softly, in wonder. Then he said to Laureline under his breath, "I told you!"

The empress had risen. Tears swam in the azure glory of her eyes. Her cheeks, too, were a soft warm rose. She stepped toward him, her tan and orange robes fluttering with the graceful movement. "My daughter…"

Valerian panicked for just an instant as the empress

reached out long-fingered, slender hands and slipped them around his. Then, suddenly, everything in him that was little and petty, insecure and self-centered, fearful and angry, seemed to simply dissolve. Calmness filled him. He breathed in and out, and it was the ancient rhythm of every sea pulled to the shore by the sweet song of its moons, every mother's kiss on the beloved child's brow, every kind laugh, every soft sigh, and the vast twinkling of every star.

For the first time in his energetic, tumultuous life, Valerian tasted peace.

He felt *her* stir within him, summoned by her mother's longing words, and Empress Aloi took a quick breath. Laureline was staring at him—no. Not at him.

At Princess Liho-Minaa.

"Oh, my dear one... I am so happy to see you," the empress... the mother whispered, her voice thick with emotion.

As am I, came the—words? Thoughts?

"Same here," stammered Valerian. "I mean, she is, too."

The empress's full-hearted smile turned slightly playful at Valerian's words, and she released his hands. He dared not look at Laureline. Not yet. One of the Pearls brought them drinks. Laureline and Valerian accepted the beverage, but did not drink.

The emperor raised his glass. "To my daughter's memory!"

The two humans paused with their drinks at their lips. Valerian pointed to the commander. "If we drink with you, should we expect to suffer the same fate?"

He had to ask, but he knew the answer. He had known it, really, ever since he had woken from the "dream" of a world destroyed.

The emperor must have seen it in his face. He smiled, his eyes twinkling with amusement. "Your friend is merely sleeping. Do you want us to wake him up?"

Valerian glanced again at the commander, and started to grin when he heard Filitt's soft snoring.

"It can wait. And I wouldn't call him my friend." Valerian gazed intently at the emperor, sobering slightly. "Where do you come from?"

"Ah, I thought you had worked that out."

He had. But it was one thing to think it, another to speak it.

"Planet Mül," Valerian said quietly.

Laureline's eyes were wide. The emperor continued to speak, and as he did so, Valerian saw in his mind, as real as if it were all playing out before him in reality, everything the Pearl said.

"Our planet was a true paradise, in which we lived in harmony with the elements."

Valerian saw the Twelve Wise Sisters, as the Pearls called the dozen moons that orbited their world, hovering protectively over their child, the sea. Fishermen were hauling nets swollen with pearls, which they spread on the sand and, laughing, began to sort.

"Our main activity was fishing for the pearls which possessed phenomenal energy. They fertilized our lands, controlled the winds and tides…"

Carrying woven baskets of the precious objects, the Pearls strode inland, heading to a small crater. They upended their baskets, pouring thousands of harvested pearls into the crater's mouth.

"Three times a year, we gave to the earth what the

sea had given us. And so we had lived, in harmony, for centuries incalculable." His voice turned heavy. "Until the day it all ended."

Valerian tensed. He did not want to see this again. Did not want to see laughing children, chasing one another along the white sand beach, stop and stare as a meteorite streaked across the heavens, followed by thousands of others.

"In the sky over Mül," said the emperor, "other people blindly fought out a brutal war. A war that wasn't ours."

"Your daughter died during the battle," Valerian said. It was a statement, not a question.

"Yes," said the emperor, his voice heavy with sorrow. "She died… along with six million others."

There was silence. Laureline stared in horror, then chugged her cocktail. Valerian peered at her. "What are you doing?"

"I don't know," Laureline replied, defensively. "I… I was thirsty! Can I get another wonderful house cocktail please?" She didn't look like she thought it was wonderful. She looked sick and shaken by the realizations that were coming thick and fast.

And Valerian realized that he, too, could use a drink.

CHAPTER
TWENTY-FOUR

Noïntan Okto-Bar prided himself on being in control and operating by the book. No flashy, dramatic gestures, just hard work, a keen eye for gathering the up-and-coming as staff members, and a cool head when things got hot.

But now, though, he found himself holding an empty shot glass that had very recently contained Scotch to calm nerves that were more jangled than he could ever remember. He stared dolefully at the screen, resisting the temptation for another drink. *One shot steadies nerves, a second gets on them*, he told himself.

All at once, streams of data flashed on the screen.

"We have contact, General," Neza informed him. He looked as pleased and relieved as Okto-Bar felt.

About time, the general thought. He plunked the empty shot glass down and straightened.

"All right, Captain Kris," he said, his voice as calm and steady as ever, "we are locked onto you."

"We see no signs of radiation or contamination," came Kris's voice. "Can you confirm?"

Okto-Bar's gaze moved over the screen. "Sounds crazy, but yes… confirmed. Zero trace of either."

"Make note that we are proceeding without our gas masks. Moving forward."

Okto-Bar's eyes flickered to the empty glass, then back to the screen. *What the hell is going on down there?*

The Pearls had brought Valerian and Laureline more drinks. They were cool, and sweet, and soothing, much like the Pearls themselves, and Valerian and Laureline drank gratefully. At last, Valerian asked, "What happened after the explosion? How did you survive?"

"We drifted in space for many years, in a spaceship that wasn't ours. To survive, we needed to learn. So we studied your civilization, down to the smallest detail, searching for anything that could be of use, that could keep us alive. We found a portion of the ship that housed living plants. And so, we planted shoots, collected droplets of water on leaves. We analyzed your computer, and learned by trial and error how to operate it.

"Then, one day, we were picked up by scrap dealers traveling the galaxies. After a few years, their hold was full, and they went off to sell the cargo on a huge construction site."

"Alpha," Valerian breathed.

The emperor nodded. "The city of a thousand planets, where for hundreds of years so many species have shared their knowledge and intelligence with each other. Patiently and discreetly, we learned from each of them, and we pieced together our own vessel. Our planet is gone forever, but now, we are able to virtually reconstitute our world."

"Amazing," Valerian exclaimed.

"There are only two things that we lack," the emperor continued.

"A Mül converter," Laureline said.

"And a pearl," said Valerian.

"The only one Tsûuri managed to salvage," the emperor said.

Valerian was starting to fill in the blank spaces in the narrative. "So, a year ago, you signal your existence, and you make contact with us," he said, working it out.

Laureline was piecing it together, too. "And the only thing you ask for in compensation for all you have lost is the last converter alive in order to mass-produce your pearl," said Laureline.

"Yes," replied the emperor. "That was all. We could do the rest." A shadow settled upon his beautiful face. "But during the handover, things did not go as planned."

"What happened?"

He paused for a moment, clearly still feeling the pain of what happened. "A unit came to negotiate with us outside the wall—where you stood just now. Tsûuri stepped through the wall to speak with them. We were all so pleased that, at last, we could honor those who had died by rebuilding the world we had so loved.

"A young captain met us there. He had a metallic box at his side—we believe it was the converter. He seemed uneasy, and spoke to someone who was not present. This person— the commander of the mission—asked how many of us there were. When the captain replied, he gave his orders."

The emperor paused. "The commander of the mission said, 'I want no survivors. Annihilate them all!'"

Valerian and Laureline stared at him. Valerian didn't want to believe it. His people? Why?

The emperor smiled sadly. "The unfortunate captain looked confused, but he obeyed his order. Many of my people were fatally wounded. A few, including Tsûuri, managed to make it back through the wall alive.

"What… why…" Laureline stammered, shocked beyond the ability to form a coherent question.

The emperor continued. "After—after the attack, we continued to observe what was happening on the other side of the wall, hoping we could somehow rescue our injured brethren. But we could not—and we were not the only ones who were betrayed that terrible day. The poor captain received another transmission. The commanding officer spoke. 'I said: no survivors. Annihilate them all!' And so, the captain and his men fell—killed by hidden black-armored robots, tall, sleek, and merciless."

K-TRONs, Valerian thought, feeling ill. *K-TRONs under the command of whoever was heading that mission.*

Valerian and Laureline could say nothing. What was there to say? It was too awful to comprehend.

"We are survivors, but that makes us witnesses," the emperor said quietly. "Witnesses of the past that humans want to erase and forget forever."

"We can forgive," the empress said, "but how can we forget?"

Valerian and Laureline exchanged sick, sad glances. Then Laureline spoke. Her voice was raw, almost as if she had been crying. "So they… *we*… left you no choice but to steal the converter from us. Tsûuri hired a professional to do the job…"

"Igon Siruss!" yelped Valerian. It all came together.

"But," Laureline continued, "zealous Major Valerian intervenes during the transaction, and retrieves the converter."

"You'd exhausted all your options by that point," Valerian said. "The only thing you could do to get the converter was to kidnap the commander and force him to tell the truth."

The emperor nodded. "You know our story now. Our destiny is in your hands."

The emperor motioned to his wife. Empress Aloi nodded and knelt beside the slumbering form of Commander Filitt. Gentle, even now, she ran a long-fingered hand over his brow. He woke with a panic-stricken start and leapt to his feet.

"Where am I? Men!" His gaze fell on Valerian. "Major?"

He rushed over to the two agents and put them between him and the emperor. "Major! Arrest these creatures immediately! They kidnapped me! They're extremely dangerous!"

"They are Pearls from planet Mül," said Valerian, coldly.

Filitt stared at him. Something flickered, frightened and ugly, in the depths of his eyes, to be replaced by the more familiar hardness. "Yes—they are. They told me their ridiculous story. But it's impossible. Mül was uninhabited."

Laureline scoffed, and pointed to the Pearls. "Their existence proves the contrary, doesn't it?"

Filitt flushed darkly, and his expression grew dangerous. "There was no life on the planet, I'm telling you. The detectors were categorical. Arrest them—and that's an order!"

Valerian's eyes narrowed. "How can you be so sure?"

Filitt's eyes slid away. "Because I—I read the reports, and—"

Valerian finished for him. "And you were on board."

He'd seen his share of cornered criminals. He knew what would come next. Anger, justification, perhaps pleading.

Filitt did not disappoint. "Yes," he snapped. "I *was* on board. And we had plenty more to worry about! Our cruisers were being decimated. We lost five hundred thousand soldiers in one day. *Half a million of our people*, Agent! It was complete carnage!"

Valerian shoved his face to within an inch of the commander's. "And you were so preoccupied that you didn't see the detector indicating signs of life on the planet."

The commander looked confused.

"Or even worse," Laureline put in, "perhaps you knew the planet was inhabited and deliberately sacrificed it."

Too much had happened to Arun Filitt. He stared at the young agents, wondering how they had found him, wondering where he was, wondering what had happened. How it had gone so wrong. It wasn't wrong, what he did, it was necessary. How could they possibly understand? They weren't there, having to make decisions that affected millions.

And there had been no life on the planet. This couldn't be real.

And yet…

The memory, until now distorted, revised, shoved away to the back of his mind, descended like a creature too long leashed and now set free—angry, and too powerful to resist.

"Engage fusio-missiles!" Commander Filitt shouted, screaming to be heard over the din of attack, the crackle and spitting of damaged equipment, and the screams of the dying. Through the cacophony of battle, somehow he heard Major Samk's panic-stricken voice.

"Commander?" The major stood at his post, which was operating the detector that scanned for any and all forms of life.

"What is it?" The ship took another hit and everyone stumbled, clutching at chairs or consoles to stay on their feet.

"The planet is inhabited!" Samk shouted.

Filitt spared a glance from the hell manifesting on the viewing screens to look at the major. Samk's eyes were wide and he looked distraught.

"We know, by primitive life forms!" Filitt snapped. Why was Samk wasting his time? People were dying on this ship, dying on the other hundreds of vessels in the fleet—

"No, Commander," Samk replied, speaking quickly. "By sentient beings!"

Filitt stared at him. This wasn't possible. That planet was uninhabited. Needed to be uninhabited...

You have to be quiet, Samk, he thought wildly. I can't hear this. Not now.

But Samk pressed on. "I have detected a complex language and huge cerebral energy."

The words galvanized Filitt into action. He strode to

*the major and snatched his badge. The detector abruptly
ceased functioning.*

*"Major Samk," he growled through clenched teeth,
"history is on the march. Neither you, nor a bunch of
savages can stand in its way!"*

*But Samk, apparently, was going to try. "It's an intelligent
species, Commander. I'm sorry to insist, but their DNA
print is bigger than ours."*

*"And so our victory will be twice as big." The commander
returned to his post. He did not waver. Staring out on the
screen, seeing ships catch fire and be blown to bits—he hit
the button that unleashed the apocalypse.*

*He watched with cold pleasure and a sense of justice
done as the gigantic enemy flagship was hit, spiraled out
of control, and crashed into Mül. He felt only the slightest
twinge as the planet was wrapped by an explosion that
cracked its blue-green orb into pieces.*

It had been a pretty planet… but war had casualties.

A cold, hard, male voice jolted him out of the memory.

"So when you found out that survivors from planet
Mül were living in the heart of Alpha, you decided to
erase any trace of your mistake, rather than accept the
consequences. Right?"

Filitt heard again his own voice in memory, now, as he
watched the Pearls emerge from behind their wall. *I want
no survivors. Annihilate them all!*

And the young captain, gone too. No voices left to
speak against him. K-TRONs. Better than humans. No
loyalty, no ideology, no judgment. Just programming, and

obeying that programming. Simple. Clean.

"And you destroyed all evidence Major Samk had against you."

No. He didn't want to see this. But the speaker had said the words, and the images came, unbidden, and he was unable to drive them back into the safe darkness where they had dwelt for the last year.

He had overridden the lock on Major Samk's door and entered quietly, so very quietly. He checked before he acted—a brief glimpse at the screen confirmed that Samk was, indeed, typing a report on what had happened above planet Mül.

It was a shame.

Filitt had lifted the muzzle to the back of Samk's head and pulled the trigger.

"It was the only way!" Filitt exploded. The words of justification he had hoped he would never have to speak were ripped from him. He stared wildly at the two agents, whose faces might as well have been carved into stone.

"Don't you see?" he pleaded. "Admitting to an error on this scale would have exposed our government to colossal damages and compensation claims. Our economy would never recover!"

The faces only grew harder, more judgmental. They were willfully choosing not to understand. His voice rose in desperation.

"In one instant, we would have lost our supremacy, our *leadership*. There would have been immediate sanctions, and it's a pretty good bet we would have been banished from Alpha—the very station we *created*, dammit—and been deprived of access to the galaxy's greatest market of knowledge and intelligence. Is that what you would have wanted for your fellow citizens?"

Filitt looked from Valerian to Laureline, and found no sympathy there.

He did not dare look at the Pearls. He could not permit himself to think of them as anything other than obstacles to humanity.

"Is it?" he pressed. Spittle flew from his mouth. "Leading them into ruin and degradation? Forcing them to go a thousand years backward? The Council saw fit to protect our fellow citizens. First and foremost. Is that not its *duty*?"

He thumped his chest hard as he said, "And mine? And *yours*? Isn't it, agents? Or would you rather we risk wrecking our economy for the sake of a bunch of…" He wheeled on the emperor, looking at him with a mix of loathing and resentment, words failing him.

"Savages?" offered Laureline.

Filitt wheeled on her. "Sergeant! You are totally under the influence of this creature! Don't confuse the issue. He's the threat! He's our enemy!"

The emperor, still impossibly patient, stepped forward toward the commander, placing his forefinger on the man's chest.

"*You* are your own worst enemy, Commander," he said compassionately. "Unless you make peace with your past, you won't have a future."

The commander backed away, dazed by the emperor's words. No. He was wrong. He had to be. The only way for humanity to be safe, for himself to be safe, was if this problem went away now. It could. It almost had. He had almost wiped them from the universe's memory.

He could still do it. "Major!" Filitt barked. "I order you to arrest this man. Do you hear me?"

"Can we talk man to man for a second?" Valerian asked.

Slightly wild-eyed, Filitt turned to stare at him. "What?"

The punch came so swiftly Commander Arun Filitt didn't even have time to blink.

CHAPTER
TWENTY-FIVE

The commander crumpled to the floor. Valerian winced and
shook his aching hand. He'd put a *lot* of feeling into that blow.

"Good talk," he said to the unconscious form. He
turned to the emperor. "Look, this was fun, but we need
to report back to our people. Here. This is yours."

He took out the pearl and handed it to the emperor.
He stared at the tiny, perfect orb nestled in his palm, then
closed his fingers around it and lifted shining, grateful eyes
to Valerian.

"We'll make this right," Valerian assured him. "You have
my word." He glanced back down at the commander and a
smile quirked his lips. "Let me take this guy off your hands."

As he turned, he noticed Laureline speaking with the
empress. The Pearl's eyes were full of tears, and Laureline
was reaching into her belt. Her hands came out holding
the converter.

"Hey!" Valerian shouted. "What are you doing?"

Laureline said, as if it were self-explanatory, "You gave
them the pearl. They also need the converter."

"I know, but—" He turned to the emperor and gave
him a smile that was more like a grimace. "Will you
excuse us a second?"

Valerian marched over to his partner, grabbed her arm, and steered her away. "Listen," he said, keeping his voice low, "the converter is government property. And most likely it's the last one in the whole universe."

"Oh," Laureline said, her eyes narrowing in anger, "so you buy into the commander's what's-mine-is-mine-and-what's-yours-is-mine philosophy? Is *that* what you're saying?"

"No," Valerian shot back, stung, "I 'buy into' my oath of allegiance! We have no authority to hand this over to the Pearls."

"Valerian, the Federation messed up and must make amends." Laureline was adamant.

"I agree, but that's not for us to decide. We have to leave it to the courts."

He knew Laureline well enough to know when she was hanging onto her temper by a thread. Right now, that thread snapped. "They're eighteen light years away, Valerian! Only *we* can make this right!"

He pressed his lips together tightly. "Laureline, I'm a soldier. I play by the rules. It's what makes me who I am."

There was a long pause. The righteous anger faded from Laureline's face. Then she said quietly, a trace of sorrow lacing her words, "You see? That's why I don't want to marry you. Because you don't really know what love is."

"Come on!" exclaimed Valerian, fear making his words sharp. "This situation has nothing to do with love, or even you and me!"

Tears glistened in Laureline's eyes. "That's where you're wrong. Love, real love, it's more powerful than anything else, Valerian. It's more powerful than rules and laws. More powerful than any army or government."

She looked over at the empress. "Look at her," she said, her voice full of admiration. "She had her whole people and one of her children taken from her, and she's prepared to forgive. *That's* love. It's the trust you place in someone." Laureline turned back to him. "And I thought *I* could be that someone. That… that I could be the most important thing in your life, Valerian."

"You are," Valerian said, his voice hoarse with emotion. "I'd die for you."

But that was not the right answer. Laureline shook her blonde head, frustrated. "You don't understand. I'm not asking you to die for me. I'm asking you to *trust* me."

They stared at one another. Her face was radiant with intensity, with longing—a yearning for connection. Valerian wanted very badly to be what she needed. To really understand what she needed.

Finally, Valerian said, hesitantly, "Are you sure you know what you're doing?"

"No," Laureline said bluntly, startling him. "But I know that if a whole race is wiped out because you have no faith in me, I'll never be able to look at you again."

And then, Valerian understood. Trust. Of course it would be trust, wouldn't it? Courage, loyalty, even love—he could give those easily. But he had known betrayal, and trust—real, perfect trust—came harder to him than anything else.

But he trusted Laureline.

Valerian nodded tentatively. "All right," he said at last. "Give it to them."

Laureline smiled. Not with her lips, or even her eyes, but her whole face—her whole being—lit up like a sun.

And Valerian knew, whatever happened, that he had made the right choice. She wiped at her eyes, then stepped forward and kissed him.

Her lips were warm and soft, and there was something sweet and powerful in that kiss. Valerian felt dizzy and clear-minded all at once. He had trusted Laureline, and now she had offered him a kiss that was stirring, sweet, unguarded, and absolutely real. He melted into it, offering himself up to her in the same way, and when she pulled back and whispered, "Thank you," it was all right. She was Laureline, and he trusted her.

She held the converter in her arms, and walked over to the empress. With a final, farewell pat, she held the little creature out to Aloi. It chirped and squirmed happily as it ducked its head under the empress's throat.

"Here," Laureline said. "We are to blame for the loss of your planet. We would be honored to help you get it back."

"*Melinama!*" said the empress, tears in her own eyes as she embraced the converter.

"It means 'thank you,'" Valerian said.

"Come with us," the emperor said. "You should see what your compassion will accomplish."

The two agents followed him as he approached a small crater. Valerian was reminded of a similar one on Mül, where the fishermen emptied their catch. The emperor handed the pearl to his wife. She held it in one hand, the Mül converter in the other. The little animal sniffed at the pearl, then opened its narrow snout and swallowed. Valerian watched as its reptilian top portion changed colors, like a sunset bleeding from one hue into the next. He couldn't seem to tear his eyes from it and was only dimly aware that the rest of the Pearls had come up to them, enclosing them inside a circle of joined hands.

The empress stroked the converter with affection, then held it out over the crater. It shivered and grew larger—and then began to eject perfect, lustrous pearls into the crater.

A strange, haunting, beautiful sound rose around Valerian, and he realized the Pearls were beginning to sing. His heart was racing and his breath was shallow with wonder.

A bright, clean, white light emanated from the crater. Then, like an erupting volcano spewing lightning instead of lava, fingers of white crackled through the air, racing along the curving sides of the zeppelin. A wind picked up out of quite literally nowhere, whipping Valerian and Laureline's hair. Colors, the radiant hues of an opalescent shell, snaked over and along and around them, and then the grids along the side of the zeppelin were obscured. Sky burst into being over their heads—a sky Valerian recognized, filled with rounded moons and a slight freckling of stars in the darker blue.

Rocks jutted upward as if sketched into existence by the dancing strands of light. Valerian felt the hardness of the flooring give slightly beneath his feet as it was transformed into sand.

He and Laureline were watching the birth of a world.

The crackling of the creative force ceased, and the wind died down to a gentle breeze. Soft, gentle rain pattered down on Valerian's upturned face and he closed his eyes briefly, then opened them to discover there was nothing left to be seen of the walls of the zeppelin.

Instead, Valerian beheld myriad rainbows, sparkling

everywhere after the rain. With a faint rustling sound almost inaudible to his ears, lush vegetation started to grow from the rocks, sending forth questing roots and bursting leaves and flowers. All the pair of astonished spatio-temporal agents could see now were endless panoramas with clear blue sky stretching to the horizon.

Valerian and Laureline stood back to back, each beholding the wonder exploding into being around them. Impulsively Valerian extended his hand, reaching for Laureline's.

She was already reaching for him. Their hands met and clasped, fingers entwining, the simple touch of human flesh in its own way as beautiful and magical as what was happening around them.

The empress still held the converter. It had returned to its normal size, its ears and tail drooping as if from exhaustion. Valerian couldn't blame the little fellow. He'd just completed quite a task.

No, he wasn't done yet. There was a final cough, and a few more pearls fell into the crater.

They heard it before they saw it: a rushing, deep, primal sound. And then, the sea, so beloved by the Pearls, could be glimpsed as a sliver of silver on the horizon, surging forward, its waves high. For an instant, Valerian was terrified the Pearls had inadvertently created a tsunami, but even as the thought formed, the sea was tamed, and by the time it reached the white stretch of sand beneath their feet, it lapped gently.

He smiled a little. These were Pearls. Their whole culture, their whole world, was based upon harmony and tranquility. All that had ever been harsh on Mül had come from outside. They would never birth a world with harm in it.

Laureline squeezed his hand, then turned toward him, grinning. "Didn't you say you wanted to go to the beach?"

The empress walked toward them, reaching out her long, pale fingers to Valerian. Laureline released his hand, allowing the Aloi to take both of Valerian's in hers.

She smiled serenely at him. "Our daughter made a good choice. She can rest in peace now."

The smile Valerian gave her was shaky with emotion, and he felt heat rise in his cheeks. Laureline smiled too, catching him blushing. He took a deep breath and knew the empress was right. As he exhaled, he felt a tingling along his entire body and a gentle but excited trembling in the pit of his stomach. No fear, only peace. And then the blue wave rippled through, around, and from him, momentarily coloring his vision the same exquisite hue as the new world's sky.

All that was Lïho-Minaa slipped away, like a leaf borne on the last of autumn's wind. She was gone, and Valerian knew she was, indeed, at peace.

But there was an emptiness he had not known he possessed until a Pearl's spirit had filled it, and he felt oddly bereft.

"We must leave now," said the emperor. Valerian nodded, and the empress squeezed his hands one final time, then released them, stepping back to stand beside her husband. "May you and your people live in peace, wherever you may venture in space and time."

Tsûuri's voice came, quick and sharp, disrupting the calm atmosphere. "Father, there are hundreds of soldiers surrounding the ship. They've placed explosives on our walls!"

"We will be gone in a minute," his father reassured him.

But Valerian and Laureline were not reassured at all. They knew exactly what Tsûuri's words meant. "If the troops are in position," Valerian said quickly, "you don't *have* a minute. You have no means of communication with the outside world?"

"We do, but we have been jamming signals," Tsûuri said. "If we stop that, we are defenseless."

"If you don't allow me to communicate with them, you will be defenseless forever!" Valerian said. He looked around desperately, and his gaze fell on the *Destiny* capsule lying on the soft sand. It was old, but it would do.

"Just one call," he said.

The emperor searched his eyes, then nodded. To his son, he said, "They have proven worthy of our trust. Disarm the signal."

The wall abruptly stopped moving.

Captain Kris glanced at the dozens of mines that had been affixed to the wall a few moments earlier. He had contacted General Okto-Bar and informed him that the explosives would be detonated on the general's command.

Now he stared at the suddenly still wall, then his gaze flickered around at the hundreds of troops lying in wait behind him.

"Unit in position," he reported to Okto-Bar. "But the wall has stopped moving. Something's going on."

Okto-Bar's sigh was audible over the radio. "Our countdown is at six minutes and counting. Maintain your position. We're trying to analyze what's happening."

All at once, the K-TRONs snapped to attention, their rifles clattering in their metallic hands as they took aim at a handful of the mysterious aliens who had abruptly materialized in front of them, calmly regarding the robots, the soldiers, and Kris himself.

"K-TRON warriors at attention. Contact with the enemy. It's the same creatures who kidnapped the commander."

"Are they showing signs of hostility?" Okto-Bar demanded.

"Not really," Kris had to admit, adding, "Not so far."

Help us. You have what we need.

The dying alien's words had haunted Okto-Bar since he first heard them uttered. He couldn't shake them, and now, here the beings were again.

"General?" said Neza, breaking into Okto-Bar's thoughts. "I can't believe this but—we're picking up a radio signal." He looked over at the general, his eyes wide. "From the 2005 *Destiny* module."

"*What?*" Okto-Bar was incredulous.

"It—sir, it sounds like Major Valerian!" the soldier said.

Okto-Bar couldn't believe his ears. "Patch him through."

The seconds seemed to last forever, and then:

"Hello?"

It was, indeed, Valerian's voice. Okto-Bar let out a short bark of astonishment. "Major?"

"Yes, sir!" The voice was full of relief. "Major Valerian and Sergeant Laureline here! We're alive and on the inside, on the other side of the wall. Call off the assault immediately!"

"Major," Okto-Bar said, hating every word, "I'd like to believe it's you, but I can't read your DNA code, and you know the procedure. I need proof that this is not a hoax, and that—"

"This is no time for dumbass procedures!"

Neza and Okto-Bar exchanged glances. The voice certainly sounded like Sergeant Laureline. "We're *in here*, dammit! With a whole *species* you already wiped out once! The Pearls from planet Mül. So tell your men to back off before you commit a second genocide!"

Okto-Bar was reeling. He was a calm, thoughtful man, and procedure had always served him well his entire career. Now, he was unsure as to what to do.

"That's definitely her temper," Neza observed.

Okto-Bar had to agree. "But…" he stammered, slightly dazed at the potential upending of so much he had believed to be true, "planet Mül was uninhabited!"

"You know that's not true!" Valerian shouted. "Commander Filitt was *there*. He gave the orders. And he organized this whole operation to eliminate the survivors, the living proof of his mistake. Stop the procedure!"

Neza stepped close to his commanding officer. Softly, so that he would not be overheard, he murmured, "Maybe that would explain why the commander was interrogating that creature."

It all came together in dreadful, heartbreaking sense that even now Okto-Bar wished he could deny.

He stopped the countdown at three minutes, fourteen seconds.

* * *

"Countdown paused."

Laureline and Valerian both blew out sighs of relief at the general's words. "Is the commander with you?" he continued.

Laureline and Valerian shared a glance, then, as one, got up, hauled the groggy commander to his feet, and threw him into a seat in the capsule. His head lolled and he resumed snoring.

With perhaps a bit more enjoyment than he ought to have felt, Valerian slapped Filitt's slack face.

"Come on!" Valerian said, loudly and cheerfully. "Wakey wakey! There's a call for you."

"Commander?" came Okto-Bar's voice. "Do you read me?"

Still no response.

Laureline slapped the commander harder than Valerian had. Now he did lurch awake, muttering, "Ouch!"

"Come on, my friend," Valerian said. "It's time to confess."

Filitt blinked dazedly. He frowned as he looked around, clearly puzzled that he didn't see the general. Hesitantly, he said in a slightly slurred voice, "Hel… lo?"

"Commander Filitt, this is General Okto-Bar. Do you read me? We can't get a DNA code on you, but we do have a voice wave match."

The commander sat up, wincing. His eyes became focused and his voice was clear as he responded. "I read you. What's going on?"

"We are ready to activate the explosive device in accordance with the orders you gave," came Okto-Bar's voice. "Do you confirm these orders, or do you have anything to tell me that will enable me to suspend the assault?"

The commander didn't answer at once. Valerian and Laureline tensed. He looked at them in turn, then, whatever sedative the Pearls had used on him now fully out of his system, straightened in his seat.

"I'm a soldier," he said, his voice quiet, calm, and intense. "A soldier will always choose death over humiliation. *Annihilate them all!*"

CHAPTER
TWENTY-SIX

The words, brutally clear, came over the radio. Kris and his men were stunned, but the K-TRONs, having received their orders, opened fire immediately. Bullets tore through the air, cutting down not just the delicate, beautiful creatures that were the supposed enemy, but the rest of Kris's all-too-human troops.

"Take cover!" Kris yelled to his soldiers, obeying his own order. But just as he leaped for one of the trenches, a bullet ripped through his shoulder and he landed hard and awkwardly.

"What the hell do you think you're doing?" came Major Valerian's voice.

"I gave no orders!" shouted Okto-Bar. "Kris, cease fire immediately!"

Kris pressed a hand to his wounded shoulder. Over the din of his men returning fire at the black metal robots, he shouted, "It's not us, it's the K-TRONs! They're attacking us!"

Okto-Bar was utterly stunned. The K-TRONs were under orders from Filitt and no one else, which meant—

Large black metal forms with red lights atop their

heads surged into the control room, blazing away in all directions. "Retreat!" Okto-Bar shouted. Some of his people dropped to the floor, diving for cover. Some of them fell, and did not get up. Okto-Bar placed one of the consoles between him and the door, firing over it as best he could at the implacable machines.

Under a hail of gunfire, one of the K-TRONs moved to the console and hit the button.

The countdown, stopped at 3:14, resumed.

Valerian couldn't believe it. They had come so close—

"I'll go give Tsûuri some backup," he told Laureline. He jerked his head in the direction of Filitt, who wore a look of smug triumph. "Keep an eye on him!"

"Oh, he's not going anywhere," Laureline promised. As Valerian grabbed his weapons on the way out, he looked back in time to see Laureline landing a solid punch on the commander's smirking face.

He emerged into the chaos of a battle going full force between the K-TRONs, the Pearls, and the human troops. There were several large blue cocoons lying about, which bore testament to the fact that the Pearls were putting up a good fight.

"Alex?" said Valerian, shouting to be heard over the sound of bullets, "if you can hear me, load me up with all you've got!"

A green light flashed on Valerian's gun.

"Acknowledged, Major," came Alex's welcome voice. "Here goes… fifty infras, twenty anti-flux, twelve ultra-heatseekers."

"Thanks."

"You have ten seconds left."

Ten seconds. He'd make every last one count.

Valerian leapt out from cover and opened fire. Missiles of all varieties exploded from his weapons, and the K-TRONs started to drop. Sheer force blew them apart, and then the parts were pulverized. One robot was blown back, shrapnel all that remained of it. Valerian brought his guns along in a line, firing constantly, gunning the robotic enemy down with terrible precision.

Out of the corner of his eye, Valerian saw the wall start to ripple. The Pearls inside were beginning to seal it up. Valerian was running out of ammo; he was down to the last five... two... one of the eighty-two that Alex had loaded him up with.

But the K-TRONs were down, reduced to inert hunks of smoking, melted or bullet-ridden metal.

All but their captain.

Make it count.

Valerian took aim at the largest part of the robot—its gleaming, massive chest—and fired his last frag cap. Out of ammo, and almost out of time, Valerian raced through the wall a fraction of a second before it sealed shut.

The control room clock showed 00:01.

The mine-covered wall in the dead zone turned first silver, then phosphorescent.

The entire area exploded.

* * *

00:00.

In the control room of Alpha Station, still battling two remaining K-TRONs, Okto-Bar saw the clock. *No... oh, no,* he thought, the rawness of the shock and grief startling him. *What have I done?*

The general directed his impotent grief and outrage upon the final two robots, turning on them with sudden fury—firing and firing without stopping.

The last one toppled and fell.

Neza stared at Okto-Bar, his eyes wide. A few others got to their feet, dazed, shocked, silent.

Was it true?

Had they all been party to genocide?

Was there anyone left to tell them what had happened?

The silence and the stillness after all the madness was bizarre. Captain Kris could hear his own breathing, and little more. No... there were other stirrings now as other soldiers realized that they, too, had survived.

Cautiously, Kris peered out of the trench, eyes widening at what he beheld. His radio crackled.

"Survivors?" came Okto-Bar's voice, harsh with emotion. "Captain? What's going on?"

Kris didn't reply for a moment. He was staring right at the site where the wall had been. But now, there was nothing. Not a broken wall, not the bodies of those behind it... only a vast hole, like some enormous crater at the heart of the space station.

"There's nothing left!" he managed to tell Okto-Bar. "Just a gaping hole! Everything's vanished!"

Others, too, were poking their heads out, eyeing the pieces of robots, stunned at what they beheld. "Any trace of our agents? Or the commander?"

Kris fished out his infrared binoculars and peered through them, making a slow sweep of the area. "No, nothing… hold on, I've seen something! There's a body!"

In the middle of the crater, a body was indeed suspended from somewhere far above in the deepening darkness, twisting slowly back and forth. It was swathed in a strange sort of sticky, ropy substance. As Kris's binoculars refocused, the body swung slightly, so that he could see the victim's puffy, bruised face.

"It's the commander!"

"Is he alive?" asked Okto-Bar.

The eyes, swollen to slits, opened. So did the mouth. "Get me out of here, you incompetent turds!"

Kris grinned. "Affirmative. He's alive and kicking!"

"Good," said Okto-Bar. "Arrest him!"

Laureline peered out the portal of the *Destiny*, smiling a little at the vastness of space and the twinkling of stars with no ship or station or planet in sight.

"Do you have any idea where we are?"

Valerian glanced at a monitor. "We're… two hours away from vacation!" He grinned over his shoulder at her. "I just fired the distress beacon."

"Two hours, sheesh!" she exclaimed.

"I know," he said. "Two hours alone with me, what a drag!"

"No kidding," said Laureline. She sighed melodramatically, still stargazing. "An eternity!"

"So," he said, "now that the mission is over, perhaps we can finish our conversation?"

Laureline turned around. He stood with his hands clasped behind his back. "Conversation?"

"We were talking about the future," said Valerian.

Laureline said, playfully, "Really? And what does the future hold?"

She expected a tall tale of an amazing adventure, or a flirty, less-than-subtle mention of other things best conducted in private. Instead, for one of the few times she had ever seen, Valerian seemed completely serious as he replied.

"You... me... us," Valerian said quietly.

And he held up a ring.

The ring's circle itself was as pedestrian, as ordinary a thing as could possibly be imagined: a wire loop he'd obviously just now crafted from one of her own hairpins, twisted and wrapped around the gem.

But the gem...

It was a single, small, perfect Mül pearl.

Tears stung her eyes as she gazed at it, at all it represented. All the blood and death, beauty and life. And when she gave him a tremulous smile, he saw that knowledge in her eyes.

Those eyes widened as Valerian went down on one knee. "Happy birthday," he said, holding up the ring that was at once the most banal and most beautiful thing in the universe.

"Thank you," she said. "That's very romantic. Is this your idea?"

"Yes, Laureline." He swallowed hard, and she realized the hand that presented the ring was trembling. "Will you do me the honor of becoming my wife?"

"For better or worse?" she asked.

Anxiously, Valerian said, "Is this negotiable?"

Laureline smiled. She wanted to start laughing, to start crying, to start… other things.

"No," she said.

He settled his shoulders. "All right, then," he replied.

Laureline gazed down at him for a moment, then bent and accepted the ring. His happiness at the gesture turned to puzzlement as, instead of slipping it on her finger, she placed it carefully on the console. He got to his feet, his expression questioning.

She went into his arms, kissed him, and then began to unfasten his uniform.

His bewildered expression melted into a wicked grin. "Is that a yes?" Valerian asked.

"That's a maybe," Laureline replied. She had removed one of his gloves, and got to work on the other one.

He stared at her, totally at a loss. "I'm so confused. Is this how love works?"

"No." Laureline gave him a teasing look with a hint of a smolder to it, and he inhaled swiftly. She leaned in for a kiss. As he began to enthusiastically return it, she pulled back and began to remove his jacket. When she placed her hand on his chest for a moment, she could feel his heart pouncing beneath her fingers.

"This is how *women* work. A woman lived in your body for a while. Didn't you learn anything?"

She tossed aside the jacket and started to slide her

hands up under his shirt. To her surprise, he stopped her. She looked up questioningly at him.

"I did learn something," he said, grinning.

"And what might that be?"

"Don't start something you can't finish."

She laughed a little. "We have two whole hours!"

Valerian gave her a slow, wicked smile. "Precisely," he said, pulling her close and kissing her hungrily. Her arms slipped up around his neck and she pressed herself against him.

The stars were not eternal, but they were ancient beyond reckoning. They had seen much, and would behold more. But seldom had their judgeless gazes borne witness to events as momentous as those that occurred this day. Two worlds had been born. One, a vast, exquisite planet, with sea and sky and sand and tranquility.

The other, a much smaller, but no less significant world, consisting only of two.

Acknowledgments

The author must gratefully acknowledge Valerian and Laureline's creators, Pierre Christin and Jean-Claude Mézières, and of course the astoundingly creative Luc Besson, who brings them to life on the screen. Thanks must also go to my agent, Lucienne Diver, and my editors on this project, Natalie Laverick and Ella Chappell.

About the Author

Award-winning and eight-time *New York Times* bestselling author Christie Golden has written over fifty novels and several short stories in the fields of science fiction, fantasy and horror. She has writing in such franchises as *Star Wars*, *Star Trek*, *World of Warcraft*, *StarCraft*, *Assassin's Creed*, *Halo*, and *Fable*, among many others, as well as authoring her own books.

Recent projects are two novels for the *Warcraft* movie, *Warcraft: Durotan* and *Warcraft: The Official Movie Novelization*, and *Assassin's Creed: Heresy* and *Assassin's Creed: The Official Movie Novelization*. Appearing on shelves in 2017 in addition to the novelization of *Valerian and the City of A Thousand Planets* will be *Star Wars: Battlefront II: Inferno Squad*.

Golden was awarded the International Association of Media Tie-in Writers' Faust Award 2017, conferring upon her the title of Grandmaster in acknowledgment of a quarter century of contributions to the field of media tie-in fiction.

For more fantastic fiction, author events,
competitions, limited editions and more

VISIT OUR WEBSITE
titanbooks.com

LIKE US ON FACEBOOK
facebook.com/titanbooks

FOLLOW US ON TWITTER
@TitanBooks

EMAIL US
readerfeedback@titanemail.com